Fountain of Death

JUDITH MEHL

PENNYSTONE PRESS

Also by Judith Mehl...
The Kat Everitt Handwriting Analysis Mysteries

FORMULA FOR MURDER
GAME, SET, MURDER
MURDER MOST FLORAL

Learn more at www.judymehl.com

Pennystone Press
ISBN-13: 978-0-9862766-3-7
ISBN-10: 0-9862766-3-4

Printed in the United States of America.

To Mary and Tony Milano
who introduced me to the southwest coast of Florida
and tirelessly explored Dunedin for me

And to The Pocono Herb Club
With its dedicated and knowledgeable members
on all things herbal

CHAPTER ONE

A gun sure would be handy.

Lizzie sighed. She'd left it at home. No sense in an 82-year-old woman arguing with airport security over a missing permit. Who knew she'd find a gun useful at an herbal conference? It's about peace and light and the natural way. Right? She inched closer to the shouting.

Nasty man! Wincing, she paused thirty feet away, monitoring the eruption of profane epithets aimed at Natalie. The man's face flared from red to purple. "This is a damn disaster."

The enemy volley flew by while Lizzie advanced with caution. She'd come to the vendors' hall to invite her friend to breakfast, not gun down a man her first day there, metaphorically or not. Maybe Natalie could handle it—a young conference chair didn't need an elderly woman interfering—but this old fogey itched to put the guy in his place.

In her hidden position, she eavesdropped on the one-sided conversation. Her jaw firmed as vulgar language reverberated around her. How loud it must be for poor Natalie. *Putting my past behind me will be trickier than I thought, gun or not. Asking for God's help, before I think violence, would be more in keeping with this gentle, herbal way of living.*

She repositioned her weight to peek around the corner. Not sure why she bothered with stealth. This man locked onto diatribe and couldn't see past his anticipated profit. Still, her silent monitoring left Natalie in control, though her friend spoke little.

Lizzie would let the brim fire burn down before she made a stand, but this volcanic menace evidently had limitless fuel for his anger—like a life's worth.

Get a grip. The man's trying to sell some herbal stuff. How bad can he be? Remember, new world, new rules. On the other hand, his vicious onslaught ratcheted up. She bit her lip. *Please Lord, help my friend. I'm ready as back-up. This guy truly needs to be put down, but I promise I won't kill him.*

The man slapped a huge palm on the counter, snapping her out of her monologue with God. He bellowed at Natalie, "People like you ought to be shot."

Enough. Maybe God was out on break. The man was dangerous, at least verbally. Natalie was saddled with this self-absorbed vendor. Enough of his vile language. Lizzie struck. She stepped into sight to bark, "I'm trying to be nice here, but if you keep going I'll tear your vile tongue out." Her words sliced sharp and more lethal than his. It took years to hone her skills. *You missed civility by a bit there, Lizzie. Try again.*

She dialed it down. "We don't talk filthy around here." Her friend turned but Lizzie saw the smile she attempted to hide. She refocused on the man who'd just become her enemy.

He snarled, "What the hell?" His harangue froze when he saw her. He unbent his threatening stance, eyes widening.

Humph, I bet he didn't expect an old woman who sounded like a drill sergeant.

His train of thought sidetracked only for a minute. He gestured toward Natalie.

"This dumb broad needs to change the location of my booth. Right now. What business is it of yours?"

Lizzie reached into her pocket. She'd worn a long skirt to blend with the conference theme of living naturally. It brought her back to the earth movement days. But now, the deep pocket served a deceptive purpose as she pressed a couple of fingers forward.

Maybe I could just break his arm if he gets worse; no gun needed. It wouldn't delay the conference, would it? Breathe. Use your words, Lizzie.

"Dagnabbit! Clamp shut the foul mouth," she said. "What's her business is my business."

He withered.

Wow. My words worked. Or he fears I'm holding a gun. Whatever helps.

Shoulders back, head held high, Natalie withstood his outbursts and Lizzie's show of force. She said, "This man thinks he deserves the prime spot." She whirled to face him. "Even though he's a new vendor and squeaked in just before the deadline."

Lizzie admired her friend as she traded verbal assaults with the lanky man. He looked like a scientist and talked like a longshoreman. His porcelain-white skin reminded her of the pasty inventor slaving in the lab all night like those portrayed in horror movies.

Natalie breathed deep, motioned toward the booth, and edged a soft voice with ice. "You registered so late you're lucky I assigned you more than a tiny hole."

That a way, girl. You tell him.

With full light, the hall could overwhelm with sensory perception. As Lizzie listened, she also absorbed the scents around her. They maintained a pleasing aromatic blend with hints of zestful spices. The lemon balm and tarragon were a pungent distraction. She noticed most of his bottles and containers sat among a nest of packing material on the floor. He must have stopped setting up to demand the location change when he saw Natalie. Surprised he waited this late to complain, Lizzie figured he arrived just under the wire and needed to set up or lose out.

She glanced around the hall. Everything was in place, except for this last booth. He'd managed to plonk down a small placard stating, "Alexander Howell, Proprietor." Only one row of bottles stood on the counter awaiting their mates. Natalie must have come to the hall early this morning to check the empty spot from last night, and found him.

The bottles intrigued with their simplicity. They drew her and Natalie to take another look. Lizzie interjected a question in an attempt to subdue his tirade, and he moved in for the sales pitch. She remembered such products claimed to inhibit the enzyme telomerase, which causes aging and disease, so she monitored the ensuing discussion between him and Natalie. *Who knows, maybe I can learn a thing or two about aging before it gets to me. Not that I do so bad. Still, I'm getting on in years.* Wouldn't hurt to listen to this jerk. In case he knew something worthwhile.

He said, "Some reputable firms are confirming similar results, and formulating commercial plans. However, my Telomerase Might is pure. Produced under the same stiff requirements. I did it sooner. A lot less expensive."

Lizzie watched his chest expand in proportion to his pride.

Natalie feathered the air in front of the bottles with her fingertips. "They're all clear glass."

It amazed Lizzie how Howell tamped down his anger and moved in to clinch a sale. He rattled on, "Right. Light doesn't affect my merchandise but I use a sterile, glass pharmaceutical container for strength and purity. This conference will launch my product if I get the best location. I need the more visible spot. It's near the herbal stuff. Away from my competitors."

His voice rose. Lizzie resumed her cautious stance. His product results seem iffy. This man should be delighted he was admitted at all. She raised her eyes heavenward. *Remember Lizzie girl, you've come to address herbalists. To help friends. Keep your lip buttoned here.*

She hoped this Howell guy would calm down before his blood pressure spurted like Mount Vesuvius. Ah, maybe he would deflate and save us some trouble. Not the nicest thought, but there it stood, naked and true.

"Dammit! I have to have this location." His voice rose in a crescendo of angry words as he recovered from his fear of Lizzie and approached Natalie with an arrogant step and a repeat outburst, as if his boasting about his product reminded him what he wanted.

Lizzie moved back, again, letting her friend control the moment, for now. The man didn't complement this immaculate and organized hall, sporting blooming pots of herbs throughout. *He sure ruffles my ire. Still, I hope you're noticing, God. I'm keeping my cool.*

Natalie remained firm. Her face reflected warmth, even in the lowered lighting in the yet-to-open hall. As chair, she'd have researched every vendor. She said, "This Telomerase Might borders on inappropriate for this type of conference. Count your blessings you're standing here." His rants escalated when Natalie told him this. He lunged to grab her arm. She stood her ground but Lizzie saw her indecision on how to control the irate vendor as his spewed string of obscenities turned physical.

Lizzie kept her eyes on Howell and couldn't see what Natalie looked like. Her face probably dripped with spittle from the man's words erupting like the volcanic ash of sound. More filthy language interrupted Lizzie's thoughts and churned her temper.

"Motherf. . . ."

This time, he'd crossed the line of propriety.

She stepped close before he continued. With a practiced scowl and her fingers jamming her pocket forward, she said, "Don't."

He dropped Natalie's arm and swung at Lizzie. She ducked out of range, her movements graceful and clean. His elbow nicked one of the containers on the counter, starting a chain reaction. Natalie reached to stop them from falling over.

Howell swatted at her hands. "Don't touch my stuff!"

Natalie jerked away.

Lizzie grabbed his arm and twisted. On the surface it looked gentle. She didn't want her friend disturbed by a surprising display of might. Natalie was the daughter of one of her dearest friends. A beautiful child who became a woman who exuded kindness.

One who'd treated this vulgar man with patience and calm, yet bile leaked out with each of his words. He was an unvarnished man. Some men just exhibited rough edges but held an inner core of decency. Alexander Howell not only lacked veneer, he lacked moral integrity. It was all Lizzie could do not to smack the guy upside his head, but as chair, it was Natalie's call. Lizzie bit her tongue.

Natalie straightened her spine and said, "That's it. Set up or pack up. I'm sending someone in to supervise. No more invective attacks and tantrums or you're out."

Howell backed down.

This Health Naturally Conference was yet to officially open, but Lizzie saw the beginning bubbles of trouble brewing. Natalie rushed out into the corridor, followed by Lizzie. As she turned her head to see what Howell was doing she saw him standing, legs spread and arms akimbo. His heated glare could set her hair aflame. "Watch out in dark parking lots," he shouted.

How infantile. Besides, I work best in the dark. Did. Did work best in the dark. Now I like the sun. Remember, Lizzie, it's why you're here in Florida.

CHAPTER TWO

Lizzie heard the little squeak in his voice as they left the vendor hall. Maybe he and his product were deeply vulnerable. *Open mind, Lizzie, open mind. Open mind, my eye. Bullies always turn my stomach.* She raced to catch up with her friend.

"I don't know how to work with him," Natalie hissed. "He wanted the prime spot near the entrance door. Everybody knows you sign up a year in advance for the door location." She glanced at her friend. "This is my first year as conference chair and what a beginning. Do you think I can resign yet?"

Lizzie sensed a crack in Natalie's demeanor and moved to diffuse it. "I've known numerous people in my life, all kinds of hoity-toity dignitaries and top notch government uppity-ups and none of them could hold a candle to you in cool. You never raised your voice."

She continued, "The Health Naturally Conference draws hundreds of attendees, mostly herbalists from around the country, and a hundred or so vendors. It's a monumental task, yet you stand here poised, every hair neat and pinned in place. Not touched by Mr. volcano."

They moved through the roofed patio area toward the outdoors, one of the many advantages to living in this part of the sun belt. She put her arm around Natalie's shoulders for a second and squeezed in a quick hug. "You'll do great. By the way, how *did* you stay so calm in there. I was ready to deck the guy."

Hesitating as they walked out of the building, Natalie shrugged the single shoulder signifying, 'I don't know,' then looked up and down at her elderly friend. She moved forward with a bounce in her step. "I just bet you could deck him."

Natalie, like most others, knew nothing about her true life history. Lizzie ignored what lay beneath the surface of her comment. She marched outdoors and only caught a glimpse of azure skies and sandy beaches. That was okay for her, though many participants counted on the sun between herbal sessions. Today, she wanted to assist Natalie any way she could, but vowed, again, to stay in the background. Not an easy task for her. *No one ever called me reticent.*

Natalie interrupted her thoughts. "Why did you pretend to have a gun?"

"How do you know I was pretending?"

"I didn't, until you pulled your hand out to stop him. The pocket went flat."

Lizzie humphed. "Some people are too observant for their own good. Anyway, when he grabbed your arm, that's when I wished I had my gun. It just materialized in my pocket, so to speak."

"Your gun?"

"A gun. I meant 'a gun.'"

Natalie's humor appeared restored. She moved on. "Let's go find if the resort helps out with recalcitrant vendors. Their event planner gave us a great rate and terrific rooms for the main speakers. We'll see if he can deal with trouble, too."

"Sounds good. So, this is the man to thank? Our accommodations here at the Neptune's Oasis Resort are fantastic. Quiet, and away from the crowds. Yet near enough to everything." Okay, so not everyone might appreciate the peacefulness, but there was plenty of riotous activity throughout the resort to suit the others. From here she could hear a beach volleyball game in full swing despite the early hour.

"I've been thinking. Each year we switch locations for this conference," Natalie said. It already stands out as the only indoor herbal conference situated in classy hotels or resorts. What would you think of scheduling it here every year?"

"Sounds the cat's meow. Or is 'awesome' more up to date?"

Natalie's chuckle merged into a loud chortle before she calmed and said, "You're awesome, and if you like my idea, 'cool' or 'smooth' works well, too."

Lizzie slowed down for her friend. She'd established a brisk walk years ago out of necessity. Now, she needed to learn to saunter, as the others did. "This conference stands out because it addresses a wide range of herbal healing." She stopped for a minute to feel the sun on her face. "Especially since it gives each herbalist a chance to enjoy their life's work in a warm setting."

"So many attendees come from the North. Living here year round, I can't imagine being so cold, but I sympathize."

Lizzie automatically scanned the two women heading for a walk on the beach in sneakers and swimsuits. "Usually it's the only time each year many herbalists are pampered."

"Remember the good old days, when we either froze or got drenched or, at times, enjoyed sleeping in tents outdoors?"

"You mean like the one I attended in October where the freezing rain and wind almost blew us away?" Lizzie shivered with the thought. "Still, a worthwhile conference. Each one brims with new information." Reflecting on Natalie's life, Lizzie realized how intertwined it had been with all things holistic. She remembered the young woman at her mother's knee spending time with the other herbalists in the farm yard and the campus fields of the early herbal meets Lizzie attended between trips away for her job. Typical scenarios for those conferences. Most were still held in outdoor locations to provide the therapeutic and restorative nature of the open air.

Natalie justified these decisions, but put in a plug for the current event. "Holding the meetings in the countryside did have curative value, at times. But here, we have the beach for our communing around the circle of stones. More comfortable than sitting on the hard ground."

Tall and lean, Lizzie towered over Natalie and scrunched down to meet her face to face, like a proud mama. "You are a born leader."

Natalie said, "It's not me. More something like, 'The resort may heal the healers?'"

Lizzie appreciated her friend's humility as they walked the

outside path to the front office, enjoying the exuberant feeling only warm sunshine brings. *Could I ever retire to a place like Florida? The sun was beneficial. I'd get wrinkles. But then she laughed at herself.*

Natalie jostled her back to the present when a group of women crowded the walkway as they passed. "What's not to like? Lizzie asked. The fruit basket in our room rivals Seattle's space needle in height. You ever been to Seattle?"

"No. Florida's incredible." She waved her hand in all directions, pointing to balmy weather, happy people, a serene setting. "I've never had a desire to leave except for the herbal get-togethers. Besides, we have some tall buildings, too. Well, in Miami, not so much here in St. Pete Beach, where we cater to ocean views and large expanses of white sand."

"Maybe you'd learn to enjoy the tranquility of rural Pennsylvania. You know I would love to have you visit. Anytime."

"I'll see about a trip later." Natalie gave Lizzie a fast hug before they entered the office of the resort event planner. They stood to the side while he served an irate customer. Nodding toward him, Lizzie whispered, "He has those dark and bold gecko eyes."

"I know," Natalie marveled. "And he never blinks. Always looks so innocent. I wonder if he is?" Lizzie observed the man. He held the firm stature of an ancient Egyptian, tall and chocolaty smooth skin, and his nature alone soothed the grumbler out of his complaint. The guest even smiled walking away. Then she watched Natalie switch to her professional mode with a straightening of her shoulders and an extended hand to the man when he approached.

"Hello, Michael. This is Elizabeth Ort, an old friend and expert herbalist here to speak at the conference." She delved into her concern about Alexander Howell and his efforts to change booths this morning. "Is there anything you can do to back us up and make sure he doesn't cause trouble?"

He said, "Of course. You have several options. You want me to call security?" Lizzie, fluent in many languages, noted the nasal vowels from his Haitian Creole past blending into lovely French accented English.

Natalie looked down and shuffled her folder from one arm to the next in hesitation. She answered, "Not yet. Is there a more gentle way to just monitor his behavior?"

Lizzie noticed his rapid assessment of the situation. She could hear his thinking. Was this young woman able to evaluate the man's danger? If the resort kept back, would they be liable for any disturbance this Howell could cause?

He reached a conclusion and she sensed he would follow Natalie's lead. He offered, "I could stop at his booth as reinforcement. Let me check out all his information." After a minute on the computer, he said, "Okay, we'll stand guard in the convention hall now. I'll visit him in his room later, and remind Mr. Howell he is still responsible for his hotel invoice even if you kick him out of the conference. Sometimes when you march into these bullies' personal space they shift to a lower gear."

Lizzie looked over the large man. He'd have no need of a gun, pretend or otherwise. "You could be extremely intimidating. But don't smile. Your eyes already look too nice." She grinned when she said it.

He accommodated her with a frown.

"Love it." She wove her arm through Natalie's. "This man has it covered. Can we *finally* go to breakfast?"

Natalie rolled her eyes. "It's not even eight a.m."

Lizzie realized it was true. For many, the day hadn't begun. For herself and Natalie, it opened with a vengeance. Was it a sign of more to come? Or a final parlay in preparation for the grand event? She may be wise and a woman of the world, but the conference was ultimately out of her hands. She needed to keep that in mind. She strengthened her stride and charged forward. Natalie kept up. Maybe she was just hungry. *For me, it's a new beginning.*

They wound their way across the courtyard to a collection of open patio restaurants. Lizzie found it difficult deciding where to eat. The Neptune's Oasis Resort enticed the palate while exciting the eyes, and not only with the many dining establishments. The resort offered a private curve of shoreline on a peninsula off Florida's west coast. It served as a beautiful haven for vacationers and herbalists alike. Natalie nudged her toward an outdoor eating area facing the ocean. A delight, even this early in the morning.

Lizzie chatted with her friend at the table. She ate and waited for Natalie to finish, inhaling the scent of her coffee before each invigorating sip. Beyond, people tried out the beach. The soft sand encased their feet in an icy blanket. She knew because she'd walked in it the morning she arrived. No one minded the chill as far as she could tell. Like her, they looked happy to enjoy the warm sunshine on this February morning. White and wild, the ocean encouraged roaming. The rushing water removed all signs of existence in an insistent wave, the palette clean and ripe for another foot tale. *This just could be the ideal place to redefine my soul. I'd better get some beach shoes.*

An exuberant hail from their friend Abby at a nearby table interrupted before her thoughts turned into a deep philosophy on life. This energetic young lady popped out of her chair and dashed over.

Abby Weiss served as a volunteer for the conference since its inception. Considering its age, she must have been a child. Because of her career, Lizzie had not attended every year, but she did remember this young lady grinning and handing out fliers by the time she'd learned to read.

They discussed this year's conference program for a few minutes. Abby bubbled with enthusiasm, her feet bouncing to an internal rhythm. But she ended on a sour note. "I saw you in the vendor hall with the nauseating Mr. Howell. Are you okay?"

Lizzie responded, "Sure am, but what do *you* know about the man?"

"He rushed in the front door earlier, arms piled with boxes. Bowled over a small woman bringing in speaker supplies. He didn't stop, or apologize. Just left her there to pick up the papers."

Abby scurried back to where a group leader waited with patience. She hesitated after two steps and looked over her shoulder at her friends. "Be careful. I sense that man is evil. Pure evil."

CHAPTER THREE

The enthusiastic crowd surged from the room following the opening speech of the 2016 Health Naturally Conference. A thwack on her back jostled Abby from her good mood as she left the main hall. She swirled, fearing an attack she didn't understand.

"Sorry. Sorry. What a group," a young woman said as she seized Abby's arm this time in an obvious attempt to prevent another shove to her back. She smoothed over the spot on the sleeve and smiled. "Wow. Wasn't he the most exciting speaker you've ever heard?"

Abby kept walking while enjoying the animation in the woman's voice, and agreed wholeheartedly. "He knew so much. A real eye opener first thing in the morning."

They turned the corner toward the vendor hall for a break between sessions, almost knocking into Lizzie. Instead, Abby reached for her arm and brought her along. "What did you think?"

"Wesley Martell's knowledge of goldenseal and astragalus is exceptional. We all know how the native Americans used it for infection, but he revealed the latest research. A superior talk."

"I agree. He stressed how the herbs aren't a cure, but can change the body's responses to limit symptoms," Abby said.

The other woman nodded as she moved down the left corridor. "Not to mention his charisma." She waved goodbye. "See you later."

Abby continued to rave about the speaker.

Lizzie's sister, Delia O'Leary, whisked in between them and with a smooth gesture broke Abby's handhold. "Hi folks. We have a meeting, Lizzie."

Lizzie hunched up, ready to sidetrack her attendance.

Delia cut her off. "The chairman has the final report for the committee on security. I was at the early session and I know the resort promised guards and patrols, especially near the vendor hall. But you're on the committee and have to attend."

Lizzie remembered Howell's anger and shifted from disgust at the trivial meeting to agreement. She had just watched a woman give one of those to-du-loo waves but couldn't stomach doing it. She said a simple, "I'm out of here, but I enjoyed the speech, too. I could just smell the slight narcotic odor of the fresh goldenseal rhizome."

"It's such a gorgeous plant that it's a shame to dig up the roots," Abby said. "It always reminded me of licorice."

Lizzie's laugh sounded more like a bark and people turned. She ignored them. "I'm afraid such things happens with old age. If I ever start reeking of licorice, please let me know right away."

Abby tried to muffle her mirth as she walked down the vendors' aisle. This looked like serious stuff. These were not the dried wreaths found in many herb shops. She strolled down one side, noting several theme-based outlets, rather than a hodgepodge of popular herbs. The nearest booth featured herbs for the sports minded. Her eyes zipped across the bottles. *But quick eye movement is the best speed you'll get out of me. An athlete I'm not.*

A man bumped into her as he walked down the opposite side of the aisle. She glanced back but saw him as the victim of a push, also. Not bad looking. Her thoughts bounced around while she righted herself. Face strained though. Maybe a grump.

"Kind of tight quarters here, aren't they," she heard him say to the man who nudged him.

Seems polite. I'll let it go.

She continued looking, grateful there was a full hour before the next workshop she wanted to attend. So much to see. One booth held only versions of herbs to influence neurotransmitters. Again, not her. She walked further, nearing the end of the first aisle. Aah, here's one. "Herbs for Inflammation." She knew a lot of people, like the elderly, who could use help with swollen joints. Maybe she'd buy some of these products as gifts for friends. A fellow herbalist was in front of her talking to the vendor. She eavesdropped, learning about the anti-inflammatory herbs. She heard her friend tell the merchant, "I know many of those herbs, like garlic and basil, ginger and turmeric. I never heard rosemary was."

"It is, and a great one. Rosemary has many marvelous healing properties. It's not only a strong antioxidant but good for muscle stability. Some non-herb foods have similar strong properties, like the quercetin in apples and onion skins," the vendor said.

Abby scooted to her friend's side. "Hey, I didn't know that. Sorry, Julie. I'll wait till you've finished your purchases before I horn in further."

"No problem. It is fascinating. For now, I'm buying this combination herb bottle."

Before Abby got close enough to hear the sales pitch, the same man entered her personal space again. She overheard him grumble this time and turned her head to see the cause, just catching the last of his words about wishing people would go to the beach.

A man at his shoulder nodded. "If this crowd doesn't thin soon *I'm* going to grab some rays on the beach."

Now, with the chance to watch the guy, she realized the man who bumped her was, indeed, on the handsome side, like a whipcord lean Frenchman. His speech echoed pure American slang, though. An odd mix. He walked in stilted steps and observed details all around him. Not just the tins of salve and bottles of vitamins but the booth displays, everything. He paced a little further and halted again, as if so taken with each booth he had to study it. He didn't initiate any conversation with the vendors.

Strange. Still it could get interesting. Should I introduce myself? She thought about it while she completed her purchases. The combination bottle contained at least ten of the herbs she knew to combat inflammation. A perfect gift for several of her elder friends. Abby glanced out of the side of her eyes to locate the man she'd dubbed as the American-Frenchman, but stopped walking when she saw the next vendor spot. It was horrid Howell's telomerase booth.

A hard thunk in the middle of her back pushed her forward, but strong arms around her waist kept her from falling.

"I'm so sorry," the mystery man said. "I take full responsibility. I must have been walking too close to you. A sad state of affairs. A little more distance and I could have had a better view of such a beautiful woman. And I wouldn't have tackled you. Maybe."

Abby stuttered. "I stopped suddenly when I saw his booth."

"Something wrong with the wares?" he asked. "I don't believe in his Telomerase Might's effect on telomeres but this man is one of several touting those products just now."

They walked together past Alexander Howell's booth into the wider corridor. He motioned to the outside patio where small tables allowed shoppers to rest for a bit. She grabbed a chair, anxious to continue a conversation with a man who knew what telomeres were.

She settled her skirt under her with a few snaps of the fabric and asked, "What's your concern?"

He dropped his folder on the table and studied her.

"I don't question that telomerase can mitigate the bits of DNA and stall shortening of life."

"But???"

"He's a quack."

The 'quack' startled her and she leaned back. "Strange. I believe he's evil, and he's rude to boot."

"Whoa, that's huge. What brought that on?"

She quivered. "The things people say about him. And you'll think I'm crazy, but I get these vibes from him. Occurred again when we were in front of his booth."

"Does this happen often?"

She shook off the shivers. "Fortunately, no."

She added, "You may be correct about his merchandise. Plus, I think before we accept products that purport to be the panacea for aging we need to complete a lot more research."

He grunted. "Huh." But didn't interrupt further.

She made her point. "Safe herbs can be used, for now, to create the same effect."

"You gotta be kiddin' me. You can't believe what you just said."

They argued about telomeres. She touted how eating proper food with quality herbs can promote telomere length without drugs. He disagreed. Attendees moved around them as they came and went from the herbal sessions to the vendors' hall. Most ignored them. A scruffy looking man, one of her favorite herbalists, stopped and smiled.

"Abby, how are you?"

She rose and hugged him. "Glenn, good to see you." She turned to present her new friend and realized she didn't know his name. He'd risen when Glenn moved forward. His height dwarfed Glenn, but he thrust out his hand in a friendly gesture. "Hi. I'm Jacob Zebadiah Meindl. Abby and I just met and we're already embroiled in an argument."

She liked how he'd picked up on her name, oozing charm as he and Glenn talked.

"So you're German? Like Gregor Mendel?"

"Just a tad South German, but I do admire how the man knew his peas in a pod."

Glenn laughed. They all chatted until he said he had to move on. "See you later."

She stayed standing and said to Jacob, "I don't want to miss the program on herbal first aids."

He motioned her forward. "Maybe we can fight over herbal values later."

As they walked, she continued, "Herbs do have an affect. A chemical in astragalus appears to increase production of telomerase. Can we agree the enzyme telomerase helps convey the replacement of those bits of DNA?"

"Yeah, we can, on that, but who's going to believe an herb can make you live longer. Besides, some forms of the stuff are toxic."

She fisted her hands on her hips. "You're an herbalist. How can you think that way?" They entered the break-out room for the first aid program. "This subject is a weak spot in my herbal knowledge. The talk should be great. The speaker's renowned in the field."

Andrew Bonita stood at the podium and jumped right in to his topic. "The correct herbs can save lives. Take the ones that heal second degree burns in twenty-four hours, or those that repair surface wounds so fast they beat the healing of inner wounds if you're not careful."

Silence fell.

The man continued. "Herbs save lives. Many of you are familiar with adaptogens and their role in returning the body to health, and also of restorative tonic herbs and demulcent herbs which help normalize the blood lipid and sugar levels. But today we deal with the first aid herbs."

Abby settled in and barely breathed. This was what she wanted.

"You may all be familiar with the popular herbal throat sprays and immunity boosters. These do the job in a safe way. But there are many more."

An hour and a half later Abby sat stunned at all she'd learned. Thank heavens he'd handed everyone information sheets or her pen would have run out of ink with the notes of all she wanted to remember.

Without a whisper, Jacob rose to leave while she moved forward with a quiet reverence to shake the speaker's hand. She was grateful Jacob was gone, and decided for once she'd been wise with a guy and hadn't provided her last name. There was something just a little off with him. He appeared intelligent, but confused on some of his beliefs. She shrugged it off. All of us feel the same way sometimes.

She left the hall in a crowd, but Jacob had waited at the door for her. "Let's get lunch and talk some more."

It was a plea she couldn't ignore. They chose the beach-side bar to enjoy the gorgeous day. Abby sat still, closed her eyes, and breathed in the scent of the white jasmine bordering the eating area. Lizzie and Delia brushed past. Abby swung out her hand just in time and grabbed Lizzie's arm. Once more, the woman in question twirled around and broke into a broad grin when she saw who it was. She asked, "Did you love the program as much as the rest of us?"

Abby beamed. "It beat magnificent by a mile. How is your speech on ancient remedies going to top that one?"

Lizzie simpered. An obvious ruse, but those who saw it restrained from comment as she said, "Just you wait. I'm sure I'll keep you awake."

Abby turned to Jacob. "Lizzie, I'd like you to meet Jacob. Jacob Meindl, Lizzie is one of our main speakers this year. And Delia, her sister, is on the conference committee."

They looked around. Delia was long gone. Lizzie laughingly said, "That's my sister for you. Always on the run, even if she does it in slow motion. You can catch up with us later."

Abby wouldn't let go of her hand. "Wait, I need a second opinion. Jacob doesn't think you can affect telomeres with herbs. I mentioned astragalus and he said there are toxic forms of it. What's your opinion?

Lizzie faced Jacob squarely and frowned. "Don't use the toxic stuff. Check your species. And if you can't tolerate astragalus. Consider the hawthorn berry. You must have seen news of how the hawthorn berry can combat angina. You know, less chest pain. More able to exercise. Slow aging."

"I do believe in herbs. But as the fountain of youth? Come again."

CHAPTER FOUR

Miranda Pennywinkle streaked out of the vendor hall and slammed into Lizzie's chest. She hiccuped and wheezed, spurting out words in a frenzy. "He's dead. I know he's dead." Her Texas twang registered as her voice rose.

Lizzie knew fear when she saw it. But she also knew what to do. She wrapped her arm around the young woman's shoulders and asked, "Anyone else in there?"

Miranda held in a scream, shuddered, then squealed, "Oh God. No. I think. No, just him."

The sound trailed off to nothing. Lizzie watched her eyes travel back toward the room she'd raced out of.

"Move her," Delia said, standing just behind her. "Before those eyes start rolling."

Lizzie realized Delia had overheard it all. She glanced inside and motioned to her sister to enter and lock the door. While she guided the shaking woman next door to a small break-out room—empty this early in the morning.

"Who was it?"

Miranda's eyes widened but she didn't answer. Like she couldn't understand the question.

Bluntness being part of her nature, Lizzie asked, "Who did you find dead?"

"Jeez, you nuts?" Miranda's voice shrilled so high the last word barely escaped.

"It's okay, sweetie. I just thought it would help if you knew who it was. We'll check it out."

Miranda sniffled. "Sor . . .ry," she stuttered. "I didn't look at him." Hiccuping, she added. "His head was covered in blood."

Lizzie pondered what to do next. Her experience with these types of interviews didn't involve young innocent women. *Don't frighten her. Calm and guide. Use empathy, not logic.* She held Miranda's hand. *I only know logic. Intuition maybe, but a little short on the soothing side. What now?*

When Miranda whimpered again, Lizzie urged deep breaths, gave her a quick hug, and praised her. "You're doing fine. I admire you for being so stoic." She walked her to the corner area with cushy seating. "Tell me what you remember. What you saw."

Miranda nodded, and nodded, and nodded. Finally, Lizzie eased her into a chair, then moved away to think.

A strangled cry stopped her. Miranda wheezed out some words. "Don't leave. Um. White. Face white. Stringy hair. All bloodyyy. . ." The wailing began again.

Bad idea. Don't ask her to remember anything about the body. She knew one person with a white face. But there were hundreds of attendees and vendors at the conference. And it could mean he'd been dead a while. Nah, It had to happen during the night. People were in there all day yesterday. Now what? Okay, one more try. Then find help.

"A quick question, sweetie, and I'll leave you alone."

Miranda gazed up at her, still trembling, and nodded. Lizzie placed her hand under the woman's chin and quieted the nodding. "Okay, this should be easy. Where exactly did you see the body?"

The whimpering returned but the head stayed still.

Lizzie tried to regroup. Miranda stopped whining and nodding. This was progress, but she needed more. "Was it near the raised speaker area in the corner?"

Miranda stared, her eyes wide.

"You know, the place with the microphone to announce winners of the giveaways?"

The stare continued.

"Was it by a vendor booth?"

She saw a flicker of change in Miranda's eyes. "Was it near this door you just came out of?"

Miranda shook her head. "No, over there."

She pointed, which did no good, but Lizzie felt encouraged. If the twang didn't detour her. She'd talked with Miranda before, and never noticed it. Stress induced? Who knew. Back to the gentle questions. "By the far door?"

Miranda nodded for real this time. Lizzie could tell because it exhibited more vigor.

She stepped aside to call Natalie Truman on her cell phone. As conference chair, the woman needed to know about the dead man immediately, but she would also stay controlled and call resort security and the local police.

To Miranda she said, "Okay. It will be okay." She pulled open the door. Thank heavens she saw Abby walking by. A charming and refreshing person. Someone who would be good with Miranda. Like a babysitter. People sitter? Who knew what they were called. She grabbed her arm and said. "Emergency. You stay here with Miranda and don't either of you move."

Abby closed her phone and tucked it into her purse. "What?"

"I need your help. It's an emergency." Better not tell her about the body. No time for more wailing. She paused for effect. "Very serious. Deadly."

"*What?*"

The word erupted a little too loud. Lizzie shushed her. "And whatever you do, don't ask her questions." They both glanced over to Miranda curled up in a corner of the loveseat. "Miranda's had a scare. Please stay with her till I return. No matter what. And don't let her talk to anyone."

She ran out as she shuffled Abby in, keeping the door as closed as possible in the process. She exited, then wheeled around. "And do *not* allow her to leave this room."

Abby must have seen her tense expression because she didn't ask even one question. She sat next to Miranda. "Go."

Holding her stride in check, Lizzie walked casually down the corridor in case someone came by and saw her. No need. It was too early in the morning for much traffic. Good, since she didn't want a crowd rushing in when the vendor doors opened.

Lizzie's sister, followed orders well, so she knew the doors would remain locked until the officials came. But she knew Delia didn't do bodies, and wouldn't go near the man. She needed to see the body before the police arrived and mucked everything up. She rapped their secret knock on the door and Delia opened it. She scurried through, motioning behind her back for Delia to lock the door again. She was out of time. Everyone would be there soon.

She headed in the direction Miranda indicated earlier. Racing past a few aisles she jerked to a stop. The man was positioned near the rear of a booth, mostly hidden by the back partition. Whoa, that was one messed up head. But she didn't doubt it was Alexander Howell, proprietor no more. Miranda had that right. The man *was* dead. Saying a brief prayer, she stopped moving and whispered to God. "No matter what the man has done, he didn't deserve this. I learned tolerance from you. May his soul be with you now. I'll try to help on this end, dealing with the body, and the killer."

And so she did. She stayed out of the immediate area, glad she still had great eyesight. There was no way *she* would destroy the scene for the police.

She stood still and studied the body—inch by inch. Hmm, doesn't look like any injuries other than the head. Looks like a natural fall. Well, as natural as you can be when you're dying. Certainly doesn't appear as if he was dragged here.

She examined the location. He was in the back of his vendor booth. The area was neat and well organized, unlike when she saw it the morning with Natalie. Unlike what she saw behind it. A few boxes scattered around on the floor. A dead body. *Maybe I do need a gun around here. It's not an herbal conference any more. It's a murder. Or more. What could have caused this?* She'd have to ponder the weapon later. After she gathered as much information from the scene as she could.

A partially full box sat open behind the booth. Maybe he was restocking. A theft gone bad? How would they know if anything was missing? Or what the bottles contained? I'll leave testing for the police. Right now, find why he was killed.

She made a semi-list, a means of thinking it through. Just the one injury might mean we can eliminate passion as a cause. But if it was a woman, it could have been an impulsive attack, followed by a frightening realization of what she'd done. Or not. She did the mental equivalent of pulling her hair. No time for the reality. She talked to herself, lacking any help. This part wavered from her normal procedure. I'm not usually aftermath, cleanup and all. Think.

Hmm. Not beaten, dead or alive. She only saw the one injury. But bludgeoned? Maybe.

She changed her viewing angle a little, squatting to scrutinize the wound. It looked like he was struck down from the side near the top of his head and he fell right here. He must have died instantly. There was blood, as Miranda said, or wailed, as the case may be. But not rivers of it. Well, she'd wait for the coroner's report. Or did they have a medical examiner here? She'd find out soon enough. No sense in speculating when the facts would be determined later.

She stood and mentally measured Howell's height. She studied the wound location again. She doubted if it had been a woman after all. The killer had to be quite tall for a woman. Not impossible, but it went further down on her list.

More important—what was the weapon? Could the killing have been premeditated? With the weapon brought in and removed afterwards? Not likely. How did the killer and Howell manage to stay inside when the security people locked up for the night? It couldn't have occurred before closing. Someone would have seen what was going on and shout out an alarm. She added to the mental list. Check with security. Or let the cops do it. No time now.

Lizzie heard noise by the door. Delia still had it locked but it sounded like her free access to the scene was at an end. She stepped back to get a larger view. Was she missing something? She saw Delia fling her arms in the air and shrug, looking for direction. Lizzie mouthed, "Stall." She knew Delia had honed the skill to perfection. It only gave her a few more minutes.

The door clicked open. As she half listened to Delia she took in the booth and surrounding area. She stepped back. It strained her neck to look above the booths, but she studied the banners hanging across each one with the booth name and number.

She heard, "What do you mean I have to leave right away? I'm doing exactly what you just said." Delia inched the door closed, though it was stopped by a beefy hand. She heard Delia's sweet voice as it wafted out the door.

"You wanted the area secure. I've been guarding it ever since Miranda said she saw a body. The police are on their way, now."

He stammered. "I know that. Wait, Miranda? Who's she? Is she inside?"

"Of course not, she came running out screaming. We placed her in a safe room so no one would talk with her and confuse her testimony before the police spoke with her."

Lizzie owed Delia big time. What a trooper. She had what she needed. A number of people stood on the other side, trying to push past Delia into the room. Her dear sister said, "Don't you want this area to stay secure until the police arrive?"

A booming and angry voice shouted, "I'm the chief of security here. I'll guard the area my way. Move it lady."

So much for stammering. And no tact, Lizzie thought. Delia would object but without Lizzie's combat skills she wouldn't last any longer. Her sister only knew self-defense. There wasn't an aggressive bone in her body. Lizzie stepped close to the left pole that secured the banner and nodded her head. She turned around to approach the door. Delia needed reinforcements and she'd do her best.

She was finished here.

CHAPTER FIVE

Detective Corporal William Milano's car screeched under the portico of the Neptune's Oasis Resort. He left the lights flashing. Jeesh, they'd reported a dead body, and headquarters just got around to informing him. Okay, so the detective they called got sick on his way in. *I'm hungry, so shoot me for being nasty*. His feet hit the ground and he slammed the door shut. Maybe he could salvage some of the crime scene.

"Where's the Chief of Security?"

"He's in the Conference Center in Building Three." The man behind the counter barely glanced at the badge but responded with respect. Milano hoped it was the authority in his voice. He was proud of the firm tone. It took him years to develop it. He'd needed to, since his promotion came so young. But it came in handy even now.

Milano saw the man's name on his ID tag and used it as a courtesy. "Burt, point me in the right direction."

Burt whipped out a map from under the counter and circled the area like he must have done thousands of times before. He straightened his shoulders. Milano figured he'd probably never done it for a crime scene.

"You might want to move your car to this parking lot, here, sir." He X'd the one nearest Building Three. "The Hyacinth," he added. And showed him the quickest walkway to the side entrance. "It will take you to the Conference Center hall that houses the vendors."

When Milano stormed into the hall, all the voices stopped simultaneously. The chief of security rushed over, ready to threaten him for interfering in an investigation. Disadvantages of having a badge and not a uniform. Ah, the good old days when he wore a uniform to draw instant respect and attention. Ah, the bad old days, when he wore a starched shirt, heavy shoes, and ridiculous belt with every possible means of destruction attached.

Several people hung by the main door, not acknowledging him, maybe not sure who he was, or in shock. Milano didn't care. He shouted out, "What are you people doing contaminating my crime scene?"

The rest stopped moving—like he'd hit freeze frame. He would have laughed—if it hadn't been a crime scene. He wondered how long they were wandering around destroying evidence. What a headache.

He didn't need a close inspection of the body to see the man was dead. He wanted to protect the integrity of the scene and evidence, but without any backup and all these people milling around, he was stretched too thin. Where in the heck was Guetierrez? His partner was new to the force but he had appeared competent. He should have been here for crowd control.

Meanwhile, the security chief's chest puffed out like a rooster's. "I'm in charge here. He reached his right hand forward to shake, oblivious of Milano's anger. Milano shook his hand, but hung his head in despair. *I'm supposed to be home eating bacon and eggs and here I am. And somehow, I'm sure my day isn't going to get better.* He pulled out his own identification, established himself as the lead investigator, and asked for the man's cooperation.

He motioned the others to stay by the main door, while demanding the security guy explain what happened. The man obliged, or tried to. He didn't know much. Instead, he flung out his arm and motioned to an elderly woman, tiny but erect. "She was here when I got here. "Ask her."

Milano was no rookie and saw the guy's effort to accept no blame, even though it was his responsibility to secure the place before anyone came in. Probably wanted to finish *his* eggs and bacon before he meandered over. He took a deep breath and attempted to stifle his mental wanderings. Maybe the smell of bacon was just his imagination.

Turning to the door, he studied the woman in question. A little fussy. Kept twitching at the scarf around the younger woman's shoulders. Good grief. Somebody persnickety who wouldn't help at all.

He knew it was time to introduce himself and discover who these people were who trooped into the room before he could secure it. He observed all the rows at the cavernous center, with over a hundred booths and a gazillion hiding places.

He looked the security chief in the eyes. "Have you checked out the entire area and secured the scene?"

"I just got here before you arrived."

Milano asked him to guard the door at the rear of the booths. The one opposite the main door where he, and apparently everyone else, had entered. "Nod if it's locked."

The guy trudged over there, as if his limited gear dragged him down. But he did a quick visual of each row as he passed and indicated the door was locked when he got there.

"Make sure it stays that way."

He motioned to the elderly woman to approach. He hoped he was far enough away from the body to not contaminate any evidence himself. If the team had arrived he could have left the crime scene and moved these people elsewhere. After a brief discussion, he discovered this woman, who introduced herself as Delia O'Leary, had not discovered the body.

With hesitation she said, "My sister. Elizabeth Ort's her name. She saw a woman run from the room."

"And your sister did what?"

"Well she calmed her down. Heard she'd found a body in here, and told me to keep the door locked till the police arrived."

Milano starred into her eyes. No guile there. Pure honesty. "And that's what you did?"

"Yes. I locked the door as soon as Miranda came out so no one would contaminate the crime scene. I kind of stood inside here and glanced around. The room felt empty, so I locked it."

Oh brother. Not another CSI fanatic. "What do you know of crime scenes?"

Delia stared right back. "Only what my sister tells me?"

"What does she know of crime scenes?"

The woman shuddered this time.

He decided to let it go for now and settled for pinpointing what had happened. "You walked right in? Not knowing if the killer was still in here?"

Delia fluttered her hands. "She just said he was dead."

"And it never occurred to you how he might have died?"

"Well, I kept scanning the room, but I did stay by the entry. You know, it's safer to keep my 'back to the door' theory?"

Someone with sense. Maybe things were looking up. He could only hope. "You saw no movement anywhere as you looked around?" He checked the area from where he stood.

She shook her head fiercely. "No, thank heavens."

He heard a slight shiver but when he turned back to her she'd already righted herself.

Milano looked around at the group of people standing in the room. He raised his eyebrows but before he could speak, Mrs. O'Leary did. "I tried. I did. But they practically broke the door down."

He acknowledged his understanding with a silent look.

She continued. "I did keep them away from the area as much as possible." She waved toward the booth with the dead guy behind it. "They stayed right by the door when I strongly suggested it."

The woman smirked a little. "The security guy was ready to tramp through here when you arrived though. Good timing. You kept him from marching over to the body."

The detective asked where he could find the person who discovered the body.

"Her name is Miranda Pennywinkle. My sister said she was quite upset so she closeted her in one of the nearby breakout rooms. Maybe Miranda's calmed down a little, the poor thing."

He grimaced. "I want to look around here and meet the medical examiner when he comes. Would you stay over by the entrance in case I need you again?"

After Mrs. O'Leary agreed, he stopped at the front of the booth in question. Above was a banner announcing "Telomerase Might," whatever the heck it was. A more discreet placard, on the front counter, read, "Alexander Howell, Proprietor." Could he be the dead guy?

He studied the two people left. The man looked like a linebacker, but maybe too foreign. The other was the woman Mrs. O'Leary fussed over. He'd tackle the linebacker first. He pulled the guy aside as much as possible without losing sight of the immediate crime scene. He identified himself and, tilting his head back a notch, studied the chocolaty brown face. He saw an open-faced gentleman with friendly eyes. He asked for the man's name and why he was there.

"My name's Michael. I'm the resort event planner. Like a liaison between the groups and the resort. I received the call about the body. I notified the security office and the conference chair. And ran over here."

"What time was it?"

Seven thirty exactly.

Milano appreciated his efficient answers and made notes. "What's your last name, Michael?"

"I just go by Michael."

The detective scowled. "I need your last name."

The Egyptian leaned closer and whispered it. "Please don't pass it around."

Milano laughed. "Don't worry. I can't spell it or say it."

Michael turned the notebook around and printed the name for him.

When he returned it, the detective motioned to the lone woman at the door. "The conference chair?"

"Yes sir. Her name is Natalie Truman."

He asked Michael if he wouldn't mind standing by outside the entrance and keeping anyone from coming in until the rest of his team arrived. Keys seem to proliferate considering how many people had access.

With any luck the conference chair could help him. From where she was located though, he wasn't sure if she'd been close enough to see anything of value. Once he got her identification, he asked, "Can you tell me how many keys there are to this room and who has them?"

She appeared to think for a moment, as if counting them, scrunching up her eyes up and said, "No. I can think of three but there could be many more."

Strike one. "Okay, Miss Truman, do you know the victim?"

"Not sure. He's behind the booth of Alexander Howell, but I didn't get any closer than the door when Delia asked us to stay right there."

He thought, strike two, but he said, "You trust Delia O'Leary?"

"Absolutely. Her and her sister, Lizzie, are the best. They know as much about life, and villains, as they do about herbs."

The detective frowned.

Natalie Truman continued, "Lizzie's one of our main speakers this week. And Delia's on the advisory committee."

Intrigued more with her comment about Lizzie and villains, he glanced at his notes and asked, "You're referring to Elizabeth Ort? Is she speaking about herbs or villains?"

Natalie cringed inside. "Yes. It's Elizabeth Ort. Sorry, everyone knows her as Lizzie. And she's speaking this time about ancient herbal remedies."

He waited for her to continue, pen posed.

"I don't know why I said that about villains. She knows more than most about those things." She waved her arm toward the booth in question.

He asked her if there were any other entrances to the room. She pointed to the one hidden behind the booth. "The service door is supposed to be secured at all times."

H'd already checked. It was unlocked. "Thanks for your help. Would you please sit here by the main entrance and not offer any information yet about what you saw? I'll get your official statement as soon as possible."

He poked around, bent down out of sight studying the floor, moved to the back of the booth, staying away from any area near the body. He'd want every inch of it covered for evidence collection. The groove in the side of the man's head provided a clue to his death but Milano would wait for confirmation. Instead, he sought infinitesimal signs of the presence of others. Nothing lay around to indicate something fell on the man. Besides, it would have had to hit him hard to make such a dent. Signs of a killer? Killers? Where was the ME? And his team?

And what was that scent? A floral sweet smell. He stood up and glanced around the booth. It didn't emanate from here. He headed toward the next vendor area, looking for a flower display or something. This was an herb conference after all. Didn't they have flowers? What good were herbs if not? They finally registered, the live ones anyway, placed here and there throughout.

Lizzie moved in from the sideline. Milano saw her as he inspected the crime scene and surrounding area. He stepped back a little and visually checked the nearby booths for any sign of disturbance. Acknowledging her presence without even turning around, he made a wild guess.

"Miss Elizabeth 'Lizzie' Ort, I presume?" Still studying the nearest booth, he could see from the corner of his eye, she was startled.

She recovered quickly. "See any signs of disruption?"

"Not by you, I'm sure. What have you been up to, lurking back there?"

"How would you know I wouldn't muddle your precious area?"

The detective faced her, and raised one skeptical eyebrow. "According to one of your fans, you are quite educated about such things."

He only received a harrumph as a reply. He gave her points for being there right after it happened, and sequestering the witness. Maybe he should deputize her. His second in command was looking at a demotion if he didn't arrive soon. He held his tongue, yet it was time to put *her* in her place.

Impatient, Lizzie walked in closer, measuring his height against her five feet ten inches. Taller than most of her acquaintances. She raised her head to look into the eyes of this lean man who must have run six feet two or more. Before she could speak, he braced his hands on his hips and said, "What are you still doing here?"

She placed her hands on her hips replicating his move, and

stretching her neck even longer to record her defiance, snipped. "Don't you want to know how he died?"

CHAPTER SIX

"Move back, please, I'm Detective Grant Guetierrez," said the man who rammed through the door past the guard. Michael winced and shrugged his shoulders.

"Who called the police?" The detective enunciated clearly in a loud voice as if the room held hundreds of people. Studying his face, Lizzie thought it must be fun trying to see in here with those sunglasses on.

She noticed Milano moved back behind the booth, probably hoping to determine means of death before he had to ask her. On the other hand, maybe he wasn't the man in charge. Who's this guy?

She decided to find out. "I asked the conference people to call the police, sir. The victim is Alexander Howell. He was found this morning before anyone else was in the room as far as we know." She pointed. He inched closer and looked. She watched as his swarthy young face turned white and rippled into a frown.

He took a breath to recover. "Alright. Everybody sit over there. Don't move. I'm in charge now and we'll get to each one of you as we can."

Lizzie looked around. There was only her, Michael, Delia and Natalie. Oh well. The others stepped back. If there was a vote, she'd pick the first cop who came in.

A muffled voice from behind the vendor's booth spoke abruptly. "I'm in charge here, Guetierrez. What took you so long?"

Milano moved into sight. He looked ticked off. At her? At the new guy? At the dead guy? It appeared the man in the steel-cut Aviator sunglasses might be the one to take the bullet this time. At least the old detective's eyes seem to bore into the new detective's eyes —right through those Ray Bans.

The man grinned and whipped off the Aviators. "I just heard the ME is on his way. Sorry for the delay. A major traffic accident tied up the streets and we lost a couple of men to helping out." He shivered. "There was blood everywhere."

Lizzie noticed no stains on his pristine suit. But she hadn't forgotten Milano's fierce stare. She decided not to wait around and find out the cause, and slid away toward the door.

"Not so fast, Mzzz. Ort."

What? He made fun of her name, now? Maybe she should leave it alone. She strolled back to center stage. "Yes?"

"This is Detective Grant Guetierrez." He waved his arm, pointing out the fastidious gentlemen who had wiped the sweat from his face and folded the handkerchief precisely before pocketing it. "He will assist me in this investigation."

He added, "Guetierrez, Miss Elizabeth Ort here, will lead you to the location of our one witness. Let me clarify, the woman may have been the one to find the body. It would seem she did not witness the event. Correct, ma'am?"

"Yes." She offered the young detective a gracious smile and ushered him to the door. Miss Miranda Pennywinkle saw the body around seven fifteen this morning. She has been secluded with a friend of ours, Abigail Weiss, until you arrived to question her."

"Thank you ma'am." He oozed charm and Lizzie wasn't too worried, but cautioned anyway. "Please be gentle with her. She's a sensitive person."

They walked together toward the door, chatting amiably as they left. Lizzie responded to the agreeableness, offering friendship and interest. "Isn't Guetierrez an old Visigoth name?"

He puffed up with pride. "Well, ma'am, you sure know your history. It comes from Gunthair and means battle sword."

"The name is reminiscent of war and glory, and control. Quite appropriate for a policeman."

"Yes, it is. And that's why I feel I must pursue a career in this honorable profession and be the best detective I can."

Milano stifled a grunt at the man's audacity. He said, "Miss Ort, ma'am. I'll wait for the ME. Would you mind returning immediately after introducing my assistant to Miss Pennywinkle? We have unfinished business."

* * *

Abby opened the door a crack at the knock. Happy to see she was still there, Lizzie asked, "How's Miranda?"

"Recovered nicely, yet becoming twitchy at the same time, I'm afraid. She told me what happened in a clear voice once the whimpering stopped." Abby let them in.

Lizzie made introductions around and Miranda perked up immensely at the entry of the suave detective. Guetierrez whipped off the thin-as-a-blade Ray Bans again, with a flourish this time, and bowed.

Miranda's bright purplish-blue eyes twinkled. Lizzie muffled a snort as the detective made his move. "Those beautiful eyes remind me of, what's the little flower with the trailing stems? Periwinkle, I think it's called. Do you know it?"

"Yes, pennywinkle is another name for periwinkle. Well, the flower is called many things. Myrtle is one more term." She giggled nervously, not quite forgetting about the body that had her screaming out the door an hour ago. Those nerves escalated as the young woman's voice rose even higher. "So my mom named me Miranda Myrtle Pennywinkle."

He laughed, "It could be worse. I know some one with the initials MNM. Everybody calls her M and M for the candy. I bet you're just as sweet though."

Lizzie noticed a slight shift in the detective's demeanor as he continued, "Would you mind sitting down here and answering a few questions for us?"

Lizzie pulled Abby aside to leave when Detective Milano walked in. "The ME and his crew finally arrived so I came to assist in the interrogation.

Miranda stumbled backward into the offered chair. Guetierrez raised *his* eyes to heaven. Lizzie read his thoughts in his gesture. He'd just calmed her considerably with a quiet discussion and now "the boss" had to ruin everything. She bit her tongue, but not for long. One glance at Abby and her mouth hung open. The girl looked stunned. But the stricken look on *his* face touched her. Detective William Milano was smitten. No doubt in her mind. How strange. The guy had to be almost forty, and must meet a lot of people. Of course, in his line of work, maybe none of them were as appealing as sweet Abby.

Her contagious smile prompted friendliness in others. One to brighten your day. One to make you want to keep her as a friend for your whole life, just to take out and savor on bad days. Lizzie knew it was such an innate part of Abby, she didn't even have to do it anymore to cheer people up. You just knew she smiled inside and that was enough. But not today.

Today, Abby glowed. She slid to the doorway where the detective stood still. Entranced. Abby proffered her hand, in a regal gesture, not unlike one could imagine the Old Testament King David's wife, Abigail, doing centuries ago. "Welcome, my name is Abigail Weiss. And you are?"

Milano, who'd probably stopped cold some of the deadliest beings with his voice alone, stuttered out his name and title.

Lizzie heard Guetierrez clear his throat to speak. Fearing a cutting retort to break the mood, she stared him down. It took but a second. He turned back to Miranda and quietly asked for some basic information to start the interview. Lizzie did a quick mental pat on her own back and moved out of the new couple's line of vision to watch the meeting.

Milano took Abby's hand and spoke. "Maybe you could help us with this investigation?" The voice of the crude interrogator had melted into butter.

Lizzie glanced at the floor, almost expecting to find him there in a puddle. Should she remind these four people about the body in the next room? Or just let things unfold. *Oh what's a body between friends? This is more intriguing.*

Detective Guetierrez stayed with Miranda to finish his questioning while Detective Milano captured Abby's complete attention. Lizzie knew those with the name Abigail tended to be creative and skilled at expressing themselves. Her friend could probably hold her own. She concentrated on the detective.

"Did you know this Alexander Howell?"

How he managed to be suave while discussing a murder victim she didn't know. But he accomplished it. He still gripped the regal hand Abigail offered, and moved her to a secluded chair in the corner as if she was a fragile egg needing protection from the rest of them. "Come. Do you mind telling me a little about him?"

"Why, he's never been here before, but have *I* heard stories. He arrived late. So he wasn't involved in any of the socializing some of the rest of us do before the conference opens."

"He managed to be nasty in just the two days since you opened?"

"Yes, he practically drop-kicked a poor old woman carrying supplies into the main conference room even before we opened. I heard he didn't pick up one thing off the floor, including the poor woman, and just went on his way. It was Delia O'Leary but she leapt up so I didn't get involved."

Lizzie's eavesdropping tripped her into a stifled laugh. Little did they realize even Delia knew self-defense. She wiped the enjoyment off her face before it took voice. *Should I ever tell my dear sister, Delia that she's a "poor old woman"?*

Milano patted Abby's hand and asked her to continue. She said, "I understand he ripped Natalie Turner apart. She's the conference chair and wouldn't let him move his booth to the main entrance at the last minute."

Milano jotted down a note next to the woman's name. She hadn't mentioned the fight when they spoke earlier. Lizzie wondered if he thought it was enough to get the man murdered. Maybe she should warn Natalie. On the other hand, she didn't want him to think she was sneaking out to run away from the police. Funny as it seemed to her— a good upstanding citizen of the USA.

Abby interrupted her thoughts. "Miss Ort there can tell you more. I understand she sure gave him a comeuppance."

Terrific. Now I'm on the spot. I should have been paying attention. But Milano just made a note without even looking at her. *Probably already thought I was a suspect so this didn't surprise him.*

He either had learned that Abby knew little about the "evil ways" of the victim, or planned to talk with her more later. Without removing his eyes from Abby's, he asked for her personal information, not only where and how he could find her during the conference, but her home address. No one could miss the sparkle of joy on his face when he learned she lived in the area.

Requesting that Lizzie sit in front of him after Abby left, he said, "Miss Abigail Weiss claimed she was unfamiliar with this Howell's work. It is *Miss* Weiss, right? She's not married?"

"Correct, she's single."

He returned his eyes to the notepad. "What's this about a 'comeuppance?' "

"He spouted too much vile language to Natalie Turner. I told him to stop. We all departed unscathed."

She knew he'd check with Natalie on her end of the story so left it at that.

Detective Milano persisted. "Are you able to tell me briefly what Telomerase Might is?"

Lizzie sucked in a breath through pursed lips. "I'll try. As a person matures through the stages of life his metabolism changes even though the DNA doesn't. Different genes are triggered at those stages and they control growth, physical, mental, and sexual maturity, and possibly aging. That's the big popular subject now. Aging. With the search through the years, I guess that's not so new after all. Just our knowledge changes. Are you with me so far?"

Milano sat back, straightened his spine and looked down his nose at her, but this time with respect. "Seems like you know your stuff."

"Not like these researchers do."

"Am I missing a motive to kill someone here?"

Lizzie shrugged. "It's new science, just being on the edge of final results in many companies now. Howell, apparently owner of a small, independent company, has pulled out ahead of the pack and produced something for sale."

Milano stood up abruptly. "Now it sounds like a motive for murder."

Lizzie rose also, hands on hips. "Don't jump your guns. Just because some believe that the length of telomeres affect age doesn't mean that whatever he's selling in that little bottle will help you live longer."

Milano tucked the notebook into his shirt pocket. "Ahhh, doesn't matter. As long as someone thought it would. One good point, we found his packing list. Should be able to tell if any is missing."

Lizzie's eyebrows rose. She was going to leave it at that but couldn't resist saying, "Glad I could help detective. No need to thank me."

"Oh, don't you worry. I'll let you know if I want to thank you or arrest you. Because you know of telomeres doesn't let you off the hook. It puts you right in my sights."

He plucked his hat off the table and said. "Guetierrez, come on. You get anything from that interview? Or were you just making eyes at that beautiful woman the whole time?"

The assistant smiled at Lizzie, but trailed Milano out the door. "Yep. She found the body. Doesn't know if any one else saw him before she did. She opened the door with a key. Went in to distribute flyers and stopped when she got to Howell. Can't remember doing anything but scream after that."

"Great! We're just full of facts today." Milano encircled Lizzie's wrist with a firm hand as she followed out the door and attempted to head in the other direction. Let's go this way, back to the crime scene. They should be finishing up by now. We can revisit your last statement. You know. The one about how he died?"

She walked right up to the booth as the ME rose off the floor. She was dying to ask what he discovered but bit her lip. Maybe later. She stopped when Milano jerked on her arm. She'd forgotten he'd grabbed her wrist and hadn't let it go. *I suppose it's better than a handcuff.*

"Stand here and don't move." He motioned the ME to turn their backs to the few remaining men at work, and especially Lizzie. After a couple of minutes of mumbling Milano went back to Lizzie. "Give."

This wasn't time to be coy. She pointed out the skewed nature of the banner and the pole that it was attached to on the left side of the booth. "Take the pole apart—the top part just lifts off."

He told Guetierrez to do it.

"Careful now. Don't touch it," she snapped." They saw what appeared to be blood as soon as the two parts separated. They all looked at Lizzie. Milano said with a deep frown and a scowl, "Mz. Ort?"

She opened her eyes wide. "Power of deduction. It was the only skewed banner in the area. The pole appears to have been replaced improperly."

He circled his hand. "Continue."

"Since there was blood on the back of his neck, that could be his."

They all stared at her.

"I'm just saying. There might be prints on the pole."

It dropped from Guetierrez's hand.

Milano's scowl couldn't get any deeper. He shewed her out the door. "Be seeing you, *ma'am*."

CHAPTER SEVEN

"Guetierrez, quit dragging. We have to make some decisions, quick. Where are you parked?" Milano rushed from the vendor hall with his detective close behind. He walked backwards in front of him, waiting for an answer. Guetierrez stopped and pointed to his car. Milano skidded into a turn when he saw the vehicle.

The man in the neon tie with hair styled just so, rested his elbow in a proud gesture on the hood of an old yellow car. Milano circled it. Something out of a junk yard, maybe? No, it gleamed. He didn't have time to be polite. "Why would you bring this scrap of metal to an investigation? And how did you manage to park on the sidewalk, here, without it getting hauled away or ticketed?"

"This is an oldie known as a 1972 Chrysler Imperial LeBaron. He touched it with a fingertip. The fabric roof is in supreme condition. I've been working on the rest a little at a time. It's like an antique." He pursed his lips in a pout as he rubbed the hood with his shirt sleeve. "And I didn't have time to go pick up a squad car." I thought you'd want me here as soon as possible."

Milano barked. "You were late. I came before you and I had to park in the lot."

"Well, this wonderful woman in a uniform did come by as I got out. I flashed her my badge and she smiled and said she would watch it on her rounds for me."

"It was probably that shit-eating grin you flashed. Now high tail it to the office so we can discuss our next move. I'll meet you there."

Argh. He'd forgotten the accident pile-up. His only consolation—the back roads would have taken just as much time.

Drumming his fingers on the steering wheel while he waited, he rethought the situation in the vendor hall. He probably should have sat down with those sisters, individually, and drilled them on the events and their knowledge of the deceased. He had his best officer finding next of kin, residence and business relationships of the victim. Michael what's-his-name offered to help. They ran back to the office when the tech guys came. He'd heard what he needed to know from the preliminary examination by the time he left. Meanwhile the ME and the tech team stayed behind to finish details and remove the body.

Milano grabbed a mug of coffee on the way to his desk, wishing it was a full egg breakfast but knowing it would have to do. It could be hours before he got autopsy results. He saw his partner on the case slink down the side aisle. "Gutz, get over here."

The man scrambled this time. "Stop calling me Gutz. I don't want the other guys to hear."

One of these days I'm going to slip and call him golden boy. Can't wait till the guys pick that up. "Let's settle down and get something done here. What do you have?"

Before his ass hit the chair his partner had the notebook out, wet his thumb and paged to the spot. "What I've got: "Miranda Pennywinkle didn't do it."

Milano chugged his coffee. "Good. One suspect eliminated. Why?"

"Her eyes. They were too innocent. She was scared, white in the face. Didn't wait to see if the guy was dead. She said when he didn't move and she saw his open eyes she screamed and ran."

"I know you're a cop and all, Guetierrez, but it apparently will surprise you to hear seemingly innocent people, did it, and got scared when they realized what they'd done."

"*I know that.* But she didn't even know who he was. She was sent into the room to drop a flyer on each booth. I checked it out before we left. I picked one up. It looked like about half the booths were covered. She had the rest of the flyers with her in the room where the sisters sequestered her."

"Okay. Continue."

"She shivered whenever we mentioned the body. Her eyes reflect her soul. There was no dead guy in the mirror."

Rubbing his jaw, Milano studied his notes. It was going to be a long day. "We'll move on. Call the resort. See if she has a roommate."

Guetierrez kept his voice low and his head stationed on his notebook. Pen ready. "What do you want me to ask?"

God help me. This is the best you could provide for a partner when good old Jimmy retired? He shook his head and said, "Maybe she or he, can verify whether Miss Pennywinkle was in the room last night. Fat chance since it's a wide expanse of hours until we hear further from the ME. Right now we're guessing anywhere from eleven in the evening till three in the morning. For all we know, the killer could be in Georgia by now."

Laughing as he wrote down the hours, Guetierrez said, "Who in their right mind would go to Georgia heading into the muggy season?"

"Georgia is beautiful in February." Milano paused a second. "Except when they're having a blizzard like a couple years ago. Anyway, think Gutz. Who says the killer is in his right mind?"

Gutz gulped. Milano finished. "Besides, I didn't specifically mean Georgia. Just anywhere but here."

"Oh."

Milano plowed on, hoping for the best. "We also need another interview with Miss Ort. And it wouldn't hurt to talk with her sister again, Mrs. O'Leary. There's something fishy about the two of them. Especially that Ort lady. Did you see her tell me where the murder weapon was?"

Eyes wide, Guetierrez kept a straight face. "The nerve of her."

Milano's growl didn't come from his stomach, even though it could have. He turned the page. "Items to check. You're on for these unless I say otherwise.

Find out what happened with the surveillance cameras. The officer I sent to get a copy said the cameras weren't functioning. We need more specifics. And who was responsible to keep them functioning? Find that out."

"You must have sent Jerry to check, right?"

"You're learning Gutz."

"Boss, please. No Gutz. It's Grant, Guetierrez, partner. No Gutz."

Milano flipped the page in his notebook and kept writing. He took a second to give the man a grin. Okay. I'll try Grant. Now, were all the doors into the room locked last night and this morning? By whom?"

"Miranda said . . ."

His words were interrupted by a loud whoa from Milano. "Hey man, we're on a case here. I believe her name is Miranda Pennywinkle, which means Miss Pennywinkle to you."

"But she said to call her Miranda. Did you know she was a specialist in nutritional herbology?"

"Will the tea leaves tell us who the killer was?"

Grant couldn't miss his torrid glare. "And as I was about to say, she said she was given a key to the room by the chair of the event, Natalie Truman, uh, Miss Truman, who was there in the hall."

Milano shook his head. He saw Grant writing notes. Milano watched, happy the man was catching on. "One more question. How did Howell get in if all the doors are locked?"

"The security guard said if he was killed last night before midnight, he must have been inside, maybe with the killer. He said he checked himself, and all the doors were locked. He went off duty shortly after, so we don't know about the early hours of the morning."

"Okay. Some progress. Where's the person in charge after that?"

"I'm waiting for the call. Guess they had to find him. He stays here at the resort. A few of the employees prefer to do that. He wasn't in his room."

"Anyone find that suspicious?"

"I did ask. I got a chuckle bordering on a snort."

"When we get the official autopsy report, find the man. Can't pin him down until we know more on the time."

Guetierrez closed his notebook and looked up. "Know how he died?"

"I'm betting on a bash to the head from the banner pole. But again, we wait for the autopsy."

His partner rose.

"Sit. we need to compile a list of all the people he knew. We start interviewing right away."

Guetierrez sat. "Do we start with the old ladies? Or maybe Abigail Weiss? They knew the guy.

Milano stretched out his legs. "I need more ammo for those three. Let's begin with the chair of the conference. She's the person who sent Miss Pennywinkle in there this morning. And she was inside the room when I arrived."

"That doesn't mean she didn't kill him earlier."

"True. The others said she'd just arrived. We'll confirm the meeting she claims she was in. She left before the tech team came but asked permission to leave to handle repercussions regarding Howell's death."

A shout crossed the room. "Milano, call for you. The conference chair has some urgent questions. Can you pick up?"

Milano reached for the phone. "Perfect timing."

Beefy ole Harry from the reception desk bellowed in just as the other cop quit. "And the head of the Neptune's Oasis Resort is on line two."

"Okay, Harry. I'm right here. You know you don't have to tell the whole office."

"Sorry, I forget."

"Grant, take the resort call. I'll snag the this one."

He turned away from his partner and gave a firm, but polite, hello. The woman sounded so much in control he thought she might pass out from the strain. Her worry palpitated the line. He responded quickly. "Yes, I know my men have blocked off the vendor hall. Someone was killed in there."

Her crisp words sharpened even more but the speed increased and the sound rose high. He cut her off. "I realize you have a conference to run. Can't you route everything around the vendor hall?"

Her response wailed through the line. He interrupted again. "Ma'am hold the committee off for a few more hours. Meanwhile, we need to talk with you. Could you come to the department immediately?"

When he finally hung up he noticed Grant's mile-wide grin. "What's with you?"

"I got the easy call. He wanted to know what was going on and could we get rid of the cop cars. They were scaring people away."

"And . . .what did you tell him?" He shoved his hands in his pockets to prevent strangling his partner.

"Like I said, easy. I told him I didn't know, and I didn't know. He'll probably be back on the line in less than ten minutes. You need an answer."

Milano threw his pen on the desk. "I'm getting something to eat. When Miss Truman comes in, could you please make her comfortable in an interrogation room? And if your friend, Resort Guy, calls back, tell him we're investigating a murder and no, the cop cars stay. Eventually, we'll park them in a more discreet location. Make that answer work."

Detective Corporal Milano knew better than to leave his young detective alone too long with a woman, any woman. He'd been starved but raced through lunch so fast he wasn't sure what he ate. His stomach had stopped rumbling and he made it back in fifteen minutes. Even the gallivant Guetierrez couldn't do harm so quickly.

However, one step toward the interrogation room and he had second thoughts. He engineered a knock and shuffle at the door to barely resemble a polite entry. Thank heavens he hadn't taken time to chew his food. He introduced himself ever so agreeably. "May I borrow Detective Guetierrez for a moment? We'll be right back."

He ushered out his partner and the man knew what was coming. He held his hands defensively in front of him and said, "I behaved. Honest."

Milano looked in his eyes and believed him. He knew the Hun and Visegoth in the man was well buried over the centuries, but it didn't stop him from wondering how often the present man needed to own up to his libidinous nature in confession.

Instead his partner asked, "What do you think of her smile? The best, huh?"

"She wasn't smiling when I talked with her this morning."

"Hey, I didn't step out of line. I'm a professional cop!"

"Gutz!"

"Okay, but all I did was appreciate. Didn't even speak out of line. Her smile appears such an innate part of her you knew she couldn't fake such gentle sweetness. She didn't do it."

Milano shook his head. It would fall off if he spent much more time around his partner without a break. "What questions have you asked her?"

"Just the opening ones. She claims she was in a meeting late, than dealing with confused attendees. Figured we could check those out later. But she brought along the victim's vendor registration. Pretty smart, huh."

"Any more?"

"Getting to it when you barged in."

With raised eyebrows, Milano opened the door and immediately initiated the official interview.

Natalie Truman provided crisp answers with no subterfuge. She'd apparently never met the guy before the morning when he showed up late to set up his booth. "That man was rude, bad-mannered and foul-mouthed. I'm glad Lizzie came by."

Her tale of the confrontation between her and Howell and Miss Elizabeth "Lizzie" Ort was a doozy.

Guetierrez couldn't resist. "Did she really fake having a gun?"

The smile teased back out again for a second, until seriousness blanketed it. "Sure did. And she looked comfortable."

Before Milano could question her firm statement, she defended her friend, "I've never seen her with a gun. And she put him to shame over his offensive language. She's one of the finest people I know."

"This is the first year you've been chair of the what-cha-call-it —" He looked at his notes. "The Health Naturally Conference?"

"Yes, but I've worked on it for years. My mother developed the conference when I was young."

He glanced at his partner, who wiggled his brows. She didn't look a day over thirty.

"Was this man at any of the earlier conferences?"

"No; besides, his product is too new to have been all over yet. It certainly wasn't available last year."

When asked about the product itself, she hesitated. "I'm afraid I don't understand a lot of it. Most of our vendors sell herbal items or formulations. The 'Telomerase Might' is more complex. And the main ingredient is considered an herb."

She offered them copies of his submission information and a few articles she'd printed off the internet for them. Milano glanced at them, before looking back up at her. "So you only understand some of this, huh?" He smiled. It felt like the first one of his day considering how his lips cracked. But she got the idea.

"Ask me which herb helps your digestion or eases a bruise and I'm right there, but this stuff? No way." She shook her head in apparent dismay. "Beyond me."

Milano's stomach grumbled. "What do I do for digestion?"

She responded, "Eat."

They laughed but she immediately added, "Try bromelain, or eat pineapple."

"Thanks. Now I'm curious. What do you do to ease a bruise, like if I hit my partner here and he wants to hide it?"

Guetierrez reared back in a joking gesture. Natalie's face lit up, but her voice spoke in serious tones. "Arnica gel is great, but St. John's wort oil shrinks tissue, too."

He pointed to Guetierrez and said, "Make note, just in case." He handed him the papers she'd brought and said, "Please take these to Timothy. If he can't decipher it, no one here can."

When the door closed, he pivoted back to her and saw the scowl. "What?"

"Is it my turn yet? Because I need to know *now* what to do with this conference. Are you shutting us down?"

CHAPTER EIGHT

Despite the temptations out the wide window facing her, Lizzie sat focused at the quaint desk in the corner of their suite. Her pencil stub flew across the sheet as she made notes for her speech the next day. The computer never talked to her like paper and pencil did, and today she needed inspiration.

"Lizzy, why don't you fix your messy bun?"

"My hair's not messy. What's gotten into you?" Lizzie scratched out the last word as she spoke.

Delia walked behind her at the table and poked at her hair. She explained, "It is falling out more than it should. But I meant the messy bun style doesn't suit you."

"Okay, stop calling my hair messy. Because you like the sleek and formal look doesn't mean I have to."

Delia sniffed. "That just goes to show you're not sophisticated, or even up on the latest hair styles. The messy bun is a style. Looks less formal. The old buns pulled women's hair so tight their eyes looked Oriental even on salt-of-the-earth Americans."

Lizzy spun around on the desk chair so fast she went 360 degrees before stopping.

She grabbed Delia's hand as an anchor.

"That was fun." She put on her serious face. "I wore these buns years before they became the craze. And this fad will move on into twilight hair or some such nonsense and I'll still be wearing my hair this way."

Delia looked out the bank of windows. Lizzie knew she wished to be out there in the sun. Her sister looked like the typical old lady, no way to hide the skin wrinkled by years of living. She may appear staid, but instead she was steadfast. People could trust her with their lives. And for Lizzie, more importantly, with their secrets. She needed to remember how important Delia was to her, and give in a little. Spend time with her. The years moved too fast to wait.

Eyes wide and steady, Delia looked at Lizzie, "Sister, dear, leave your speech writing for a little while. We could go check out some of the wonderful salons." She swirled her long skirt around as she turned, her whole face lighting up with an obvious new enticement. "And restaurants. They have marvelous sea food in the area."

She stepped to the side and offered her hand, as if she felt her younger, agile sister, needed help out of the chair. You choose where to eat, and you could have your hair snipped a little, maybe styled a little, for your talk tomorrow."

Lizzy rose and placing hands at her waist, stretched. "We took a walk on the beach yesterday. Won't that do?"

Delia came over and rubbed her sister's back. She nestled her head between Lizzie's shoulder blades and wheedled, "Please?"

Turning slowly, Lizzie tilted her face to look down at her shorter sister. "Can't we do something else? You get me out on a commercial strip and you'll end up wandering into each store even though there is nothing you need to buy."

"I won't. I promise. We can go out for a quick lunch, have your hair done, and come back. You don't need to prepare for your talk. You've presented it dozens of times."

Lizzie reached for her light weight jacket and humphed, "Don't dawdle. What's keeping you?"

Some would not think a jacket essential on this balmy day. Her old body could move like the wind when it needed to, but it still liked a little help keeping those bones warm. She swung her enormous bag over her shoulder and marched out.

Delia patted her hair and smiled. "Great, we'll be just in time for your appointment."

Lizzie narrowed her eyes at the subterfuge, and searched the busy street for the least commercial strip. She people-watched as they strolled toward the restaurants. "St. Pete Beach sure has everything right here, from beachcombers and businessmen to shops for hot yoga, and tattoos. Just look at those tattoos." Her head swiveled to follow one inked guy in what they called a beater shirt in days gone by, but knew they no longer used such terms. *Strange. You couldn't use the word, but it was apparently still okay to do the deed. Life around her was changing. She wondered if any of it was for the good.*

Delia laughed as Lizzie prodded her along with a gentle but firm touch at the elbow. She'd been staring at two women in the hair salon they passed, and commented, "And the hottest hair stylists this side of the equator."

The frown on Lizzie's face said it all. Before she could complain, Delia promised, "Don't worry, I didn't tell them to turn your hair into purple spikes."

"Pshaw. You can see those back home, too. Learn to look beneath to the brain."

"Sometimes I think the brains shrink during teen years," Delia said as she visually followed a teenage girl.

They studied menus posted in restaurant windows and only glanced at other stores. It was Lizzie's turn to gawk but she kept walking. "Was that a gun shop we just passed?"

"No, dear. It was a novelty store with toy guns for kids."

Lizzie sniffed. "You're moving too fast. How can I see anything?"

"If I'd known you wanted to saunter along like a tourist I would have allowed more time. But we need to find a good restaurant to serve us fast, before your appointment." Her words sliced, but Lizzie saw the smile lurking behind them. Delia probably figured they'd traded places, tourist-wise.

Lizzie picked up her pace. "Okay. I guess I have guns on my mind. And I know there's over fifty gun shops around here. I was just surprised to see what looked like one between a restaurant and a deli."

"How do you know how many? Never mind. Maybe you should find a local shop. The real thing looks much better in your pocket."

Lizzie stuffed her hands in her pockets and studied the look. "Delia, you heard about that?"

"Of course. I"m your older sister. People tell me about you."

"You know I rarely keep my gun in a pocket."

Delia answered, "Well, it sounds like you think there are people here who inspire such thoughts. Any others besides Mr. Howell?" She quickly backed off from Lizzie's frown, hands held up. Sorry, I haven't met any one else so far. . . .and to be frank, I didn't find him that offensive the one time I met him."

Lizzie dropped the frown, it was fake anyway. Telling Delia it was Howell who knocked her over was not an option. Bad discussion in public. She studied the sidewalk as they moved along. "It's early days yet. I sure hope his death doesn't cause trouble."

Totally ignoring the murder, Delia said, "Thank heavens that nice detective didn't close down the conference and opened the vendor hall later the same day."

"Delia, I can't pin anything down, but something's bothering me."

"You're being a little ominous for a lighthearted herbal conference. Anything specific?"

"No,. But it's hanging heavy on me. Since Abby lives in town, you think she has her car at the conference?"

"Who knows. We've only been here a few days. Are you feeling hemmed in already? I mean, we're only bordered by the whole ocean on one side. Should be enough room, don't you think?"

As usual, Lizzie ignored the snide question from her older sister. That woman just wouldn't let go of the, "I'm the eldest, I have to take care of you," thing. Do the math. What difference could one year over a span of eighty matter? So instead, she tucked Abby's possible car idea away for another time.

In between smart food banter and reading about the listed menus, they talked of Lizzie's speech. Despite Delia's comment about Lizzie knowing the topic quite well, Lizzie always attempted a unique introduction and some new and profound information.

"And what is the shocker this time?" Delia asked. She'd stopped dead still on the sidewalk and let others walk around her as she waited for Lizzie's answer.

Her sister saw her puckered brow and knew the cause but played dumb. "You have a concern?"

"Yeah, sis. I sure do. What goes? You seem more smug than usual."

Lizzie hammed it up, clutching her hands to her chest. "You wound me." She dropped the drama and continued walking before too many people had to step aside. Delia followed and they studied more menus. She was anxious to try out the highly-acclaimed local fish, whereas Delia inserted her reading glasses low on her nose each time and looked for Italian—anything Italian. You'd think they'd had different parents the way they held such diverse interests, even in food. Well, not in herbs. They both loved anything herbal.

They found the perfect dining spot featuring each of their preferences. As they were seated at a sidewalk table off the main street, Lizzie commented, "Food dominates my thoughts lately. Maybe we could find time for laps in the pool early tomorrow morning?"

She felt Delia hesitate. Finally, her wise sister asked, "How early is early?"

Shaking with laughter, Lizzie said, "Okay, I'll compromise. Say, eight?"

Delia shivered and opened her menu. Lizzie executed her normal haggling over what herbs should be used, stressing the addition of lots of oregano.

Lizzie stared at the folks strolling down the main street. "Look at all the white hair. We fit in perfectly."

Her sister giggled, "Yeah, but there's a lot of bald heads, too. It could be worse." "Those who sport braids and surfer hair stand out like pumpernickel bread on a burger. The Health Naturally Conference attracts many types of people—but I didn't notice any of the surfer hair."

Delia may look scatter-brained but Lizzie knew better. And she never let go of an idea, like now. She tore off a piece of bread with nonchalance before the frontal attack. "What sort of scandal will you cause with your speech, this time?"

"No scandal, but don't you wonder how many ancient peoples survived when imbibing herbs? Some hit the top of the list of poisons these days."

"So you're going to tell the audience members how to poison themselves?"

Lizzie grunted. "Of course not. But you know we tell how herbs were used as medicine in the Old Testament, and ancient Egypt around 1000 B.C. We tout it to prove herbs must have value since their uses have endured for so long."

The arrival of their food only caused a blip in Lizzie's tale. She was on a tear. A slight smile to the waitress and she continued, "Now they're saying pollen from eight plant species found in the 60,000-year-old Neanderthal burial site was from burrows of small rodents rather than from relatives of the deceased as a send-off. We all hoped they were herbs."

When Delia looked at her but didn't say anything, she added, "You know, the SHANIDAR-4 in Iraq?"

"Sure, sis. 60,000-year-old Iraq is always on my night-time reading list."

"It should be. It puts me in a real bind. Here I am, scheduled to talk about ancient herbal remedies and that news quite softens the information."

Delia was delicately picking out the offending bits of okra in her salad but managed to say. "Sister, you know there is tons of data to back up your premise. The highly touted Smithsonian reported archaeologists finding evidence of flowers in 12,000-year-old cemetery graves. Isn't that old enough for you?"

"Or I could just say, 'Rodents liked herbs 60,000 years ago and those critters are still around. Herbs for longevity.' "

Lizzie could tell her rant had lost its steam so she finished off her lunch with relish. She studied the dessert table like it was a computer formula in need of decoding. Delia must have misunderstood her intense expression. "Something else bothering you Lizzie? You haven't been yourself since you returned home this last time."

When I looked at her I realized how deep my thoughts have been, over more than the lemon crème pie versus the chocolate mousse. Maybe I could share a little. How to begin? "You know I've had nightmares since I returned from Southeast Asia."

"Have you had them here, in Florida?"

Lizzie pointed out the pie to the server and offered the mousse to Delia. She took it graciously and waited.

"No. No nightmares here. It got me thinking. I really want to help with this investigation. Must help. Yet I want to heal, too. And I need to do good, make retribution."

"Lizzie, you have done good all your life. Your work, which you did tirelessly, helped thousands of people, hundreds of thousands."

"But Burma. . ."

"No but Burma. That guy in Burma was not your fault. Sleep dreamlessly."

"Dreamlessly? No one eye open in case something is happening around me?"

"Right. Now let's go and enjoy ourselves."

Lizzie rose, left some bills for a tip and went to pay at the front desk. "Easy for you to say. You're not going to put *your* head under the knife."

"Scissors. Not a knife."

"I've done some pretty serious things with scissors."

Delia linked arms and laughed instead of following the thread. Fun, remember."

They joined the streams of people on the sidewalk and rushed to keep the salon appointment. "It's nice to see such a range of ages. Maybe there's someone here for dear Natalie. Or delightful Abby. I'd put Detective Milano in the running for her."

Delia giggled. "Do we look like matchmakers? If so, we need to get another line of work." She raised her eyebrows and marched ahead. But she added, "The old dudes stroll in the sun. The young dudes flaunt their abs on the beach and at the bar. For a few years there I wondered if any new blood would step up at the conference with an infusion before us old timers all died off. I'm glad we have some younger people like Natalie and Abby taking leadership roles."

Lizzie threw in an exasperated sigh about the constant age reminder, but agreed. "It looks like this year's conference will be the most exciting ever."

CHAPTER NINE

"Lizzie, for heaven's sake. Hurry up."

"Keep quiet. Someone will hear you. It takes more than a second to pick a lock, Delia."

Delia craned her neck to see past the corner of the hallway, then swiveled her head in a rapid check of the other direction. "Why didn't we just ask our friend Geraldine to get us a key?"

"And give her a megaphone at the same time?"

Lizzie turned the knob and strode through the door, jerking Delia in behind her. She peered out the crack she'd left. Didn't see a soul. Not even a soft click signaled the closing. *Humph. I'm still good at some things.* "Delia, how many people do you think we should tell we're searching Howell's room?"

Her sister sniffed, nose in the air. "Why, none of course."

"You get my point. Please stand by the door and let me get a feel for things."

"Hey, this is your game. I'm a bystander sucked in. Just tell me if you need my help."

Lizzie stood in silence and absorbed. Scents, feelings and vibes lingered from the past few days. She'd allowed the cops a day to do their search, since she wasn't interfering. Now the accumulated personalities filtering throughout the room twanged the vibes beyond communication. *So much for not interfering.*

Still, Lizzie smelled tomatoes, and said so. Strange. The man hadn't been there for a day. "Would the cops bring food in here? Dumb question. I'm sure not. I'm rushing, not thinking. Hopefully, Detective Milano searched the room before they cleaned."

Delia moved closer to the trash can. "Looks like they halted the cleaning all together for now. Though there's only one paper plate in the can. Smells like the source of your tomato scent."

Lizzie agreed, while frisking half-heartedly through the suitcase open on the bed. She knew the sheriff's office had already been here so figured there wasn't anything in it. She still hoped she'd find a significant note, an item, a tiny piece of evidence to lead her in a direction toward the killer.

"Start searching the drawers, dear."

"What is it we hope to find?"

Lizzie offered a few of her jumbled thoughts in an effort to keep Delia in the loop. But she wasn't used to working with a partner on such things, and she didn't have a loop. Yet. "I'd like to learn as much as we can about Alexander Howell. What brought him here, what he wanted to gain from the conference, how he spent his time in the few days since he arrived."

Delia methodically worked her way through each item in the top drawer. "Well, if it helps, he wore boxer shorts. Other than that I'm not gathering much about the guy from here. I'll keep looking."

Attempting to squelch a laugh, Lizzie stood back and studied the desk top. It sat bare, unrevealing of any breakthrough science. She searched the small drawer. It held only a wrinkled napkin. Maybe the police didn't bar the cleaning crew from touching the room. The napkin, once unfurled, held nothing—not one smudge and certainly no clue. The hotel portfolio of amenities available, and places to visit, contained a few nooks and crannies. With meticulous care, she pulled out each section, but only found a note that Crabby Bills couldn't be beat for a fine place to eat.

"Delia, guess what?"

Her sister looked up with bright attention. "You found something."

"Sorry, didn't mean to ring a false alarm. Just wanted to say this guy thought Crabby Bills was great. We both love Crabby Bills but I doubt if this is a break-through clue. Remind me to plan a meal there real soon, though."

"Oh bother." Delia riffled another drawer. "This one's empty."

She closed it with barely a sound. "I'd love to go there." Her voice came out muted as she leaned down to tug on the bottom drawer. "But next time let's hope you've found something. You know I hate this breaking in. This is a great resort. I'd be horrified if they banned us from coming here again."

Lizzie snorted and returned to the portfolio, seeking anything unusual. She closed it in defeat and flipped through the notepad the resort provided at each phone. She held it sideways to the light. Not an etch mark on it. Either he never used the thing, or he wrote with such a gentle touch it didn't go through the paper. Sitting down on the bed she cleared her mind to think. "We're out of leads. Well, we really haven't had any, have we?"

Delia didn't answer.

Still pondering, Lizzie mumbled a list of their attempts at finding the killer. "Miranda couldn't remember anything more than she'd already told us. Natalie said Howell requested to stay late in the hall rearranging his booth. The security guy supposedly locked all the doors after everyone else left. Was the killer still in there?"

She rose and continued, "This search was my last hope. I wonder if the police confiscated his papers, or if someone else did."

Delia, still hunched over the lower drawers closed the bottom one in a smooth and silent move, then stretched her spine. "You mean right after they killed him and before the police got here?" Her eyes followed Lizzie to the closet. "The timing is off dear. That is quite unlikely. Besides, how do you know he had any notes?"

She received a quick glare over her sister's shoulder before Lizzie said, "He may have been many things, but he was a scientist. I doubt if he could live a day without at least doodling the periodic table."

Delia sniffed, "The police probably found his notebooks. She stooped to strip the bed, searched it and remade it while her sister explored the closet. Lizzie stopped for a moment to watch in amazement. Such things were beyond her. She could have stripped it in seconds. Putting it back together neatly took her much longer. But she knew how to search, and did so efficiently through every inch of the closet. She'd even tried to pry up the carpeting in the corners—prime hiding spots. She pulled out some dry cleaning still in the bag.

From the date, she could tell it had been delivered past noon today. It must have come after the police searched the room. What luck.

But what were the odds it was a clue? She remembered the scene in the hotel room in *North by Northwest*. Right away they learned the clothes were much too short to fit Cary Grant. She pictured how high Howell reached when they'd talked in the vendors' hall. "I think he was about five foot seven inches tall. These look just right. No clue here."

She saw Delia shake her head in consternation and move on to the refrigerator, while she removed the suit from underneath the cleaning bag and found a note from the cleaner pinned to the top. It said they found a scrap of paper in the pocket. They attached it with their cleaning company note. The small scrap held a Chicago phone number on it.

"Let's hustle. Maybe this number will lead us somewhere."

Delia closed the refrigerator door after checking the freezer. "Well, at least you found something. The refrigerator only held beer —and the cheap kind, too. Looks like the guy put all his money into his product."

They both looked around with care, saw nothing was amiss, and tiptoed to the door. Lizzie opened it one crack at a time, but swooshed it closed with quiet force. It almost took off Delia's nose since she'd peeked out underneath Lizzie's arm. Her sister back-peddled but pursed her lips to keep from making any noise. Lizzie raised her eyes to heaven and whispered a "Thank you, God, for such a smart sister." They moved to a corner of the room and Lizzie hissed, "I hear voices out there down the hall. Call me crazy, but one sounded like that detective."

Delia said, "Let me rush down the hall the other way."

"And, that helps how?"

"We could both run and try to leave. But if he caught you with the note he'd arrest you."

"Okay, got it. Then what will you do?"

"I'll stand in front of one of those doors way down near the corner. When they confront me I'll cause a commotion. With luck, you can sneak out. You know, *before* he sees you."

Lizzie looked upward, "And God, thank you for making her a quick thinker." She patted Delia on the back while moving her to the door. "Go for it."

Delia escaped unseen and walked a dozen doors down in her ballet-slipper shoes, then marched back and forth, back and forth, patting her watch, and glancing up and down the hall. Detective Milano couldn't help but see her and stopped. Lizzie heard the whole performance from the crack in her door. But she couldn't discern emotion, or intent, just words. Delia put on a prime performance. "Too bad you already have a case, officer."

He waited.

She nodded, like he should know how she'd finish. Finally, she added, "Or I could hire you to find my sister. I can't imagine where she is."

Delia glanced at her watch. Peeked down the hall. "She's late. She's late. We were to meet." Lizzie could sense her trying to draw the man and his assistant in the other direction as the voices faded. She looked him in the eye. "To meet with the executive board."

Hah! He was falling for it. Detective Corporal William Milano braced her arm as if she was about to faint, and assured her not to worry. He had to spoil it by saying, "You don't *hire* the police, ma'am. And I'm sure your sister isn't lost."

With his hand shoring her up, Delia turned them both to walk down the hall and around the corner where the nearest elevator was located. She barely heard Delia say she'd wait a while longer and he and two men descended. Lizzie heard nothing more.

A couple of restless minutes later, Delia rapped the secret knock lightly on Howell's door and Lizzie darted out. They raced down the hall in the opposite direction, only to bump head first into Milano, who was standing there waiting for them.

Lizzie stopped so abruptly, her Deer Stag shoes, designed for stealth, squeaked. *Jeesh, the man must have wings.* Delia managed a little more aplomb and shuffled to a standstill before running him over.

He smirked. There was no disguising it. Not a polite smile. It was a smirk. Lizzie just waited. He said, "I thought it would be more beneficial to see what you found. Better than trapping you sitting in his room twiddling your thumbs, or eating a clue before I got in."

She noticed Delia shrug and open her eyes wide, trying to indicate she didn't have any idea what he was talking about. He ignored her, anyway, and zeroed in on Lizzie. He held out his hand, palm up. She stalled. *Will they search me?* They'd find whose phone it was easier than she could. Cell phones made such things more difficult. And she could inveigle the info out of him later.

He didn't appear to like her stalling tactics. Grabbing Lizzie's arm, none too gently, he walked her into the elevator, and once on the main floor, out the door. Delia followed with the officer.

Lizzie was more concerned with what he may have found in the room. When he wouldn't answer her questions but steered her toward his car, she said, "Did you check the Bible?"

The look he gave her could frizz her hair. Too bad she hated perms.

He glanced over at the officer with him, raising one eyebrow. The man made a barely imperceptible nod. Milano turned back to Lizzie. "What do you think I am? Of course I checked it. And I ask the questions here. Move forward. We're taking you in."

"Just asking. There wasn't anything in there when I looked. What did you find?"

"Nothing," he blurted.

She had him shouting. *Good. Rattled is good. Maybe he'll let something leak.*

"Heck. You should look again. You'll find worthwhile stuff in there, like in Matthew 6:14. Jesus shows us what forgiveness is: 'For if you forgive others their trespasses, your heavenly Father will also forgive you.' Just saying. Words worth thinking about."

She peeked under her lashes at him as they walked. Oops. It didn't work. Not rattled. Furious. Well, it had been worth a try. Could be he didn't catch the similarities to the Bible quote in this situation.

When they arrived at his car he ducked her head into his back seat. The other detective told Delia to stay out of trouble and motioned her to walk away. She stood her ground. "How come you're taking Lizzie and not me?"

The officer shrugged.

Lizzie raised her eyes to the car roof. *Dumb, sister. Dumb. Take off before they change their mind.* Meanwhile, Milano answered before he climbed into the car. "So I suppose it was all your idea?" Confusion flooded her face. Lizzie could see her debating whether to lie. Fortunately, her sister knew better than to lie this time. She didn't do it well. She waved goodbye.

Lizzie looked around inside the car. It wasn't super clean. Still, no weapon in sight. Strange. No cage. Was she being arrested? Maybe he's having second thoughts? Or maybe he just thinks an old lady won't give him much of a fight. *Heck. Won't need a weapon. With his neck right in front of me.* She noticed a slight smile and a twinkle in his eyes when he glanced in at her, then shut the door.

CHAPTER TEN

"Well now, Miz Elizabeth 'Lizzie' Ort, would you like to tell me what you were doing in Alexander Howell's room?"

"Just looking around."

Detective Corporal William Milano stood, arms braced behind his back. He reined in his anger, yet couldn't help but raise his voice. "Someone killed this man. This could put you at the top of the suspect list. Should I take you to an interrogation room and record your confession?"

When she didn't answer, he approached her chair, where she sat relaxed in his office. An officer had placed her there just minutes ago and stood with her until Milano could interview her. He wanted her to stew but didn't have the time. Maybe he *should* have her installed in a proper interrogation room to instill some fear. Yet, if he judged her correctly, this woman feared little, and certainly not him.

He needed a way to reach her, already a burr in his side and he'd barely met her. Anger wouldn't work, though it came with no effort right now. Maybe camaraderie.

"Do we do a search or do you want to tell me what you found?" Milano realized he hadn't quite mastered the friendly approach as he twirled the pen in his hand, and turned his back to her. He gave her a minute to answer, then turned to face her.

She fixed him with a glance so sharp it could skewer a flea. "What makes you think I found something?" She didn't look away.

He walked around the desk and sat across from her. "Playing games? My men are researching your entire background now. I don't need their report to know you are not just some old lady herbalist."

Both eyebrows reached to her hairline and her lips pursed, but she didn't respond to his "old lady" comment. He knew it could be considered rude. Lady was polite under the circumstances. On the other hand, she'd passed her eightieth birthday. He already had that much info. Some would consider her old. He had the feeling that she didn't.

She said, "Explain how you know I found something."

He'd asked her not to play games. He decided it was time for him to talk straight, too. "Okay, you are someone who knows what she's doing. You break into a hotel room, leave not a mark, and send out your sister as a decoy while you try to escape with the crucial find."

She kept silent. He continued. "Now you could be devious enough to give your sister the evidence, knowing I'd go after you, but I don't think so."

She settled back. And dropped her guard. She might actually tell him the truth for once. She asked, "Why go after me and not Delia?"

He held out his hand, palm up, and notched fingers into his fist as he counted. "You reportedly had an altercation with the man when he arrived. Maybe even had a gun."

The second finger went in. "You knew he had blood on his neck, not visible seeing him from above as he lay."

The third finger followed. "You knew where the murder weapon was."

She interrupted. "But, I did tell you where it was, maybe saving you days of searching."

"Could have been a ploy, to throw my suspicions off."

She smiled. "Is that it, or are you going to complete a fist and hit me with it?"

He rose and took slow steps to her side of the desk. "We don't work that way any more. Not a rubber hose in sight."

Her laugh cracked for a second, then disappeared. "Detective, do you suspect me of this murder?"

"Ma'am, I don't know what to think. I heard you intimidated the man the day before he died. Even a pretend gun is a threat."

Lizzie wiggled around in the chair. I'll never live down that fake gun. A real one would have been less of a problem."

"Why the need for a gun?"

"His language offended me on Natalie's behalf. But when I saw him move to grab her, he displayed a dangerous glare in his eyes. I thought the gun intruded less than a karate chop to the neck."

He stared at her, mouth open. Clamping it shut, he said, "Oh, okay."

She nodded, as if he finally understood. He added, "And you want to know why I suspect you of killing him? But I haven't forgotten the immediate reason why we're here. He opened his fist and held his hand right up to her face. "Hand over whatever you found. Now." He was startled when the woman seemed amused.

She didn't move.

Without taking his eyes off her, he phoned an officer to request the report on Miss Ort. A woman in uniform approached the desk with an accelerated walk just a minute later. He made introductions. "Miss Ort, this is Officer Laurie Nederhoff."

She handed the report over. "Sorry, boss. This is all we could get." She left a lot faster than she came. Milano didn't have to look at the folder to know it would be bad news. The woman's earlier tight lips burst into a full-fledged smile while he studied the report.

"Ma'am, in your earlier career . . ."

She sputtered. He heard the sound in her throat but she restrained it. He wondered what she thought he was going to say, but continued as he'd begun. "In your earlier career, before hampering my life and my investigation, did you know what redacting is?"

"Of course."

He slammed the pages down. Though they made little noise, he felt better. A bit. "Most of these pages are blacked out. What little there is here. You have anything to say?"

"I'm one of the good guys?"

"Was the question mark for me, or are you unsure?"

She stood abruptly and looked out his tiny window. He let her.

"I may not be lily white, but I have been one of the good guys for a very long time, or so they claimed. Right now, I'm an herbalist. One who feels this serene and healing world should not have been tainted with murder. I want to find who did this as much as you do." She faced him.

He saw the truth in her whole demeanor. The trouble was, what did he do about it? And was this another dead end?

She whirled around and pulled a scrap of paper from a hidden pocket in her skirt. She stuck out her hand. "Here it is. Just a phone number, but a useful one," she said with a hopeful inflection. "It's not on any of his literature."

He glanced at the number and didn't even ask how she knew. He called in Nederhoff again. "Contact the Chicago police. Find out what you can about this. It's connected with the Howell case. And urgent." Officer Nederhoff looked at the number as she double-timed out of the room. "On it, boss."

Before Milano could speak, Lizzie asked, "Did you discover anything from the search of his home and business?"

He settled back in his chair and crossed his right leg over his knee. "Chicago's out of our jurisdiction."

"But you had it searched. What did they find?"

"I'm supposed to ask the questions here. Let's start. Who are you?"

"I'm one of the main speakers at this conference because of my expertise in herbs and herbal history."

He stared at her. She knew the technique. Probably used it herself. But she finally answered the unasked question.

Her secret smile was now only half ambiguous. "I worked with the government a while back."

Officer Nederhoff knocked this time and rushed in, delaying his decision.

"What now ???"

The woman offered him a sheaf of papers. "You know Venezia, sir. He can decipher anything to discern answers. He gathered a ton of stuff on this telomerase from Howell and a few hundred other scientists, but finding what it has to do with this conference and his death, well, you look at it. Maybe you can tell him where to go from here.

Milano studied the papers and grimaced. The double-time had

slowed to half-time as the officer realized he wouldn't have an answer soon and left the room. He continued to read, this time out loud. "Telomeres are necessary for gene stability. They protect the ends of chromosomes from degradation."

He lifted his head and stared at her. "You have a handle on this stuff?"

Her face tightened, revealing the wrinkles of age, but opened, as she decided to cooperate. "I'm sorry. I'm an herbalist. This only borders on herbal subjects. I do know a little, because, as when drugs are involved, herbs long ago had already done some of the work."

Milano frowned. "Could you attempt to target the situation for our purposes?"

She continued, "Ignoring as much of it as we can, it's a question of how does the body know how old it is? Our metabolism changes as we age. Since genes control growth and development, they control aging."

She had his attention now. "Before I jump to conclusions, can you tell me a little more?"

"These enzymes perform a number of important functions in different situations. They regulate cellular aging. As telomeres shorten over time, cells can no longer divide and this correlates with physical aging." She walked in circles as she talked, her speech stilted, as if translating from a foreign language.

"Telomerase is a protein complex, an activator, that adds length to telomeres with each cell division—stalling or prolonging the aging process."

His eyes widened. "Are we talking the fountain of youth?"

"Not in those words, but the concept fits. Could be we're talking the fountain of death depending on how his science, his product, plays into this."

Her pause was not lost on him. He merely nodded.

She continued, "Scientists are working to find the clock that controls our lives. They feel telomeres affect the clock."

Milano rose with a clatter. "Was Howell one of those to believe the theory?"

"She didn't dither. "Most certainly. How successful is the big question. They still don't have an absolute on curing disease with this research, let alone the more complex aging process. I assume the question for us, is, 'Who may have feared he succeeded?' "

He followed the thinking. "We're not just looking for someone who had a run-in with him, but a true enemy."

He walked around the office, speculating. "A competitor. An investor of a competitor."

She added, "We could complicate things and add, someone who took his product with bad results, or no results."

"Thanks. I needed this to be even more difficult to pin down."

She sat, feet firmly placed in front of her. "Let's start. What did you find in Chicago?"

Settling back in his chair, he decided, why not? This woman was not the enemy. He might as well discuss some possibilities. The thought barely ratcheted around his brain before the decision to trust her popped out fully formed.

"We didn't find one useful thing in his lab. Someone had searched the office in a hurry. The Chicago police said they had no idea what was taken. The place was neat except for the computer smashed beyond repair and some papers on the floor."

Puzzlement conflicted her facial features. She asked, "I can't figure the timeline. Could the same person who ransacked his office be here at the conference?"

"Tough question. There are direct flights to Tampa International Airport from Chicago. It's about a forty-five-minute drive from there to this resort." Milano called Nederhoff on the phone this time and requested all flight schedules from Tampa to Chicago, and back. Within minutes she'd sent him an e-mail with the answers.

Milano absorbed it all, then said, "Our killer could leave Tampa anytime from five in the morning and return anytime in the afternoon, until almost midnight. Or he could leave Tampa one evening at eleven and return to the resort by lunch time."

Realizing he could confide in her on the rest of the case, he assured her they would check the registration lists against the airline ones and let her know what they found. "Try to stay out of trouble until then."

She rose. "You've a lot to do. I'll leave."

When she turned to say goodbye his face revealed his inner turmoil.

He swallowed, then voiced it. "If you're not the enemy, who is?"

CHAPTER ELEVEN

"The dead will keep you healthy."

Lizzie paused to see the effect of the opening line in her Ancient Herbal Remedies talk. Good, shock predominated their expressions.

"What? you say. The dead?"

When the muttering died down, Lizzie continued. "Many herbal uses today were discovered in ancient times. We only know this from their ruins or gravesites. Evidence of flowers in the graves of a twelve-thousand-year-old cemetery revealed knowledge of, and reverence for, herbs still in use now. How they used them is unknown, but preserving them with humans for the afterlife communicates their value. After finding them, healers examined the plants and found many benefits for us, today."

She looked over the crowd with confidence. This group reflected the best minds in the herbal industry. Many of them didn't recognize their worth. Herbs healed. But only if people knew how and when to use them. That was the job of these fine participants. Hers was to boost their morale, inspire them, and strengthen their knowledge base. Oh yeah, and to keep their minds off the dead body found in the vendor hall. Oops. A touch more difficult.

"I'm not speaking today to honor the dead. We are all here to venerate herbs. We follow a long, long line of herbal educators. Many here serve as vendors. But never forget to enlighten as you sell."

Lizzie had requested the lights be dimmed. So she could see individuals in the crowd. It helped her to know their response from facial expressions. So far, none shifted around in their chairs. She continued while she still held their attention.

"Evidence of a bed of flowers found in a sixty-thousand-year-old Neanderthal burial site caused speculation and debate over herbal usage that long ago. However, more flowers lined the graves in a 12,000-year-old cemetery. If nothing else, this leads to an ancient background of herbology.

"Use of herbs as medicine predates documented human history. You've just discovered that caraway prevents bloating and sweetens the breath? Sumarians wrote about it five thousand years ago. And garlic, coriander, mint and other herbs were used by ancient Egyptians as medicine around 1,000 B.C."

"The Ebers Papyrus of Egypt, which dates to 1500 B.C., is believed to be the earliest surviving record of medicinal plants, and the most voluminous. The papyrus contains approximately 700 formulas and remedies. Admittedly, it includes many incantations to ward off disease-causing demons. But it also provides dozens of herbal cures and their uses."

A male vendor part-way down the room jumped up. "Any of them there incantations going ta help us sell our stuff? Half the people here won't walk down my aisle since the guy got himself killed."

Sheila, a friendly fellow vendor sitting behind him reached up her long arm and pulled him down. "Knock it off, Tim. My booth's right next to yours and I'm doing fine."

Before Tim could respond, Glenn stood up. "It's probably your nasty scowl." The crowd laughed, and settled.

The reminder that murder permeated these halls stifled Lizzie's exuberance for herbs. This time herbs had not caused the man's demise. She altered the thought in her head as she shuffled her papers, a stalling tactic but the best she had as she realized that indeed, herbs or a related product, may not have been the means of death, but still, the cause. Yet this could not turn into a negative talk. She continued.

"The Sushruta Samhita of Indian Ayurveda describes 700 medicinal plants in the sixth century. Hildegard of Bingen, the medieval healer of the Rhine, listed more than 300 herbal plants and treatments in the 1100s. In 1552 an Aztec physician wrote what was considered the first herbal of the Americas, detailing therapeutic uses of hundreds of Mexican plant species."

A sharp noise in the back of the room drew Lizzie's attention away from her talk for a second. The door finished its creaking and left a crack for Detective Grant Guetierrez to stroll in. Staying in the back and moving to the side, he kept off the center aisle. He whipped off his sunglasses and stood loosely to attention. Fortunately, most people didn't notice him and waited for the rest of her speech.

As she sipped her water she noticed Jacob, the young man Abby introduced her to the other day. He wasn't sitting with Abby, but sat alone. Lizzie didn't see Abby in the crowd. She could use some of her ebullient cheer. Maybe she could find her after the talk. She continued, "As an anti-inflammatory, meadowsweet, kept good company through the centuries. The Greeks and Romans used it. Again B.C., Hippocrates, the ancient Greek physician, discovered its use in fighting arthritis pain, while at the same time, he recommended white willow bark for pain and fever."

She scanned the crowd. She was still holding them, so added, "During the same time period, Theophrastus, whose treatise on plants is well known to many of you, grew meadowsweet himself for continued use. Later it was used for gout and skin eruptions. We use it still today. Who of you knows why and how it works?"

A dozen hands rose. Grateful, Lizzie chose a man in the back. He shouted out, "Salicylic Acid."

"Right, of course. And it's terrific for arthritis, too."

As people chuckled, she continued, "Since life began on earth, humans used plants as their primary source of healing. These ancients reflect on what we do today. Let's look at the list of plants used then."

She opened with bloodroot and told of it's fame for the blood-red sap that drips from the cut root, and how North American Indian tribes believed in its medicinal benefits from cure of coughs to healing skin lesions. After providing this example, she requested suggestions from the audience. They were wide and varied and spread across all continents. "Aloe Vera from Africa," shouted Glenn, famous for his use of any healing herb, no matter it's source. Some only used local herbs.

Others rose their hands and she picked two more. One said, "Ginko from Asia." A man new to the group, spoke in a quiet voice. "Eucalyptus from Australian aborigines."

He provided numerous uses for the oil and a long and exuberant list of benefits from increasing blood flow for healing to use as a germicide and an antiseptic, or to treat everything from joint and muscle pain to skin eruptions.

Others in the audience piped in, "I use it for my asthma."

Another added, "I give it to my patients as a stimulant to fight exhaustion."

Lizzie laughed. "Okay, we promise we'll look into eucalyptus." She pointed to the young man who started the litany. "Please provide me your name after the speech so we can ask you to develop a program on it next year."

When the audience laughter died down, she said, "When we discuss herbs and their ancient uses, I hope it opens up some ideas for you to expand what you do with herbs."

Looking around, she studied the crowd. Were they any different than those ancient peoples, seeking aids for the body and mind? She continued, "Remember Hildegard of the 1100s. She combined fennel with other herbs to treat respiratory ailments, and word was, those who took her compound with wine, stopped coughing soon after." Some titters followed.

Lizzie recognized the weak wave of a hand deep in the audience. The woman squeaked out something. She acknowledged her. "Miranda Pennywinkle, it's good to see you today. Could you shout out your question again so this old lady can hear you?" That elicited the laugh Lizzie'd hoped for. Everyone knew her hearing was off the charts. Anyone who tried to whisper around her sure did.

Miss Pennywinkle's voice rose to the occasion, despite her drawl. "We speak today as if all herbs, especially those from ancient times, were for healing. What about herbs like belladonna?"

"True, belladonna holds a varied history. With its psychoactive ingredients it held a reputation for helping witches fly. It is made up of chemicals which block some of the functions of the nervous system.

This can cure or kill. In 68 A.D. they believed it poisoned the Roman Emperor Claudius."

Her thoughts wandered for a second to the victim found in the vendor hall. She wondered if that's what prompted Miranda's question. She hoped the poor thing had recovered from her trauma of discovering the body. It was a shame Howell hadn't been poisoned with an herb. Here sat the finest minds to help discover the cause. Her head and shoulders twitched, but she continued, "Many herbs have the ability to harm. It's all about lethal doses."

Concerned she hadn't explained enough, Lizzie looked at the audience. "Any more questions?"

A new participant shouted out, "What's your favorite herb?"

The audience erupted. Some of them already knowing the answer. As Lizzie responded, they shouted with her. "Oregano."

Once the quiet returned, she defended her choice. "Oregano's many uses over time still hold true today. It's my absolute favorite because of its strong benefits to the lungs and respiratory system."

"Did you ever have a breathing problem?" the young man asked.

"No. But I can still run like the wind and I'm not out of breath when I'm done."

Those who knew her age, laughed. The few, like Delia, who knew her ability to run, laughed with them. Lizzie chose to conclude her speech.

"It is common among almost all non-industrial societies to heal with herbs. Over time, industrialized countries exhibited pride that, instead, they could manufacture medicine for the masses. The records show, however, that in many cases these countries are not any healthier, and at a much greater cost.

"Our role today and forward is to be the best herbalists we can be. And heal."

Detective Grant Guetierrez strode down the main aisle like a king on a crusade. Lizzie saw Delia's eyebrows rise so high they reached her hairline. What now?

"Excuse me ma'am. I just need a minute of everyone's time. I'll have your audience back to you shortly. We'll keep this on schedule for you."

Lizzie bowed to him, and with a gracious motion to come on up, turned to the crowd. This is Detective Grant Guetierrez of the sheriff's department. He wishes a word with you."

Proud, with a Roman nose to match his background, the detective gripped the podium and smiled. Words rolled off his tongue like a soothing serenade, though the tone hinted of neither his German or Spanish heritage. The language came out more like a cop on a mission. Lizzie just wished she knew what his was. She stepped to the side of the stage and listened.

Like he was born to the podium, he spoke, "As Miss Ort said, my name is Detective Grant Guetierrez. It has come to the knowledge of the sheriff's office that rumors have been spreading about an incident in the vendor hall two days ago."

Lizzie rolled her eyes. *He must be an awfully new cop if he didn't even use the word death yet. Watch it Lizzie, one of these days you'll speak your thoughts out loud. Then what?*

He'd moved on, using that slippery tongue all the way. "Understandable with an intelligent group like yours. Now, Miss Ort has allowed me these few minutes of her time. I'm hear to clear up any concerns you may have."

She muffled her snort. Kind of inelegant on the stage, even if she was on the dark sideline. It would have helped if he'd asked her ahead of time. Oh well.

"You may all know one of the vendors, Alexander Howell, died here from a severe wound to the head. We are looking for anyone who can help us know more about this man, his product, and who may have been near him near the closing hours, day before yesterday."

This time Lizzie stepped into the curve of the curtain. No need to let everyone see her uncontrolled facial expressions. *My heavens, I used to be quite skillful at composure. Is old age taking nicks out of me?*

A hand rose straight up. At first it looked like an answer already. It was Natalie Truman. She identified herself as chairman of the conference. It was wise for her to assist the police, as well as any herbalist who may be able to help. She asked, "Who should we contact if we think we know something."

"Please feel free to ask for me specifically. Again. My name is

Detective Grant Guetierrez. I left cards at the registration desk. My number is listed, or you can call the main number at the sheriff's office."

He waited a beat or two, and when no one stood up or raised his hand he left the podium. A tall man stood up, knocking into his chair. "That Howell guy was killed, wasn't he?"

She was sure Guetierrez had deliberately avoided the 'kill' word. Too late now. She tried to see who asked the question but didn't want to step out of the shadows. Did that man know something. Who was he?

The detective answered with courtly evasion. He may be a new detective, but he had that part down pat. He turned his head and nodded to indicate the podium was now hers.

She stepped near and waved goodbye to everyone to release any of those who were uncertain whether it was time to leave. The audience was no longer hers and she knew it. Seeing her reaction, Guetierrez came close, blocking her view of the audience, and she missed a better look at the clumsy man from earlier. The detective invaded Lizzie's personal space, and whispered. "You announced me with such aplomb. I would love to see you out of your comfort zone."

She stared him straight in the eyes, not taking a step back, and not blinking. "No you wouldn't."

CHAPTER TWELVE

Guetierrez knocked with zeal at seven in the morning on the door of Elizabeth Ort and Delia O'Leary.

Milano caught the man's smile and told him to turn it down a notch. "We talked about this. We're playing it severe. Official. The plan was to catch the Ort woman off-guard and bring her in to the office. They needed to ask for a favor but decided to couch it in proper police jargon to prompt her to comply without question.

The door opened and framed a surprised, but alert, Lizzie. Milano hadn't dare use her familiar name, yet, though everyone else did. What time did these people wake up? Only a tinge of pink light showed on the horizon. Guetierrez surged forward with the attack.

"Miss Elizabeth Ort? Corporal Detective William Milano would like a word with you."

Lizzie gestured them in, to a spacious suite that put Howell's room to shame. And what a view. Away from the noise, but on the ocean side. Not that Howell's room was in the weeds, Milano thought. This was a high-class resort, after all. The room difference would be between speaking and selling, it would seem. Another woman walked out of the bedroom area. As she entered the living room, Milano recognized her from the murder scene.

Placing her hand on the woman's shoulder, Lizzie introduced her. "Detectives Guetierrez and Milano, I don't know if you remember my sister, Mrs. Delia O'Leary?"

While trading pleasantries, Milano took a discreet look around. The room could serve as a sterilization test in a laboratory. Nothing. Not a speck. Not a book. Not a crumb. No resemblance to his car, or his apartment, either. He swiveled his head to the side as if to check on the whereabouts of his partner so they wouldn't see him sniff. Aah, a hint of flowers. Guetierrez would probably know. Better to wait and ask later. Fortunately, the dandy took over the conversation in the lull while he thought out the next step. Of course they remembered Mrs. O'Leary. She was on the suspect list.

The Ort woman had turned the tide on him and gone formal. *Okay, I can play this game.* Kind of a version of two teams working together. Or against each other. For now, he took over the discussion.

Guetierrez just grinned again, as if sensing his discomfort.

Milano addressed Ms. Ort. "We would like you to come to the office and answer a few questions. She looked a little puzzled, but not angry. "What kind of questions?"

He decided he'd try straight-forward honesty. "We have Howell's computer with files about his product. Found it in his room. I admit, much of the information is beyond our men. We could use a translator. We're looking for anything to give us a lead."

Mrs. O'Leary piped in. "Such as?"

"Ma'am. We'll take anything."

"Please call me Delia. Everyone does."

See how simple that was? Why couldn't Ms. Ort respond the same? But then, if he called her Lizzie all the time he'd have to find another way to express his anger. Using her full name was too amateurish for her, anyway. He feared he'd have further opportunities to perfect a killer name for her. She got under his skin. Instead, Milano turned to her sister.

"Thank you, Delia."

"Once Howell's files are deciphered we might know which direction to head," he said.

Delia responded, "You mean like whether it's safe, ineffective, or even poisonous."

Milano looked at Lizzie, maybe for confirmation. He wasn't sure, but for some reason he had the feeling she knew most answers.

Lizzie added, "Or if he noted down any deadly rivals or verbal arrows pointing to his killer?"

Milano decided to ignore her for now, even though it's what they hoped for. Delia sniffed, as if he'd hurt her by checking with Lizzie. *Oh brother. Not rivalry between sisters?*

Guetierrez had stepped back following his spate of pleasantries. Milano thought the man merely watched. But he saw his eyes roam around the room in a methodical way, inch by inch. A unique way to search but less intrusive. Especially without permission and no warrant. Maybe the guy was more than a fancy tie. He'd have to be more open to his partner.

Delia paced, and talked. "You need to check into places he sold Telomerase Might prior to this conference. Is there a store? A recent convention or product show?"

Milano's eyes widened. He glanced back and forth between her and her sister.

"Mrs. Ort, . . . He wondered why the dynamic had changed when she interrupted.

"You may call me Lizzie."

Finally. Another direction shift in the game. He was having trouble keeping up.

She continued, "If it was a bad product, it would have to be extremely quick-acting to have caused a problem after purchase here."

He remained blank for a moment.

She clarified, in case he couldn't follow. "In time to come and kill the man."

Detective Guetierrez stepped back from the desk with an awkward twist of his ankle and fell down onto his knees. Though his arms caught his fall his face dipped low for a few seconds. Delia stopped in front of him to assist. He rose in an easy movement to his full height, then took her offered hand. "I am such a klutz. Thank you for attempting to help, but I am fine." He bent and kissed her hand before letting go.

Lizzie rolled her eyes and looked at Milano.

Delia blushed, then continued pacing. Her forehead wrinkled in concentration. "And we could check the notes for use of herbs, or worse, chemicals in his product not mentioned. Did you do an analysis of any of the bottles?"

Milano snipped. "We're working on it."

Lizzie walked over to her sister and hugged her shoulder while facing him. "Delia is the expert on herbs and anything related. If you want a translator, here she is."

Milano turned his feet toward Delia in a subtle move of recognition. Lizzie saw it, and he could see from her approving expression she knew what he was doing. He ignored her and addressed Delia. "Ma'am, this may seem like a strange request. We have you on our list to interview today regarding the murder of Alexander Howell. Would you please come down to the station with us now and examine Howell's files?"

"Why, I'll gladly help."

Milano felt like he should offer his arm in southern charm. Despite the fact that Florida wasn't that kind of south, and this woman was born and bred in Pennsylvania. He'd checked. Her life held no secrets. Unlike some he could name. He shot a sly look toward the woman he meant, while Delia fetched a wrap.

Her heard Lizzie whisper to his partner. "It's okay, son. Even though Delia's feet got in the way, you wouldn't have seen anything under the desk. We're neat people. No clues here at all."

His partner's face reddened. What a shock. The guy *could* be embarrassed. And he'd tried so hard, himself, with little success. Something to know, though he may have to take lessons from Lizzie to succeed.

After they'd left the ladies' suite, Milano glanced at Guetierrez with a questioning look, and with one amazed shrug of his shoulder Guetierrez confirmed nothing untold was there. Milano had gotten the message. The room might as well have been swept clean by the CIA. But the guy had tried. And he did it in an acceptable, yet surreptitious manner. Even he thought Guetierrez disguised the search well, until her whispered comment from the phenomenal Ms. Ort revealed he'd given it away some how. More than likely, Ms. Ort was too astute. So he wouldn't deck the man just yet.

Driving to the sheriff's department, Milano glimpsed movement in the back of his car. His partner, in an uncharacteristic move, agreed to sit in back with the suspect. They didn't imagined that Mrs. O'Leary was guilty. *Yet, was the man patting her hand? God help him. Oh. She's patting his. Not any better.* He knew Delia wouldn't have killed Howell, even accidentally, but patting her hand? Why not ask her out on a date? Okay, she was older than Guetierrez's grandmother, but still. Fraternizing with suspects? Or even accomplices, to be more honest.

They delivered Delia to Milano's office so she could work in a secure location on the victim's computer. He asked Officer Laurie Nederhoff to give her anything she needed while he rounded up Officer Juan José Venezia to bring the computer in. He debated the correct approach. The officer was a genius when it came to the tech end of software, but his knowledge didn't include the depths of biology and chemistry. Hopefully, the man would offer assistance rather than being affronted by an old lady telling him what to do.

Milano caught up with Guetierrez as he walked down the hall shouting for Venezia. He slapped his partner on the back in an attempt at joviality. The guy had deserted him the second they got to the department.

"Learn anything in the back seat?"

"Yeah, she told me I need special hand cream with coconut oil mixed with healing herbs. She's making me some when she gets home."

"What?"

Before Guetierrez could see the agony contorting his boss's face, he responded, "Well, the work we do leaves oil on the skin—not always the best kind . . ."

"Not that, you numbskull. Did you learn anything about the case? You know—the murder case? Alexander Howell, who had his head bashed in?"

"Sorry, boss. She seemed too genteel to bring it up."

"Go arrange another interview with the chairman, Natalie Truman, and that guy she called to intervene if Howell caused any more trouble."

Guetierrez looked blank. "What was his name?"

"Duh, look it up on your own, please."

Venezia had come running when he heard his name. Milano explained about the victim's computer and about Delia, and the officer fetched the stuff he needed and followed him back to the office. They walked in on the woman frowning at a file on the computer. His computer had all passworded files. Venezia and Milano looked at each other simultaneously. His tech officer stepped back, passing the buck.

Before he could formulate what to say, Delia saw them and brightened. "I was bored. Thought I'd see what's happening around here. Just peeking at some of your files."

She turned back to the computer and saved something. Milano panicked. What could she have altered? Today vied for the worst day of his life. He stuttered. Where to begin?

She interrupted. "The man who owns this has serious problems. Anyone could break in."

"Ma'am, we're in a room surrounded by police officers. I doubt if someone would come in here and try to hack into my computer."

The woman didn't even turn pink. "Why, I should have known it was you. The owner was such a sweetie, even if a little transparent." She saw his purple face and realized she may have upset him. He knew it as soon as she smiled again. But then she said, "Oh, don't take me seriously about the files. My looking at your police files would be unethical." Without even a blink she asked if she could print something.

Milano jerked his head down in a silent okay, while his hand reached behind him to grab the retreating Venezia before he escaped.

Delia reached for the printout. "I wrote down anything I could remember about the morning we found poor Mr. Howell. I know you interviewed me earlier, but thought you might try again to hunt for any discrepancies or new information."

Milano held onto Venezia like a lifeline. *He recited to himself, "I'm in charge here. I'm in charge here."*

Not realizing his confidence waned, Delia added, "I asked myself any question I could think you would. And I wrote a reminder to have the tonic tested as soon as possible in case you forgot." She handed him the sheet. "Maybe you want to look at this while I'm working on Mr. Howell's files? Don't hesitate to ask anything else."

He'd ignore the whole computer hacking thing until later. And the prepared interview. He introduced his tech man as Officer Juan José Venezia.

The woman could decide what she wanted to call him. "Please, take a look and let us know what it says. English translation from the scientific, of course. The officer will stay to assist with the software technology. If you need any help, that is."

Only a few minutes later Delia issued statements. Milano grabbed a notebook and scribbled. He'd barely had a chance to review his supposed questions but everything looked complete. Who was this woman? He planned to ask her more questions as soon as he could dream some up.

A half-hour later, the woman spoke. He wrote. "Howell was a genius for sure. His grasp of disease and the body is unbelievable."

The detective waited.

"Let me try to reword this. First, one of a gene's functions is to tell cells to create something. With cancer, for instance, there is too much telomerase. So the cells keep creating new cells. That's what telomerase does."

"This is bad?"

Delia swiveled her head just enough to catch his eye. "Well, if they're *cancer* cells, yeah."

She whipped back to the computer. She mumbled so much she might have been speaking to it, coaxing it, as her fingers scrolled up and down. "Howell not only explored how to stop the telomerase in disease, but how to increase it for healthy cells."

Milano wrote in a frenzy, too cowed by her earlier comments to jettison everything on this side of the desk to reposition his computer for faster notes. He tried to catch it all. The next statement raised his concern to high alert.

"Howell questioned the results of reactivating telomerase cells. His concern was a significant one, possibly a deadly one. Would it immortalize us, or make us more vulnerable to certain diseases, one of which is cancer?"

My God. Could his tonic cause cancer? No wonder she wanted information on the contents of the bottles. His mind had drifted.

Meanwhile Delia said in wonderment, "I don't know why he was peddling stuff a bottle at a time. He could win the Nobel Prize."

She looked up at their startled gasps. "Of course, not now. He wasn't finished. And he's dead."

CHAPTER THIRTEEN

As the ocean breached the calm sand where Lizzie stood, she debated her options.

She mulled over dark thoughts and deadly deeds, while the surf worked on the best approach to assault her feet. Sometimes the water curled in shyly on a foamy foray. It would tempt with a weak sally, then leap straight forward with a frontal advance to bite her toes and hustle backwards before a return rally. She didn't enjoy the subtlety. It lacked her usual modus operandi.

But that was before. Now, retired, life required new methods. Still providing aid. Yet more open and friendly. Less lethal. She needed to scuttlebutt the tide and turn it away. Without causing disaster. *Because when given an option, God chose peace over killing every time. So should I. To move on, mentally strong and on point, I must decide. I've wavered in and out of the investigation. That's not enough.*

What are the pros and cons of becoming involved? *Okay, Lizzie, you mean more involved.* Pretending to ponder which way to go was a wasteful task. In the end, a man had been murdered and seeped up cold from the slab in the morgue. Why did she hesitate to plunge forward this time? Because she was ill-fitted for civilian life and there might be new rules she didn't understand? That never stopped her before.

There weren't any rules then, but she could adapt. Her friends were on the suspect list. Police hadn't found a clue. She needed to turn the tide and find the killer. In a way that didn't necessitate violence.

Good. I'm in. I need a checklist.

First, pick the brain of Corporal Detective William Milano. Anything he appeared to be exploring, she would leave alone. For now.

So back to the list. Second: find the clue. Only one? Was that wise? Well, maybe one at a time. Hopefully, Delia will have learned something useful. She needed a long, sharp arrow pointing the way.

Come on, Lizzie, that's not how it works. Not how it used to work. Have I lost my edge? Did age blur my brain?

Mesmerized by the ocean, she stared out over the vast blue, unbroken by even a person, a boat or an ocean liner. She pictured swimming straight out till she hit Mexico. Or, maybe with an extreme shift to the right she'd make it to New Orleans. Her brain knew her desire lacked substance or possibility. But dreaming came easier than finding a killer. Was that the new way? Not for her.

Someone approached from behind, but in that seventh sense that she'd honed over eighty years, Lizzie knew it was her sister and didn't react. Sometimes the fast swivel to defend herself manifested itself before she could think. Delia always sensed this and thought kind, sisterly thoughts as she drew forward at a slow pace.

"Are these your flip-flops covered in sand over here?"

Lizzie glanced at her feet, as if they would answer while her mind wandered elsewhere. "Yeah, I've never worn them before. Thought I should learn these things. But they hurt my toes."

Delia waited. Then Lizzie spoke, facing the ocean again. "I know, Delia, it's time to make up my mind."

"Too bad our friend, Kat Everitt, isn't here," Delia said, picking up the flip-flops and shaking off the sand. "She'd gather copies of everyone's handwriting to examine for clues to who could have done it."

"That's Kat. Always willing to help people out. Her handwriting analysis sure did bring results. But it looks like we're on our own this time."

They strolled the edge of the waves together. The water could find another victim's toes. She strode forward in a power walk. Delia kept up, filling her in. "I tried to absorb everything while at the sheriff's department. I placed myself in your brain and looked at each tidbit from an intellectual angle. By the way, I don't like being there."

"Where, the sheriff's department? What happened? Didn't they treat you right?"

Her sister's delicate laugh tinkled out with joy. "My heavens yes. They were wonderful. The woman officer that assisted brought me coffee and asked more than once if I needed anything."

"So what didn't you like?"

"Why, being in your head. You can never stop thinking. Your eyes need double vision. You have to smell without an obvious sniff. You even have to hear words beyond the doorway so you don't miss anything crucial."

Stopping where she stood, Lizzie marveled. "It couldn't have been that bad. I live in my head every day and I'm still here."

Delia paused with her. "It's not for me. Exhaustion set in after a few minutes. I was so glad to have the computer files to examine."

Lizzie waited. Her sister didn't let her down. She went right to the pertinent information. "Howell was a genius. I know there's more research needed on telomerase, but he had refined some strong possibilities. His product may just work. The sheriff's office is waiting for the test results."

"How will that help?"

Delia found an abandoned cabana, sat back, and stretched out her legs. "It will only tell us if the pills had safety issues. Won't even help with long term harm or benefits. But it's a breakthrough."

"Did you find anything we could run with?"

Her sister shook her head vehemently. "Nothing. There wasn't even a formula for what his bottles contained. When the lab tests, it may not be enough detail for replication. Besides, that's not this lab's role."

She groaned, for her, a signal of defeat. "We're not scientists."

Sitting next to Delia, Lizzie scoffed. "I'm more concerned if someone could have been poisoned."

"I'm sure the cops are too. They seem quite competent. That Officer Laurie Nederhoff wasn't only kind, she shown with intelligence. She also told me the product tests would be back later today."

They continued their walk, while Lizzie puzzled over the possibilities. "Good work. But we still can't narrow the field. I hate to consider any of our friends as suspects."

Her sister jumped in. "Oh, you don't really think so, do you?"

She tried to reassure her that it was unlikely, with hundreds of other people around. "It needn't be someone connected with the conference."

"Wouldn't that be nice for Natalie? I'm sure she's deeply worried about the lasting affect on conference attendance."

"Did the police mention how they thought the killer got in a supposedly locked room?"

"No, but we could investigate for ourselves, right? To help them out? You and I could work on this together."

Aware of the anxious need in her sister to assist, Lizzie decided they could explore from the inside, using their knowledge of the herbalists and conference schedules and expectations.

"That nice Detective Milano and his fancy sidekick can do the official work. Delia, you can be my foil while I hunt around. How would that be?"

Delia giggled, apparently forgetting for a second that they were discussing murder. Her sister followed with, "That poor man. He was more than a victim, wasn't he?" She stopped their walk with a gentle touch on Lizzie's arm, and stumbled over some words, a total digression from her normal speech. Finally, she just said, "How do you do it all the time? How do you look at a dead person and search for details?"

Lizzie faced her and spoke—slow, firm. "Nobody liked him, but he didn't deserve this. Who knows what he has done or might have done in the future to benefit mankind, or maybe just a few men. The quantity doesn't matter. The fact that the opportunity was taken away from Alexander Howell does."

"Is that what you tell yourself?"

"It's much more than that. When you study a person's body after death looking for clues, you know that it's just a container. The soul of a person is no longer there. We still respect the body, for what it once held and because it was a beautiful creation by God."

"Aah, I see. Examining a container. It's like exploring the outer wrappings of a package."

"Well put, my dear. Let's get moving. We need to find the killer to ease tension in the herb conference but also to find justice for this man."

Delia came along with much more bounce in her step. Lizzie could see that this gave her purpose. She said, "I attempted a checklist before you came upon me. Before I questioned myself and my need to become involved. We may be the only ones fighting for him. So *we* must."

"What sort of a checklist?"

"I'd only gotten to picking Detective Milano's brain. And then finding a clue."

"Not much of a start, is it?"

"But that's how it always begins. One piece of information at a time."

"Why the checklist?"

"I don't like waiting for clues to drop in on me."

She explained, "The police are pursuing several things: the safety of product ingredients, the possibility of the killer being the same person as the vandal, and how the killer got in. It would help to know what they come up with. You and Milano get along better than he and I do. You can be the contact with him when we have questions, okay?"

"Wonderful, what else?"

"Have you heard anything about the security cameras? Maybe they revealed a shot of the killer."

"Now, that's profound, dear."

"You malign me."

Delia smirked. "Not at all, just pondering your use of words. Also, if they had a clear photo of the killer they wouldn't be fussing around with scientific details."

"That could be true. I wonder what happened?"

They put it on their mental agenda to find out, and moved on to several items, such as speaking with resort officials who might have information, exploring what vendors were last in the hall the night before, and talking with fellow herbalists about "Telomerase Might."

More people strolled the beach. Must be the lunch hour. Delia followed her to a more remote spot, around the curve, close to the next resort. They discussed details. Words better left unheard by others. Still, someone came running to catch up with them. Lizzie turned, calm now.

"Why Abby, what's up? You're out of breath."

"Ms. Ort. I need to talk with you. I have a few minutes between herbal workshops and came looking. I don't want to be late, but I just needed someone to share my thoughts with." She halted; sucked in some air.

Lizzie urged her to go on.

Apprehension clouded Abby's eyes as she said, "I guess, just in case."

"My heavens. In case what, dear?"

"I'm not sure." Abby swirled her toes in the sand. Then looked up into Lizzie's eyes. "Something's haunting me. Since Mr. Howell was killed."

Delia fussed and with a gentle tug, pulled Abby away from the loose sand that filled her shoes. "Sit here in the cabana and shake them, out. Lizzie will help whatever it is that's bothering you."

Many people might have considered Delia's conviction a bit presumptuous. Not Lizzie. They knew each other too well. As a friend in agony, Abby would receive help. She followed to the cabana and knelt down in front of the young woman. She pulled her hair from her face and tucked it behind her ear.

"Tell me what's haunting you."

Abby screeched. Quiet, feeble, but a screech of fear, none-the-less. "I don't know. I feel like someone is following me. But I look behind, around, and see no one. Or I'm in a crowd of friendly herbalists, just strolling down the vendor aisles. I get this itchy feeling, but everyone is doing their thing—walking, talking, but not staring at me, or stalking me."

Lizzie lifted up her chin. "It's okay. There's probably something there, someone. You just haven't been able to figure it out, yet."

Delia said, "Do you want us to follow you?"

Both Abby and Lizzie shook their heads. Lizzie said, "When she's in the hall, with so many people around, she'll be fine. Sitting in the lectures provides the same safety feature."

Abby nodded agreement. "I'm also safe when on the discussion panels. I'd feel silly seeking an escort."

Lizzie added, "Do not, however, go out to your car at night alone, or walk around where only a few people linger."

They trudged up the sandy hill to the resort. Lizzie looked back, stunned. Didn't notice that hill on the way down. But she'd worry about the implications later. As she turned, she saw a tall woman in a weird cloche swivel to face the ocean. Strange. Considering the noon-time heat she appeared overly clothed. Oh well, to each his own. A cliché that accomplishes a lot. They accompanied Abby to the resort and the conference hall.

"Thank you. For listening. And for your advice. I'll be careful." She entered the workshop in time to find one of the few remaining seats. "The Percolation Method of Tincturing."

Delia smiled. "That always reminds me of coffee. You want to go and find some?"

Instead, Lizzie pulled Delia into an alcove. Delia looked around, eyebrows raised.

Her sister whispered, "We're alone. What do you think?"

Her eyes were more focused inward as Lizzie appeared to study the hallway. "We may have a problem. See that frail woman, the one with the greenish cloche?"

"Sure, that's Matelda Rasland."

"Matilda Rasland? Who's she?"

"Matelda, not Matilda. Whatever you do, don't say Matilda!"

"Okay, other than her name, do you know anything about her?"

"I've heard her called the mung bean lady. Unkind, but people simplify. Come to think of it, her product, a tincture I think it is, reportedly lengthens your telomeres by reducing inflammation."

"Maybe we should take some. I could always use more years."

Delia smirked. "The 'reportedly' comes directly from her. Depends on how much you believe her. What brought all this up."

Lizzie shook her head. "I got the feeling she was following us.

Didn't see her right away, but as we walked Abby back here I noticed her."

Even Delia thought it wasn't much to go on. "We'll put her on our list."

Lizzie switched back to her earlier topic of protection for Abby.

"I'll call Detective Milano. He seems lonely. And Abby could turn any head. Is that still an acceptable phrase these days?"

"Huh. More like, 'She's hot.' So, we play matchmaker. How will that help protect her?"

"She's the one who used the word, 'escort.'"

"Lizzie, have we ever succeeded in matchmaking?"

"No, but there's always a first time. And we *are* excellent at catching killers. Maybe it will rub off."

CHAPTER FOURTEEN

"There is no way I'll go to that Detective Milano and ask for help," Abby stuttered. "I don't even know if there's anything wrong to tell him."

The sisters accosted her with their lame plea the second she emerged from the second program, on neurotransmitters. She'd departed with reluctance since the speaker's ideas energized her and she'd waited for more information after the talk. Raving to the man, she said, "I'm familiar with some herbs which influence neurotransmitters, like St. John's wort and black cohosh, but others were a surprise. I'd never thought of passionflower, or wood betony. How exciting."

At least she was thrilled until Lizzie and Delia ganged up on her. Lizzie pulled her into the alcove, sparing her from being clipped by the mung bean lady. The woman trotted so close she almost stepped on Abby from behind as she left the meeting room, bumped her arm briefly, then scuttled away without an apology. Who would walk so close in this wide hall? Seeing these two right now was a real downer, but she offered a polite thanks. They were back at it, trying to pick at the fear she'd suppressed.

"But Abby, we're not suggesting you ask him for help. Just mention to him what's going on."

And what would that be? There's no way I'll bother him. He's too sexy for me. I can't think straight when I'm around him. I'd sound like an idiot.

She repeated it out loud for Lizzie and Delia to hear. "I'd sound like an idiot."

"Now Abby, you are one of the most learned and knowledgeable young women I know," Lizzie assured with a pat on her back.

Delia interspersed her comment. "She didn't mean for that to sound like you're a nerd or whatever they call them these days. You're beautiful too. And witty. I'm sure Detective Milano is very impressed. He probably would love for you to drop in. Bring him up to date on the case."

"Like what do I know about the case?"

"Familiarity with most of the herbalists. And about herbs. He might have a lot of questions you could answer. Just go and offer your help."

Looking around, Lizzie urged them out of the alcove where they'd lured their friend after the program, and spoke as they walked. "Once you're there, take a moment to bring up your fears."

Abby shook her head. *How naïve did they think she was? Of course I can't say I'm afraid. When nothing has happened.*

As if she could glean Abby's thoughts, Lizzie added, "You don't have to use the word fear. Maybe you could just strategize with him on what conference registrants can do to stay safe. Tell him you're on the new committee to inform and protect everyone under the circumstances."

"What committee?"

Delia, on the "Health Naturally Conference" board, said, "The one we are forming this afternoon. You could even invite him to come with you to the group meeting later."

Knowing the quick-thinking woman, Abby figured she'd just made up the committee idea. On the other hand, it was an excellent one. And it would feel good to be involved. Maybe she could shake this outrageous and unwarranted fear.

Delia continued," If he gives you some safety ideas, make sure you put them into effect for yourself."

Abby shook her head with vehemence this time, as if they hadn't gotten the message before. "Why do I have to go to him at all?"

Lizzie and Delia answered simultaneously, as if twins instead of sisters. "We're afraid for you."

"So I have to see the detective because it would make you feel better."

They both laughed, looking at each other in surprise this time at their similarity. Lizzie said, "And because he's a hunk."

Abby giggled. "Everybody is saying the same thing about the other detective, that Guetierrez dandy. But we're talking about Detective Milano."

"Yeah." Delia chimed in. "He could charm the socks off me."

Abby and Lizzie looked down at Delia's sock-less feet, shod in ballet slip-ons. This time Abby spoke, in a much more light-hearted tone. "Have you been seeing him lately?"

Delia just smirked. Abby let it go as she thought how great these two women were. They exuded strength and intellect, while possessing the art of interjecting calm into any situation.

Abby expressed her admiration. Yet, they said nothing. Lizzie raised her eyebrows, waiting. *What did they want from her? How could she face Milano? She'd dragged out her regal routine when she met him. No normal words entered her brain. What must he think of her?*

Delia let her off the hook in a back-handed way. "I know. You can accompany Natalie Truman when she goes for her interview this afternoon."

"How do you know about that?" Lizzie piped in.

"I overheard it in the hallway when I was pretending to be you. At the sheriff's office."

Abby's eyebrows furrowed this time. There's no way Delia could fake being Lizzie. But she better not ask. Lizzie managed to recover before she did.

"Are they using the word, interview now, instead of interrogation?"

Not waiting for an answer, Lizzie continued. "No matter. Excellent idea. You can escort Natalie. I'm sure she'd love the company."

Acting as if she'd settled the issue, Lizzie turned to Delia. "Anything else you forgot to mention going on while there?"

"Several of the security cameras were tampered with so the crucial areas revealed nothing all evening and into the morning."

Abby stood back and watched the exchange. She wasn't always present for communication between the sisters. Maybe she could learn something to help her with Detective Milano.

Lizzie exhibited more concern about the information, though it looked like she was miffed that Delia forgot to let her know.

Delia saw her reaction, miniscule as it was, and said, "Sorry, I forgot earlier."

Lizzie waved the apology aside. She was more interested in the answer. "Tampered with? Could they just have gone on the fritz?"

"No, I definitely heard 'tampered,' but I couldn't ask any questions. Since I was eavesdropping and all."

Abby left them to it. Later that day she and Natalie shared information on their way to the county sheriff's department. "Who called you in for your interview?"

Natalie drove with one hand, waving the other in the air in front of her face like a fan. "It was the adorable Detective Guetierrez."

"Just watch it. I saw him with Miranda Pennywinkle and they acted quite enamored with each other. . . " Her voice trailed off. She twisted to look through the rearview window. A black SUV inched tight to their rear bumper. Then eased back. *Just another crazy driver.*

Not sensing her concern, Natalie continued. "True. She couldn't quit talking about him. Boy, was she upset when he never called her. And I don't think she meant to discuss the body she found, if you know what I mean."

Abby gently placed Natalie's hand back on the steering wheel. She didn't need car accident problems. She already worried enough today. She responded at the same time, "Yes, I know. What can I do while we're there?"

Natalie eased the car into a narrow parking space between two sheriff's cars.

"Uh, Natalie, I don't think you're supposed to use this section."

Her friend flounced from her seat and closed the door. "If not, they can move it."

Abby wished she had that much moxie.

They both jerked their heads toward the sound of screeching tires on the street. Natalie shook hers in disgust as a SUV careened off. Abby wrinkled her brow. *What was going on? Was it the same vehicle that almost bumped into their car earlier?*

Right now, she must face Milano.

Natalie finally answered her question as they walked to the entrance. "They'll probably make me go into the interrogation room on my own. That's okay. But could you find Detective Milano if he's not there, and extend my thanks for letting the conference continue so quickly after, you know, the dead body."

Abby didn't correct her with the man's name. Some people were so sensitive to a person who has been killed, they got queasy over the mere thought of a bloody death. She wondered though, if the sisters hadn't primed Natalie with their request. Sure not going to avoid the detective. She raised her chin to meet the challenge and strode after Natalie.

The officer at the front desk directed them to wait. Both detectives came out a minute later. Guetierrez nodded to Abby but asked Natalie to come follow him and they entered a small private room. Abby saw another officer there with a computer but didn't have time to speculate what might be happening.

Detective Milano ushered her forward. "It's good to see you again, Ms. Weiss. I tried looking you up on LinkedIn. Did you know they have at least sixty professionals named Abigail Weiss? Probably a zillion more throughout the country. It made it difficult to find you."

She laughed. "I'm right here where I've lived all my life. Easy to look up."

The detective looked sheepish but raised his head to say, "I admit I wanted to know more about you, Ms. Weiss."

"Call me Abigail, or Abby please."

"Only if you drop the 'Detective.'"

Her eyes brightened but she managed to squelch the giggle. "I can't call you Milano."

"Try for William. At least when we're not on official business."

She motioned around the Sheriff's Department. "This isn't official enough?"

He waved toward the one clean chair in his office and settled behind his desk as she sat. "You showed up here so I took the opportunity to say 'Hi.' An informal one."

Much more comfortable than she expected to be, Abby

positioned herself to face him squarely and added, "Well, I do have one semi-formal statement for you."

With a scowl, he tilted his head sideways. She didn't keep him waiting. "Ms. Turner asked me to thank you for getting the conference back on schedule right away. Mr. Howell's death, though tragic and scary, hardly caused a ripple in the programming and vendor's needs because of your speed."

He smiled. Even his eyes lit up. It appeared to be with relief. *I wonder what he was expecting?* She asked, "What is happening with my friend, Natalie, I mean, Ms. Turner?"

The door of the room across the hall stayed closed. She sensed little concern though, so took a moment to study this office. Neat. Well, if you didn't count the piles of papers on the only other guest chair. Books crammed the shelves, but in an orderly way. And dusted even. She liked the two statues. The thinker and a drumming frog. She'd ask about those later if they got to know each other a bit better.

He said, "Your friend is in good hands. He and Officer Venezia are hoping to learn more about the intake procedure for vendors. Did she do deep background research on the applicants? What did they have on Mr. Howell? Did they receive a list of products sold?"

Okay, not so concerned about her friend now. "Lizzie Ort told me they didn't get complete inventory records. It sure would have helped to know if anything was stolen. I can't imagine what could prompt a person to kill for a bottle of 'Telomerase Might.'" Not when you could buy one for about $25."

He immediately responded, "We lucked out. In a box buried under the counter we found an inventory list. Looks like every item was still there or marked sold." He grinned sheepishly. She figured he'd let that slip and wasn't suppose to reveal such telling evidence. She slid past it, as if the import of the information didn't register with her.

Detective Milano asked about Mr. Howell's friends. She'd never remember to call him William, even as she rolled the name around in her mind with a smile.

Natalie walked out of the room across the hall as Abby answered, "That man couldn't have had any friends. He was curt and rude. Her ire built as she remembered a few incidents. I hated him." She whispered, "Nobody knows this, but after her confrontation with him, I heard Natalie weeping in the rest room. She waited until her breakfast with Lizzie ended, then went in alone and cried. But, I caught the sound of her agony. What a cruel man. Maybe he deserved what he got."

She should have choked on her words but they were already out. Even Detective Guetierrez heard her as he followed behind Natalie.

Abby didn't even say goodbye. She raced outside. Stopped and hung her head. *I just put myself at the top of the suspect list. And I liked calling him William.*

CHAPTER FIFTEEN

"Lizzie, I don't know what to do. Thanks for rushing over." Abby paced the living room of her cottage a block behind the resort. She circled so fast Lizzie grabbed her arm to prevent a collision with the coffee table.

"You should have come to me, dear. You know I'll help."

Abby halted. "I was so embarrassed. Why did I say something so stupid to Detective Milano? Sure, I didn't like the victim. Nobody did. But I sounded so vehement when I talked with the detective. I bet he moved me to the top of his suspect list."

"Why, You're not on his list, dear. You couldn't have said anything so terrible. He would need serious evidence to accuse you."

Abby faltered, but one hiccup and a sigh later, she said, "You mean me telling him I hated the guy isn't enough? Or the fact I was there when Miranda ran out?"

Lizzie heard the screech on the last words just as Abby paced in a rapid circle again. This time Lizzie let her work off some of the agony. She knew the girl had feelings for the detective. She'd seen it when they first met and her angst now just proved it. Thinking he suspected her would hurt.

The outburst continued. "Or that I touched Howell's booth and pole when I helped straighten up the place. You know Howell couldn't follow one rule about booth height or even set the banner right. I practically had to shimmy up the rod to level the pennant across the top." She twirled around in dismay.

"I bet he has a tail on me. Looking for evidence. Or my next victim." Her voice rose to a high-pitched squeak as she moaned, "And he was so nice to me. I think he was even flirting until I said that."

Lizzie sat Abby down, knelt in front of her and held the young woman's hands. "Take a minute and feel the peace of God within you. You know He is always there and won't desert you."

After a couple of breaths, Abby said, "You're right. I'll remember, and I'm stronger than I'm acting. But I liked the detective *so* much. When he smiled the glow caressed my face. I wanted to know more of that, of a man who generated such serenity."

In all her days on the job, Lizzie plowed through unspeakable circumstances, but this? Serenity? The guy was a cop, a detective. Must be what they call "true love." She didn't want to cut off the bud before it could develop. She'd have to watch what she said. *Hey, was this an upturn in my and Delia's matchmaking success?*

She stepped into the unfamiliar but well-organized kitchen and prepared a pot of chamomile tea to relax her friend. No crying in the next room. A good sign. She studied the area while waiting for the kettle to boil. Nice yellow and orange kitchen. *Look how the sparkling glass bowl of mangos and kiwi fruit reflect the sun through the windows. I need to bring her in here. It radiates cheer.*

The tea kettle whistled and returned her to the dilemma. Prop up Abby, find protection for her, expose the stalker, capture a killer. Hmm, get a gun. The need for one hid around the corner, but she felt its presence. And *this* was retirement!

First, get Abby back on track. A popular conference panel on recent medicinal research with herbs in a few hours included Abby. Time to strengthen her resolve.

"Here, Abb. Come get your tea. Drink it and buck up. We need a game plan."

Abby sat at the table and put honey in her mug. The sun brought out the scent of the many plants growing in the large windows of the dining alcove. *God would not abandon someone in such a room. My beliefs are strong. I need not state them, only use them to help me guide Abby.* Lizzie plopped down next to her friend and patted her hand. "Now start with your trip with Natalie. Tell every detail."

Inhaling the tea's aroma appeared to calm Abby. Lizzie hoped the steam and the mild flavor would comfort her. Fast.

Then Abby spoke. "Natalie and I talked about what information the police would want and what we had to give them. We decided they probably wouldn't allow me to sit with her. Can you believe interrogating that sweet woman?"

"Now Abby, you know they were just seeking her assistance, asking her questions to pinpoint Howell's inventory and what friends or enemies he might have. Right?"

"I know. We said I was to prod Milano into revealing information while she dealt with Guetierrez. By the way, Milano let slip that the inventory matched the list they found. Not one thing missing. Not even sales cash from the cigar box.

Lizzie took deep cleansing breaths of her tea. *Soothing young ladies is not my forte. Where's Delia when I need her? Okay, she's talking at the conference. Still, I can feel Abby's pain and want to ease it. How? Keep steady.* She continued, "Nothing earth shattering came up in your drive with Natalie?"

"No. Just a black SUV careening near our bumper."

"What? You both all right?"

"Of course. Natalie didn't even notice. She kept talking to me. "Whoever it was backed off as we got to the side street. Natalie whipped her car between two police vehicles in the parking lot and— whoosh—that SUV just roared down the street."

"Did you tell Detective Milano when you mentioned the other concerns about a stalker?"

Abby jerked out of her seat, spilling a few drops of tea. She walked to the window. "I never told him. There was no right time. I didn't want him to think I was a paranoid fool."

"But this car, Abby. It could have been the same person. The detective would provide you protection."

Abby choked, the tears coming in force. "He won't want to watch over his star suspect. Not likely." She lifted her head. "What can I do? You know I didn't kill anyone. Not even rude Howell."

"Of course not, dear. And I'm sure Detective Milano knows that. He would never consider you a suspect."

Abby came back to the table and drained her cooling tea. "I'm not about to rush over there and ask him."

Lizzie rose, mentally devising what they could do. One she wouldn't share with anyone. Well, maybe Delia. She told Abby to get a good rest, then go back and wow them with her talk on the evening panel for recent finds in medicinal herbs. Abby appeared calm and determined to concentrate on her notes. Before Lizzie left, she checked all the window and door locks.

Her brief walk back provoked a new worry. Abby's contribution to the panel involved information on a fantastic use for mung beans. This remarkable treatment, still in early stages of research, could extend life by reducing inflammation. She held her breath for a second. Wasn't there a connection between that and halting the shortening of telomeres?

Oh dear Lord. Telomeres. Telomerase. Was this why the stalker followed Abby? Was the stalker Matelda Rasland whose product used mung beans? If we see her again near Abby I'm going to alert Milano, immediately.

Did Abby know something about Howell's work even *she* didn't realize? This, nebulous as it might be, prompted a hastening of her steps. She needed to talk with Detective Milano soon. What could they do to protect Abby? She knew no manpower would be available for such an elusive reason.

She phoned the sheriff's department when she reached her room. *Dang the man.* Milano wasn't in. She considered asking for Detective Grant Guetierrez. Then again, she didn't want *him* concerned about Abby. She'd wait a little while for Milano.

Meanwhile, she'd set up an escort system for Abby among her herbal friends. Something secretive. Just some friendly people stopping by to accompany her to the panel. Asking her questions or starting discussions while they walked with her back to her home. An imperceptible web of protection. Lizzie could do this for her friend, even if the woman's heart throb turned into a heart crusher.

The more I hear, the more I fear for Abby. Purchase a gun on the spot? May not be possible.

Lizzie spent hours calling local gun shops. She rented a car and drove into St. Petersburg. Those men were blatantly rude. Officious and lacking understanding. In the end, there was no way she could circumvent the law that said non-residents couldn't buy a gun. Even if she could, they'd do a background check.

Who can I call? Now I'm *pacing. I know, Janet might help.* She lives in Dunedin, nearby.

At least my old cohort, Janet, answers her phone right away, unlike inconsiderate detectives. Her once gravelly laugh had rounded down to pebbles and a pleasing sound raced through the wires. "What can I do for you?"

"I'm here in St. Pete Beach for an herbal conference."

"How exciting! I'm a gardener myself—now that I have more freedom."

Lizzie wiggled deeper into her chair. She liked Janet, and respected her. It was time for a brief report on current events. She explained how she came to the conference unencumbered by her gun. And now she feared for Abby. No specifics, but her sixth sense spoke volumes. The pieces don't fit. *No need to reveal my plans for redemption. Bad timing while asking for a gun.*

She divulged the details, then said, "It's not as if I don't trust the police. Do you know Detective Milano of the sheriff's department?"

"William is such a sweet young man. Handsome, too."

After mentioning her matchmaking plans, Lizzie asked how Janet felt about him.

With no hesitation, she spelled out her beliefs. "He knows his job, and well. He doesn't bicker, or prevaricate. He just gets it done."

"You wouldn't happen to know his address would you? It's not listed anywhere."

"Of course it's not. He's a policeman. Lives in a small home in Bay Pines. It's off Alternate Route Nineteen. You could stop on your way here in the morning."

Lizzie's sigh reached through the phone. "I don't want to wait so long. He needs to know what is going on with Abby. Now. Can I confide in him?"

"I'd trust the man with my life."

"So I should let him do his job and back off?"

"No way. Abby's your friend. What can I do to help?"

Lizzie explained her plan and made arrangements to visit the next day. Maybe Delia would come. On the surface, Dunedin reeked of kitsch. She'd love it. Then she called the detective again. And left another voice mail. The guy was either avoiding her, or so busy he never picked up the message. Meanwhile, she'd lined up her friends for the afternoon and evening to be with Abby. After that, they needed some permanent way to keep Abby safe until finding the killer.

Dusk settled as Lizzie's agitation increased. She made plans for the morning trip. A call to the department informed her the detective was still out. It could mean he was working late, desperate to solve the murder, or doing something else. Intruding on his home barely caused her conscience a twinge. Tit-for-tat. She left a note for Delia, hopped in the rental car and drove to Detective Milano's.

Milano jerked open the door at her knock. Not very cop-like, she thought as she stood there. Why, she could have been anyone. She decided not to comment. Maybe he felt safe—being a cop and all. She waited, while his stunned expression settled to grim determination.

"What on earth?" He didn't even finish, just stared at her. Hands at his waist revealed a strong chest and firm abs. The t-shirt was not department issue. The paint streak down one side couldn't hide his fitness. She was glad. It appeared he would appeal to Abby on the physical level. Now she delved in to explore his mind and heart.

A half sentence emerged before he halted her with a raised hand. "How did you know where I live? It's classified for a reason."

"A friend told me. She's from the area. Knows your family."

A shake of his head revealed his irritation, but he motioned for her to continue. At least he knew there was no sense in asking her for her friend's name. *Smart man.* She outlined the fears Abby reported and the possible pursuit of someone in an SUV.

By the time she finished, they'd side-stepped the free weights in front of the wing chair and sat in the man's living room. Not one item shouted cop. But 'guy,' yeah. The area rugs looked like bears slept in them and a football throw hung off the edge of the sofa, but it must have come straight from the field. I guess a man wouldn't mind the loose grass in it.

He interrupted her musings. "Why didn't she say something this morning when she came in?"

Lizzie saw anger in his face and hoped it grew from worry about Abby instead of provocation at her. He continued his rant, not even stopping to get a feel for her reaction to his words.

She spoke her concern, again. "I know there's nothing specific, but I still think she's in danger." He didn't disagree. Not as good as wholehearted approval but not being a picky sort she continued. "You do know, despite her hateful comment this morning, she didn't kill Howell?"

He jumped up and stared at her in disbelief. "Like hell she killed the man. That sweet girl can't have a vicious bone in her body." He stood rock hard, ready to fight. "Who would say she did?"

Lizzie rose, also. Shrugged. Her work here was done.

CHAPTER SIXTEEN

"Delia quit your whining," Lizzie said as she floored the pedal of her Ford Mustang rental car at six the next morning. Her sister never enjoyed dawn. Lizzie attempted compassion but found little. She woke alert and rarin' to go. "It's not my fault you need to be at a talk before noon. You said you wanted to go with me to Dunedin."

Okay, so I didn't mention when we'd have to leave to get her back in time. So smack me.

This morning Lizzie rose with more than the sun. Something dark hung around and it reeked of peril. She figured it was Abby's. She could face danger, but finding it lurking around some one else changed the stakes. She operated best when the odds favored her—this didn't.

Meanwhile, Delia sounded more calm and controlled. Whining turned to light snoring. That wouldn't work either. She'd hoped her sister could help fine tune her plan. She'd taken Route Nineteen north again but it was a forty-five minute drive. Perfect time to talk. She careened around two cars crawling at the speed limit and forged ahead.

I'll be dead if I don't get her back in time for her appearance. Fortunately, even such smooth movement rattled her sister enough to bring her to attention. *Good going, Lizzie girl. You still have what it takes.* She knew how to maneuver through more than traffic.

"What's happening?"

"Nothing. I'm just trying to get there in a hurry so you'll be back in time."

"Late is better than dead." Delia sat up straight and surreptitiously straightened her clothes. "Tell me again why we're rushing to Dunedin to see your friend, Janet? No offense. I'd love to meet her. But seven in the morning is rather early for a friendly brunch."

"It's about the gun. And the stalker, and the fear swirling around Abby."

"If it's one thing you know, it's how to sense danger. Even as a kid. Do you remember grabbing me as we ran around that blind curve practicing for a race? The one you convinced me we could enter if we dressed like guys and kept our caps on."

Lizzie still had some brain cells. "No, dear, I don't recall that one."

Delia obviously knew better though, since she continued. "You pulled me over seconds before the car swerved off onto our side of the road. I would have been creamed. Lights out at eight-years-old. Sure glad you can sense danger."

Smiling, Lizzie reminisced about other childhood memories, then segued into, "I need a gun." Delia brought her back to the present. "So what if you didn't bring your gun? Security's such a pain."

"It's not that difficult to pack a gun. It's the concept I don't like."

"You mean because healing and healthy don't go with the violence of a gun?"

"Exactly. This conference is my yearly reprieve from stress. It's as relaxing as taking a lavender bath. It didn't seem right to pack a gun, even though I do have a hard-sided locked gun case. I wanted to go gunless in my first trip as a retiree on a moral mend."

"Right It's a start toward doing good in retirement. So why are we waking up Janet before dawn?"

"Don't be snippy, dear. See that bright ball of yellow over there? It's the morning sun. I realize you haven't seen it often so probably didn't recognize it."

"And who's being snippy?"

Lizzie shifted in her seat, acknowledging the truth of that. "Sorry. This whole conference has turned into a nightmare. And we need much more than a lavender bath to fix it. I'm going to Janet's to borrow her gun. Well, one of her guns. Janet has a cache."

Delia stared at her. Lizzie could feel it even though she didn't turn her head. She explained. "I tried to buy a gun in St. Petersburg yesterday. I called around. Did you know there are fifteen stores in town where you can legally buy a gun?"

Ignoring her, Delia said, "So instead we are going to your friend's. Why?"

Lizzie exited off Route Nineteen and turned left onto Main Street. Her words came in a huff. "Because they all wouldn't sell me one. Said I don't live here. I'd have to stick it out for the legal check and waiting period. When I mentioned I needed it right away, they hung up."

Her delicate and prim sister snorted inelegantly. Didn't say a word. Stylish and graceful no matter what the hour, Delia's sound startled Lizzie. She lowered her head, "I even went to visit a couple shops. They metaphorically did the same thing. I got the feeling one guy was calling the cops. They'd probably get Milano. With any luck, he'll be busy protecting Abby. He doesn't need extra work—like arresting an old lady for suspicious activity."

As they drove through Dunedin, she realized how well she remembered this quaint city. The wrought iron fences, the canopied benches. Bright pastel colors of downtown store fronts. She enjoyed her brief times here visiting with her friend. Such a glorious day. Too bad they couldn't spend more time walking around.

A few deft turns onto side streets and deeper into a secluded section of town, down the short stretch of Cider Boulevard, and there it was. The house Janet inherited from her parents. Her childhood home. In a stay with Janet years ago, it enticed them back to their youth, and they roamed like kids, seeking out the nooks and crannies, and secret hiding places. She knew Janet would love to show it off again.

Delia hopped out of the car in excitement. Lizzie followed and watched her enjoyment. Steps in long levels rose three-feet-wide to a brick path through a protected entryway. Gnarled and knotty trunks with purple-pink bougainvillea filled the areas between palm trees.

Potted plants of riotous color led up to the door which opened as they approached.

Janet raced out and hugged Lizzie. Delia stood in awe. Lizzie wasn't the hugging type, but she even returned the embrace and smiled at Janet. The old, crusty Lizzie materialized the instant she spoke. "You haven't aged a bit. I can't find one new wrinkle."

"Huh. The always suave girl. You can't get those compliments out without a twist. Besides the wrinkles blend together when you hit ninety. Just you wait." Janet pulled Lizzie around, arm on her shoulder and asked for an introduction to her sister.

The silver-haired woman smiled wide and hugged Delia, too. Lizzie studied her friend and was happy to see how well she looked. *Hard to believe she's ninety. Floral dress and slender boots. That's Janet. Always has been. Came as a bit of a shock to some people.* But Delia took her at face value and offered a genuine smile in return.

Once acquainted, they strolled up the walk, discussing flowers. Not a word about the purpose of their visit. Lizzie's old friend drew them straight to the cheerful kitchen nook. After a breakfast of tropical fruit and muffins and fluffy scrambled eggs, Janet asked Delia what she thought of Dunedin. Always honest, she responded, "Didn't see much on our whirlwind trip this morning." Her mouth formed a moue at her sister. "But I looked at the map. What's not to like about this fantastical town."

"Why, what do you mean?"

"It's delightful. It sports such streets as Isle of Sky Court and has Coconut Villas."

Though they all laughed, they sobered quickly. Janet forayed into the solemn part of their business. "I understand you have deep concerns about your friend Abby's safety?"

"I can't help but trust her instincts. She feels there's someone checking on her, tracking her. It's made me sensitive to what's happening around us. I looked to see if we were followed here."

Delia reacted. "You can't be serious. You drove like a maniac. No sane person would have kept up."

Lizzie sighed. "Let's just hope this killer is sane. Or is that an oxymoron?"

Janet shook her head. "Moving on. Even if no one is stalking her, there is still a killer at the conference."

Lizzie explained, "We don't even know if they stayed. Could have been an outside job. We can't determine motive. The police are tracking down leads but there's way too many possibilities. And worse, we can't completely understand all the options without technical knowledge of the victim's research on telomeres."

Their hostess gestured toward the next room. "You're too scientific for me. But I can help. Should we proceed?" She rose and motioned for the others to follow. She halted in front of a magnificent floor-to-ceiling bookcase in the huge study. Lizzie remembered it well. Not that they did much reading there.

Lizzie glanced around and realized the reason behind the windowless room. Her first reaction had been, 'What a cozy look.' Now she waited for Delia's response as Janet pulled out the book, "The Ancient Art of Strangulation," pushed an invisible button, and a small section of the wall opened on silent hinges. They all stepped back until Janet entered.

Delia whispered a reverent "Ohh." A light flicked on. A narrow staircase rose to the tiny hidden attic room—filled with shelves of guns. Lizzie had experienced the effect before, so turned to watch her sister, who blinked, then squealed in surprise. Janet laughed with loud delight. "Don't worry. This room is soundproof. And weatherproof and temperature controlled." Lizzie added, "Janet's father made some changes over the years."

Delia studied the guns, though not knowledgeable about such things, and nodded with heavy agreement. "I'd say. I imagine these weren't all here in your daddy's time."

"No. Granddaddy turned it into a hideout for runaway slaves. He hated slavery. He said he just added an upper car to the underground railroad. My daddy wrote it all down in his memoir so his family would know." She clapped her hands together. "So what do you need?"

Delia stepped back. She never touched the things. She wielded a mean knife, but mostly in the garden. Lizzie moved up to examine the choices. Her good old Browning was at home. This one was close.

She hefted it, twirled it, and searched around. Tried it again, and with a swift nod, said, "This'll do."

"What about a backup?" Before Lizzie could shake her head, no, Janet handed her the sweetest little pearl-handled pistol. "You might as well take it."

Delia tittered when she saw it. "They'll call you Priney Fischer."

Janet returned them to the immediate concern. "You probably won't do any more time for two guns than for one. Besides, this baby hardly counts at all."

Lizzie agreed. Then added, "Unless you get shot with it. I think I'll pass."

"Care for more coffee before you leave?"

Delia glanced at her watch, and led the march down the stairs. They drank a quick cup and none resisted another decadent scone. Knowing her sister's delight in classy restaurants, Lizzie recalled her and Janet's celebration one night at the the Bon Appetit Restaurant where they watched a beautiful sunset.

They said their goodbyes on a cheerful note but Lizzie's thoughts swiftly turned to planning additional securities if necessary against the killer. So far Milano looked to be their only strength. Delia walked to the car as raindrops fell. Lizzie thanked her friend and promised to return. Then the clouds turned to faucets and Lizzie ran.

CHAPTER SEVENTEEN

"It's time for a pow-wow. The tribes are getting restless."

Lizzie accosted Detective Milano as he entered the sheriff's office after lunch. He waved her in to his room, gracious, though not cheerful in the slightest. His lips, flatlined in an otherwise morbid face told her more than the herbalists were agitated.

Once seated, he stared at her without speaking and she continued. "The herbalists and vendors blended together in past years. Some of the vendors were our top herbalists. Now rumors of rumbling abound in both groups."

His shoulders straightened from their slumped position, signaling some interest. "Anything specific leading to our killer?"

"No. But we need a solution right away before you and your officers are inundated with calls of domestic violence, so-to-speak."

Milano pulled out his notepad from the towering pile of papers on his desk and waited. She stalled this time, hoping he would reveal information on the case's progress. He looked at her. "Details, please."

Stymied, she provided what she knew. "Sheila said she stood at a booth trying to decide which of the products to buy. The vendor got nervous and grabbed all three bottles from her hands and growled at her." Lizzie bounced up and down, hoping to make her point. She added, "Why even Glenn, one of our oldest conference participants, and the most gentle of men, reported getting blindsided with a purse swung at him by another herbalist. He'd just touched her arm to get her attention."

He pursed his lips and swirled his hand in a 'continue' motion.

"I raced here straight from the vendor hall. The lights blinked and dimmed. No shrieks—just instant, total silence. Fear palpated the air. A full minute later—one of those lasting an hour—the lights came back up. You could hear the whoosh as people breathed again. A vendor shouted. "Sorry, I overloaded the circuit. Once I unplugged my coffeepot we were fine. There'll be no more cooking in the booth, but I've got hot coffee right now. Bring your mug and come. It's free."

Not one word appeared on his notepad and Milano stared at her. "So you came to tell me things are getting unstable at the conference? And you want me to do what?"

Lizzie sprang out of her chair as if the herbalist's vibes had put her on edge. "Tell me what you learned. And how I can help."

"Sit, please. We can talk, though firm information is in short supply. "I'm still waiting for the video footage to see if it reveals anything. Unlikely, since we were told it was tampered with. Depending on what it means, Howell's death turns into premeditated murder."

She nodded, lips pursed.

Milano added, "We've eliminated the banner pole as useful in any way. The blood matched Howell's and no one else's. There were no clear prints, just the smear of a large one, probably a thumb."

"I'm so glad to hear that. Abby was sure you had her at the top of your suspect list because she'd touched the pole, trying to help the man straighten his pennant. She figured you wouldn't consider it had been an innocent gesture prior to his death."

Milano laughed. "You can tell her to rest easy. We have no proof of her, um, *nefarious* ways." When Lizzie didn't laugh with him, she saw from his startled expression he must be joking. Thank heavens. There was hope for this romance yet. Meanwhile, they *must* focus on finding the killer.

Looking at his folder now, the detective honed down what information they had. He went through a list of people who were cleared. "Those off the hook include you, Delia, Abigail Weiss, and Miranda Pennywinkle and her roommate."

She sighed with relief for a second, then frowned. "That's all? There must be more. What about Natalie, and Michael, and Glenn, the old time herbalist who would not undermine this conference with a murder!"

He waited for her to fade out, then said, "I'd thought you'd be happy you five were cleared."

She fidgeted. And she never fidgeted before. But controlled herself quickly. "How did you determine this?"

"You know why you and Delia are off the suspect list. Miranda's roommate suffered jelly fish stings the day before the conference opened. She was awake most of the night trying *not* to sleep on her back. Says Miranda was there and raced out at six a.m. shouting she had to deliver some schedules. Neither she nor Ms. Weiss have the strength, or the height, or the stomach for such a killing."

"Did you check out Abby's story that a black SUV might have been following her and Natalie Turner to your office."

Milano's body twitched as if his agitation was working it's way out into the open, but he just said. "No story. Natalie did confirm seeing the SUV spin away, substantiating Ms. Weiss's comments. Doesn't prove there's a stalker though."

Lizzie rose. With her back to him again, looking out the window, she calmed her voice and said, "What about Natalie Turner? As chairman of the conference, what would her motive be for killing someone?"

"Miss Turner may be cleared. We just have a few more questions for her. But motive? How about she didn't want the nasty man ruining her conference?"

"Natalie sees much more than the average attendee. Fortunately most vendors spew their venom on the conference chair and not the customers. Simply. She's used to it. Part of her job is to diffuse it."

"Let's move on, Milano said, shuffling some papers until he found a long list of names. "My officers are interviewing all of these people. It's a beginning. But we're on it. Others are taking the list of all attendees and focusing on those who could be feasible suspects."

He flipped to another page. "For unknown reasons there's been a delay on the flawed camera footage. We'll get back to that."

Then he said, "The inventory list he left in the booth, assuming it was his, matched with the items there. The sales receipts verified a few initial sales, but they were checked off an inventory sheet dated prior to his death. The new sheet had the date he died on it. Maybe he stayed late to prep for the next day. The sheets were handwritten."

She frowned. "If the product was a threat to another developer or supplier, thus causing the need to get rid of Howell, why wouldn't they steal his solutions to try and duplicate?"

"It's a fair question. We don't know the answer. But there are several possibilities. We are checking into any recent events, conferences, wherever people could purchase the product. Maybe a competitor already knew what was in it. Why steal it? They only wanted to stop his sales."

Lizzie sat down again, finding the guest chair more comfortable for viewing his facial expressions than trying to discern them through the faulty reflection in the window. "Any luck with the airlines?"

"No. We couldn't pass them names of hundreds of attendees. My men are working on narrowing the list. Guetierrez has a friend in TSA who might help us if we have just a few names. Or a photo or two. You have any likely suspects we can give them?"

Lizzie hung her head. "No. But I will take a look at potentials. We also have to work on mollifying the groups while they all wait for your announcement."

The detective ignored that. He reviewed a loose sheet of paper tucked half way into the folder. "We received this analysis of the bottles in Mr. Howell's inventory. There were only three different formulas, variations of the same thing."

She waited with anticipation for the rest of it. Her knee bounced of it's own will. *This might be our break-though.* He quelled that before hope could bubble up.

"The lab could not report on whether this stuff works, or improves health. However, the component list showed nothing volatile, nothing sensitive, and therefore, nothing deadly in itself."

Resigned, she said, "So Telomerase Might is safe, unless someone had an allergy to one of the herbs. That seldom is lethal. No one would have cause to kill over a rash."

Milano's head hung even lower as she said out loud what he must have been thinking. She tried to fill the dead space. "We've created a new committee to inform and protect the registrants under the circumstances."

His head jerked up. Was that his neck she heard snap? "You did *what?*"

"Calm down. We didn't exactly arm vigilantes." She hesitated for a moment after speaking. She'd just come from picking up a gun. Well, it's not the same as arming a committee. No need to mention it. She added, "We want to form a web of trusted people to wander around and be observant."

He sighed and held his head in his hands.

Detective Guetierrez busted through the door. His feet stopped as soon as he saw Lizzie but his body continued the forward momentum and he swung backwards to rebalance. "Sorry, boss. I didn't know you had company. We just got a call. Two dead men at the Ratzy Hotel."

Milano blinked. "Tell me more."

His partner swiveled his eyes. Milano realized Guetierrez had never seen all the government stuff involving her, clearing her. Or at least making her look less suspicious. Lizzie watched the scene play out between the two.

Filling in the man on her clearances and past activities didn't fit Milano's agenda today. He grunted. "She's okay. You can talk in front of her."

She noticed Guetierrez's wary expression, tilted her head sideways and gave him a gentle smile. She hoped to reassure him, but he stiffened, like out of his element, and stared at Milano while finishing his report. Don't know much more."

"You left the blood out, didn't you?"

His partner's head swung around toward her and she smiled again. She almost enjoyed this, except it entailed two people dead before their time. But Detective Guetierrez obviously didn't know how to deal with her. They both turned to Detective Milano.

He said, "It's okay, Gutz. I think she knows about blood. Check out the splatters if there are any. The tech people will probably be right on it. But make sure the photographer gets photos. Ms. Ort wouldn't mind looking at them."

Guetierrez's eyebrows rose skyward. He must have learned a lot from Milano in the short time they worked together. He didn't say a word.

Milano dismissed him, saving him the need. "Grab Jerry to go with you and find out more. With any luck they killed each other and a witness saw it all. Case closed."

His partner backpedaled out the door.

"Smart man." Milano said. "And wouldn't it be our lucky day if it really happened that way?"

Lizzie breathed deep and centered herself. He rose, paced, and continued with the litany of items on his checklist that didn't pan out. As Milano reviewed the pieces of information, most empty of clues to the killer's identity, his agitation built. They'd been playing some form of hot potato with the embarrassing lack of information—first her, then him. She realized they'd been competing and each felt more prickly as they fell short. But this wasn't a competition. It was an imperative—they should join together to find a murderer, and protect Abby, if she was in danger.

Meanwhile, Milano became more frazzled. He began to rant. We've got no leads. No suspects. No clues. Nothing. Nada. Like I said when you came in. Nada."

"We've got a dead man."

He plopped down in his non-ergonomic, non-comfortable chair. "Yeah. We've got that all right. Any ideas?"

CHAPTER EIGHTEEN

The mug smashed to the floor, coffee everywhere. In a simultaneous mojo, Guetierrez walked in with a sheaf of papers and a frown. "Bad news boss."

"Boss? What happened to partners? And whose bad news, yours or mine?" Milano swabbed up the mess with rapid swirls of napkins and stepped around the broken pottery. When no answer came, he stopped and looked up.

"Try two out of three."

Guetierrez's furrowed brow told of deep assessment before he elaborated. "Boss is good. If it was partners, it would be our bad news. I'll wait till the day improves before I'm your partner again."

Milano plopped into his chair, threw the soggy towels at the man's pristine shirt. "Spill it."

"The report on the security footage came back two days ago and got buried under these other papers."

"You're right. Wrong way to start my day. Tops breaking my favorite mug. But I'll decide if and when you become partner again. That's a big *if*." He straightened in the chair, pursed his lips in thought. "Does it tell us who killed Alexander Howell?"

"No, it says the video recordings got screwed up. It fuzzed out during the prime time. Or something like that. It's not my area of expertise."

I'm still waiting to see this guy's area of expertise. Actually, I'd accept general competence.

When Milano stared at him he continued. "The cameras in a small percentage of the vendor hall were non-functioning. They didn't notice until we asked for the video recordings."

"How could they not know?"

Guetierrez went into his story-telling mode. Milano winced, but motioned him on. "They claimed to be 'having a bad day.' Like they'd just discovered this major snafu in their system, and then I called." He continued. "This Jefferson came on the phone and said the security program was more of a recording in case they ever needed to see what was going on. So they don't review them unless it's necessary. The man added they'd never had any violence there, or . . . and then he grimaced, boss. I swear you could hear it over the line."

As 'boss,' Milano just motioned him on again.

"Like I said, the man groaned and said 'never any deaths.' "

Milano laughed. "Reminiscent of that movie, 'Blueberry Nights,' where he only watched certain videos for fun?" When Grant looked blank, he dismissed the thought. "Never mind. You would't know it. You're too young. No action, no killing."

"No killing?"

"An old man died. The viewer won't meet him, though. You just see the empty hospital room."

"Jeesh. That doesn't count."

Bringing them back on track, Guetierrez said, "I saw the time frame. Nothing there from those cameras. Just a blurry mess. Could have been a repeated loop but I couldn't tell."

Guetierrez sat down in the chair squarely in front of Milano's desk. He handed over most of the report but held back a page. "Their security system came in just after the year 2000. So they had DVRs, not DVD's. They still have DVD drives to copy the video files."

Milano sat back. "They're making us copies of lots of blur?"

His "ex" partner lowered his head. "Yeah."

Milano looked at the broken mug in the trash, and the useless security report and prayed the day would improve. He crossed his right ankle over his left knee, sat back and digested what was said. He sought clarification. "Okay, so tell me again what was wrong with the digital video recordings."

"They'd been tampered with."

"Deliberately or accidentally?"

"They think deliberately. Jefferson, their technical guy, said to give him a call. He'd explain what he can."

The phone rang. Picking it up and announcing himself was automatic. The restrained snarl was not. "No ma'am. We don't have any new information to share with you. We'll get back to you as soon as we can." In the pause he glared at Guetierrez. Then raised his voice, "What do you mean you were afraid of that? What?"

Guetierrez's eyes widened into large circles. "You hung up on her?"

"No. That Ort woman hung up on me, dammit."

He shouted out the door to Officer Laurie Nederhoff. "Why on earth did you put her through?"

"I was told to always put her through right away."

"By whom?"

Milano stared at his ex-partner as the answer drifted in. "Why, Grant, sir."

Before the man could defend himself from the piercing glare, Milano growled and moved back to the more pressing matter. Security. Or lack of it. "Do they have proof of the tampering?"

The maligned ""ex"partner hung his head. "No. But they're pretty sure."

Jumping up, Milano came around in front of Guetierrez and sat on the desk. "Wow. This killer planned so far ahead? And how could he do it? I know, call Jefferson. Okay. If he's in, inform him we'll be there in a half hour."

Guetierrez rose and turned to leave.

"Wait. Tell the folks in security it is essential to know what went on in the hall—big time necessary. We want copies of every video file from two days before till after they discovered the body."

Guetierrez made it all the way through the door this time. "Tell them it means the whole hall and the surrounding corridors."

Twenty minutes later they knocked on Jefferson's door frame and entered a cubby hole in the bowels of Neptune's Oasis Resort. Introductions brushed on the professional with no small talk. "I would like some answers. Now." Milano said. "Where are the recordings?"

Jefferson frowned. "The copies are all boxed on the shelf ready for you. What I tried to explain to your partner here, is they won't reveal anything you need."

Milano scowled. "How so?"

At any point if a camera isn't working either it's a power problem, the unit itself is faulty, or something is wrong with the video line. This wouldn't show up on the monitor. In this case, we saw the videos were functioning, not necessarily capturing something."

Milano interrupted. "Motion activated?"

"Sort of." The man pointed to the two empty chairs. Guetierrez sat. Milano clenched his jaw but finally did the same. They all huddled around a tiny table. Guetierrez smiled and asked, "Could you explain, please?"

"We have individual camera shots. Based on motion, yes," he said, and nodded to Milano.

With these, one can select the area to videotape to save memory, or adjust the sensitivity of the motion to trip the record function. That way we don't get every movement of an insect."

Then he harrumphed. "Of course, our people sterilize the place —I mean, you won't find any bugs in here. We can keep it sharp, but not for every detail at the ends of the camera range."

A tall hefty guy burst through the door. Stopped dead when he saw the cops. He looked at Jefferson. And mumbled.

"What?"

"I just wanted to tell you, um, we got all the cameras workin' again. You want 'em programmed same as before?"

Jefferson nodded.

Milano could see the guy knew the tech stuff, but from his stance, and expression, lacked people skills. Did that make him dangerous?

He studied Jefferson when the other tech guy asked, "Motion. Strong detail?"

Jefferson hung his head instead, obviously controlling his distress at the disruption. "Yep. Now get out of here."

As the man left, Milano jerked even more upright. "Who was that?"

Frowning at the door where his tech guy had been, Jefferson answered, "You mean Washburn? He's one of the junior tech guys. Sometimes I don't think he knows how to tie his shoes. But he does what he's told okay."

This man's attitude bothered him. He treated the young cleaning boy at the sheriff's office with more respect. Could this Jefferson be involved? What would he gain? On the other hand, if the system went down, who better to have caused it?

If it was totally secure, unreachable except from inside this department, then it narrows the field. But could he be that lucky? He asked, "Can the system be hacked? How?"

Jefferson scratched his head. "Yes, but it's complex, and time-consuming. A person could hack into the DVR through the network, pick individual cameras aimed at the desired areas of the vendor hall, then lower the sensitivity to the point it wouldn't record unless someone was quite close to the camera. Difficult since they're on the ceiling."

Milano's eyes widened. "Doesn't it require premeditation? And strong security knowledge."

Jefferson nodded. "Sure does. But we deal with that all the time."

"Do you have to adjust it for whatever the current user needs. Like blur everything out if you have a strip show going on in there?"

"That's a ridiculous question. This resort has impeccable clients. We've never even sold lingerie in there."

Milano saw Guetierrez's smile hidden behind the hand covering his mouth. Couldn't the man ever control himself? Though this Jefferson didn't seem to realize his statement left out numerous other options. Maybe he should look into both him and Washburn. Either of them could easily have changed the camera settings ahead of time. But what could their motive be? And how possible was it for someone else to do it?

Dreading the answer, which would determine whether it was an inside job or open to the whole universe, he asked. "Can it be done from outside, say one of the resort rooms, or even from way outside? In the next town?"

The tech man got flustered all of a sudden. He didn't answer. He rose and gathered all the boxes he'd promised the police and straightened the precarious pile on the table by the door. Neither man stood up to leave, so he turned to them. Looking down from this supposedly superior position, he said, "I don't know. It's never happened before."

Was it puzzlement on his face? Fear? Milano wondered, could it be guilt? That question hit the same rock wall. What would be the motive to kill this man, this Alexander Howell? Or perceived reason, anyway. How many rationales could there be to kill? At this point he'd be happy to find just one for this victim.

His mind had wandered long enough for his partner to feel like he should take over the interrogation. Which was fine with him. These young guys knew more about technology than he ever would.

He heard Guetierrez ask, "What do you see if the sensitivity is lowered like you mentioned?"

"It would still show recordings on the hard drive and wouldn't show any malfunctions or problems."

Jefferson appeared comfortable with straight technical types of questions. While the man was in an answering mode, Milano sought clarification. "So instead of a loop, what you'd get is smudged motion, or no motion."

Guetierrez said, "Like some of the cameras were turned on, but showing a grainy picture."

"As if nothing was happening." Milano said.

Jefferson's head swiveled back and forth between the two men. He exhibited difficulty with the ping-pong effect but looked to be keeping up with it. He head bobbed repeatedly in agreement. "Right, just as if nothing was happening."

Milano looked right at him. "Like a murder?"

Jefferson sank back into his chair. "Like a murder."

CHAPTER NINETEEN

"Let's find a killer. The police aren't getting anywhere. We need to help." Lizzie pranced in front of a small group of top herbalists, back and forth, back and forth, speaking to the floor as she verbalized thoughts. She called. They came. Now what?

They'd settled in pockets in the tiny room in the resort meeting area. Lizzie had imposed on Michael to find somewhere far removed from the conference crowd. After all, they would be discussing whether their friends and colleagues could kill, or did kill.

She approached the podium and smiled. *Start out strong, Lizzie girl. Wow them. Be succinct.* "Sorry to delay your plans and gather you here. But it's crucial." Everyone quieted down and looked expectant.

Good grief. I'm more comfortable finding the bad guys than talking about it. I like working alone. But I need this group. I can do this. I'll ease into it. "We've gathered here to find a killer."

The startled gasps proved she'd gotten their attention. *Slide Lizzie; slide into it. When will I learn social skills? Not while dealing with a murder.*

Delia rose with grace and ambled up to her sister's side as if on a walk in the park. "We asked you to join us tonight to help establish peace at this conference. Inner tranquility and healing is always our goal as herbalists, right?"

The shuffling feet and whispers settled as many nodded and relaxed. Lizzie watched in awe, and quickly learned the method. She thanked Delia and gathered sympathy for friends and sought determination to solve the puzzle. "Who would want to kill Alexander

Howell? Why? The police ask the same questions. But you, here, know most everyone at the conference."

Edie, one of the oldest and kindest herbalists, raised her hand as if in a classroom. She'd come, not out of fear, but to discover what efforts had been made. "Lizzie, people are scared. When they're not at their best, they don't learn and they don't buy. The whole conference will fail. What can I tell them to lift their spirits?"

Lizzie stood front and center. "You can tell them there is a strong, united police force working to find the killer. They follow each lead as it comes. They're checking every aspect available."

Adelaide maneuvered to a standing position in the back row despite her bum leg, as she called it. "Do you have more specifics?"

"Not right now." Lizzie turned to Delia. "It will be your responsibility. Talk with the police daily. Cozy up to that Lieutenant Guetierrez fellow, too. Not just Detective Milano."

Natalie raised her hand. "As chair of the conference, shouldn't reconnaissance with the police be my job?"

Everyone snickered. Most had seen the man around and knew Natalie's interest had veered from finding a killer. She blushed but didn't back down.

Lizzie's eyes rolled upward. She raised her head as if pleading to God, yet managed a calm answer. "Coordinate with Delia. You already have many responsibilities. Like keeping the rumors down and running the conference."

"I juggle well. I'll find time to meet with Grant, I mean Detective Guetierrez, quite often. We do need to know what's going on if we plan a frontal assault of our own."

Miranda Pennywinkle nudged into the conversation. "I'll help. I'm sure Grant will make time for me. We connected."

Natalie pouted, but she did have her hands full. "Okay, I'll feed my questions through you."

Lizzie knew keeping track of the police was crucial. Meanwhile, she'd better work out an investigation plan. "I'll review any possible suspects and do some research of my own. Then we interrogate them one way or another."

Edie raised her hand again. "What can I do?"

Lizzie did a mental run through of ideas. "You will be in charge of a coalition of your trusted cohorts. Spread the word. And the word is 'calm.' Anyway you can. Use variety. We don't want the herbalists to know this is a campaign."

Someone else shouted, "What about the vendors? They're getting antsy. I would, too, if a fellow exhibitor died within feet of me."

"Right, George. Do you feel like you can do the same technique with the vendors? Maybe arrange for a few friends to wander through in a cheerful bent. If an acquaintance mentions thought of buying a product, escort them to the correct vendor."

The man nodded, with a bit of reluctance, but then the bob gained momentum and Lizzie sensed firm agreement. She added, "Keep it professional. No strong arming."

The gaunt man in his later years chuckled. "Will do."

Lizzie walked through the small group, smiling at each person. "Let's hear back from everyone in twenty-four hours. Report how the plans are progressing."

There was little mumbling but a great deal of rustling sounds as people gathered together their notebooks and prepared to leave. Delia halted everyone. "If you have questions, call me. If you have problems, call Lizzie. If you need help, call Lizzie. Don't confront her in front of the others. This is a secret campaign. The code word is 'quiet.' " She turned to Lizzie. "And for heaven's sake, keep your phone with you."

Everyone laughed on the lighter note at the end.

Lizzie caught the look in Delia's eyes from across the room. She smiled and mouthed, "Good going." Delia mouthed back a silent, "What are sisters for?"

Lizzie stayed to talk with a few friends, but she found out soon enough that sisters were invaluable tools in ongoing investigations. Delia, who'd retired to an alcove to contact Detective Guetierrez, phoned her. She discovered a problem needing her and Lizzie's urgent attention.

Delia whispered into the phone, "Michael's in custody. For possible murder."

Lizzie, now in the corridor near the vendor hall, shouted back. "For what?"

Natalie overheard and came running. She ushered Lizzie into the nearest room and shut the door. Despite her preoccupation with the phone call, Lizzie saw Natalie didn't hesitate to stay inside with her when she slammed it closed.

"That nice detective did what?"

Natalie's bug eyes revealed her anxiety but Lizzie didn't take the time to explain. The young woman would have to wait. She turned into a corner of the room to move away from her stare. Natalie's forthright and stalwart character enabled her to become conference chair. Her innate concern for others ensured her success. Lizzie knew this and finally relented, letting her hear as much of the conversation as she could.

"I'm barely acquainted with Michael but there's no way he killed anyone, not even horrible Howell. How do I know? Because he's a resort liaison to our group. If he was going to kill the man he would have never done it inside the vendor hall. His goal is for us to be successful. Even *you* have to admit a dead body causes fissures in smooth operations."

Lizzie glared at the phone. Nothing beat an old fashioned phone. It was so difficult to slam one of these new-fangled cell phones down when someone needed to be hung up on. Instead she put it back to her ear. This wasn't Delia's fault, after all.

Lizzie fell into the nearest chair, her stiff chin and pursed lips revealed her waning patience with Delia. "I'm known for my exceptional reasoning. I'll be at the sheriff's office in a few minutes."

Natalie's eyes widened. She knew how long it should normally take to drive there. Lizzie ignored her but shook her head at Delia even though she couldn't see through the phone. "Okay, okay. Natalie will drive me."

She rose from the chair, grabbed Natalie's hand and rushed out the door. Natalie put on the brakes, risking her hand in the process. "I've got a conference to run. I can't just high-tail it out of here."

Lizzie snapped. "And Michael in jail for the murder of Howell will help the conference how?"

"My God. What are you waiting for? My cars in the lot on the left. Should we notify the resort?"

"He's been there long enough. Let's go." As Natalie pulled her car keys from her pocket, Lizzie flipped them up and into her hand as she opened the drivers door. "Get in. I'm faster."

Minutes later, Lizzie raced into the sheriff's department and straight to Milano's office. An angry couple kept the officer at the front desk preoccupied. Before he could see who whisked by she unlatched the gate, and breezed through. Natalie saluted the guy, shrugged her shoulders, and followed. When Lizzie discovered the detective wasn't in his office it slowed her little. She was on a mission to save Michael.

The detective must have sensed trouble coming since he walked fast out of a room further down the corridor and turned her way. Once he saw her, he stopped mid-step. She didn't like the look he shot down the hall to her. Closing the gap between them, she grabbed his arm. He eyed her fingers. The sinews in her arm spoke of current strength and past fortitude. She knew it, and loosened up in hopes it would mask some of her power. Milano looked up, and her eyes made a plea. She followed it up verbally. "We have to talk with Michael. We'll find out what happened for you. No need to use cop tactics."

She saw the moment he took pity. But was it enough? His words were firm, though kind. "Ms. Ort, this is not the war and we won't hurt your friend. But he was caught in unusual circumstances at night, lurking near Howell's room."

She jerked back, freeing his arm. "That doesn't prove anything."

Milano didn't budge. "He's tall and strong and capable of murder. And he hasn't said a word."

She rushed down the corridor past him as if she had access to the room at the end. "I don't talk some times. Doesn't mean I killed anyone."

Milano didn't move with her. With reluctance she stopped, turned around and placed her hands on hips. "William. You know I'm right. He's not our killer. So let me find out what happened."

"So now it's William, huh?"

Detective Guetierrez strolled out of the next room, laughing. She took advantage of the interruption. "See why I worry about violent measures?"

The man in question blinked. "What? I'm not violent. I didn't hurt him."

She noticed he was smart enough not to move out of the doorway. "Gotcha!" she thought. Now we know where Michael is. *Thank you God. He's not locked up.*

Meanwhile, Detective Guetierrez scowled and Milano stood firm. Looked like they were caging her in. She knew not to force the issue. This was a peace mission, after all.

She faced the younger man. "Why your name, Guetierrez, and heritage, is redolent of the Dark Ages. It is reminiscent of violence and war."

The man stood still, looking in awe. "E-god, can you believe her? A woman after my own heart. Someone who knows from which I came. And single, too. May I offer you my hand in marriage?"

Lizzie knew better than to blush. But she pushed her advantage. "I wish to see Michael, please."

Unbelievable, the guy just declared love and looks right past me like I'm not here. She turned to see the cause. Ah hah, Natalie followed me. He's smitten. Good. She will hold his attention. She wondered what would happen if Miranda and Natalie confronted him together. *For now, Lizzie, deal with Milano and you're in.*

He jerked his head toward Guetierrez. "Okay detective. Tell her what happened."

Guetierrez drew his attention back to his partner and Lizzie. He took a breath as if to find his place, and said, "Your friend Michael was found skulking in the Building One corridor two doors down from Alexander Howell's room."

"What difference does it make? The man wasn't still in it, was he?"

He attempted to stifle a laugh by masking it with a cough. She knew because the cough was a horrible fake. Too bad she couldn't see behind her head to what Detective Milano was doing. When she turned, he was escorting Natalie toward her. *That's promising.*

He stopped at Guetierrez and asked him to accompany Miss Turner to his office and keep her company. Milano took Lizzie to the last room, where Michael was installed in a comfortable chair in front of a stalled security video.

Milano sat her down none too gently. "Michael with no last name, tell Ms. Lizzie what you told us."

Smooth words rolled off the man's tongue. "I didn't tell you anything, sir."

Milano smirked at Lizzie and said, "One of our men who's duty included keeping tabs on the comings and goings near Howell's room, found him at 2 a.m. slinking down the hall." He waved his hand from her to Michael. "He's all yours."

She cocked her head at Michael, and waited. "I was only visiting a friend. There's no crime there. I won't give you her name. She might get in trouble. Ms. Ort, you do understand, don't you?"

"I do. But we want to clear your name so you can go back to work. What if Detective Milano agrees not to reveal the name to anyone if it's not related to this case?"

Milano nodded. Michael looked contemplative, then confessed. She's a staff employee. We meet in secret because of the company rules. No fraternizing."

Milano harrumphed." That's it? If that's all, then we'll check with her, discreetly, and you're on your way."

After an exchange of paper, Milano left. He returned a few minutes later and shook Michael's hand. "Thank you sir, for your help in this matter."

She and Michael walked past Guetierrez's office. Lizzie saw and snagged Natalie, and they headed outside. Once at the car, Lizzie said, "Michael, we broke you out of there. Now what do we do with you?"

"I'm so sorry, ma'am. And I tried to make peace." He hung his head. "I told him you asked me to check on Howell. And I did. The same night you asked, but nothing happened. Howell acted preoccupied. But decent."

"It's okay, Michael. Let's hope this is the end of it."

She turned to Natalie, "Remember when you said he always looks innocent? Well, is he just looking innocent, or is he?"

CHAPTER TWENTY

As both men watched the trio leave, Milano saw his partner's puzzled frown where he expected to see admiration, or at least, lust.

Before he could comment, Guetierrez asked, "When she came in to make her plea to reopen the vendor hall, did you interview her about her confrontation with the victim?"

"No. I thought you handled it yourself. But I also heard it was Miss Ort who assaulted the guy."

"Apparently she was defending Miss Turner when the argument escalated."

"Hmmm. I already went over it all with Miss Ort, but set up another interview with Miss Turner. We'll both be there this time. In case you didn't notice, our best candidate so far just walked out the door with those two women."

Guetierrez grunted as they moved back inside. "Okay, but I know Miss Turner didn't do it. If nothing else, maybe she can help us with a list of suspicious people from the conference."

Milano settled at his desk while Guetierrez held up the doorway, again. Milano shuffled some papers, and looked up, "We should ask Lizzie in, too. Then we could have both suspects giving us a list of possible killers. But I wouldn't tell anyone else. We'd be high on the demotion list."

Guetierrez must have caught the sarcasm because he changed the subject. "Did Nederhoff find out anything on Washburn and Jefferson?"

"She's searching now. But I don't think Washburn has the brains to do it."

"He's gotta have good technology skills to keep such a high-tech job. You heard him talk with Jefferson. He *could* do it."

"Granted, but why? Is he intelligent enough?"

Grant snickered when he said, "Guess we wait for Nederhoff. Unless you want to ask Miss Ort. What's going on with you two— what with you calling her Lizzie?" He raised his fingers in the air and made quote marks around her name to accompany his smirk.

"What do you mean?"

"Why do you use Lizzie. What happened to ma'am?"

"With that woman, calling her Lizzie is a sign of respect. It works better than ma'am. I think she considered my exaggerated deference an insult."

"And we don't want to upset her, why?"

"Because we don't have a killer in our hands and she might yet help us find one."

Guetierrez drifted out without another word.

Now what? Do my own suspect list. Or shut down that conference trying. First, check with our man viewing all the security videos. If he hasn't gone bonkers, he might have found something. He called. His luck, the man wasn't in. He left a message.

He pulled out a list of vendors situated around or near the victim. So far no one had come forth with information regarding the evening the man was killed. It was time to hunt them down. If we call them into the department it might loosen someone's tongue. Better yet, we'll escort them here. Half of them flew in and don't have transportation anyway. Nice touch, driving them away in a cop car. Might frighten even more talk from people watching them take off.

His humor restored, he asked Officer Nederhoffer to review the list, gather what information she could on phone numbers and location, then send a car to start picking people up. He added, "Schedule a meeting with each of my staff involved in the case. If there's no useable video, we'll move on to something else. The new guy who's been working the night shift for us, walking the rounds at the conference, what's-his-name, better locate him and get him in here this afternoon."

Returning to his office he thought about what they had. Good find on Michael no-name. Too bad it didn't pan out. His mind ran through other options, and added Officer Venezia to the meeting list. With any luck he'd found a big clue in the victim's computer files that would lead them to a killer. Right now he needed large red arrow pointing to someone.

He spent the rest of the day lining up hopes and possibilities. Nothing firm popped up, and breakfast proved long ago. When Guetierrez asked if he wanted to catch a burger and beer at two he jumped up in mid-sentence. They'd all been weaving around in an insane dance that mocked his efforts. Time to regroup. God forbid he'd rely on his partner for help. Still, the man couldn't be all fancy sunglasses and sporty antiques. And the beer might clear his head.

Most of the men hung out around the corner at Handcuff Hannah's but not Guetierrez. He should have known. "We just passed the bar. Where you headed?"

"This place is better, and the beer is higher quality."

"Hannah's has Yeungling as well as Miller. What's the problem?"

Guetierrez drove like an old lady in his jeep and didn't respond.

Milano managed silence for a few minutes, then blurted, "Whose funeral procession are we in?"

Guetierrez pulled into a wide parking space, his car hugging the edge of the lot. If the next guy coming in stayed on his side of the line he'd have to have a five-foot door to scratch Grant's car. "You think it's safe enough there or should you move it over another inch or two?" Milano jibed.

His partner pocketed the keys, took a second look, and walked to the bar. If you could call this upscale place a bar. "You're goin' in for a real treat here, Bill. The beer is beyond belief."

Milano jerked the man's arm back. Stood still and waited for the man's full attention. "What did you call me?"

Guetierrez shook off the hand. "My bad, sir. Slipped out."

Milano laughed. "Cut the bunk. William is fine. But I never want to hear Bill again."

His partner opened the door wide and ushered William in. "Bill? Bill who?"

The burgers were everything promised, William thought after one bite. He sat back to enjoy the meal. The beer came with an education. Grant explained many details about the place and the drinks. My level of knowledge suited me fine before, but the man couldn't seem to help it. He actually believed this highfalutin stuff. Grant sucked on a glass of Birra del Borgo Re Ale Extra, and didn't stop talking. "It's an India pale ale—brewed in Italy no less."

William sipped and grinned. "Good." He added, "I had some Yeungling India Pale Lager the other day. New. Pretty good, too.

"That might have been, but this is superb ale. I think the hops added to the end of the brewing process make the difference. I like the crisp balanced flavor."

"Okay, Grant. I appreciate the taste. Just saying. You can get lager nearer home and all."

The sarcasm skimmed past Grant's head, but William didn't care. Mellowed by the ale, he stretched back and enjoyed the rest of the meal. Ever since William heard of Miss Weiss's possible stalker he'd spent more time at the resort and the conference. An extra security guard hired by the resort patrolled the property at night. They talked about having the man keep a check on Abby when William couldn't but it wasn't always feasible. Grant concluded, "Should be enough coverage for now, considering we're not even sure she's in danger."

"But he could find her in the trees."

Grant slapped his feet flat on the floor. "What?"

"Abby takes a shortcut through the woods. It ends up at the back of her lot."

"And you know this how?"

Milano dipped his head away from Grant's scrutiny. "I walked her home last night. I told her to drive from now on but she's the pig-headed sort."

Grant barked out a belly laugh. Strange for such a refined guy. Milano didn't have to wait long for the reason. "Trust me you don't want to use that word with her," he said.

"Too late, I already did."

"God help you. I need to give you some lessons. And it wouldn't hurt to sharpen your appearance a little."

"I'm perfectly happy with my clothes and my life."

"But you wear last century t-shirts." Grant slugged down more beer. Disgust must have blurred his refinement.

"My clothes were in season once and I'll wear them till they are in season again—and it saves me from having to think when I get up in the morning."

"At least you wear band collars. There's hope."

William dashed the idea with his next sentence. "They're as close as I could come to my old Henley-Tees. I have it on good authority some of them now cost $350. Besides, these are all over the place, even on sale—ridiculous."

Grant's empty beer glass settled on the table as he shook his head and rose. "A stylish and frugal man. What's next boss."

The sun beat down on Milano as he walked to the car, the gentle breeze reminding him of lost days enjoying Florida's gulf coast in February. Maybe when this case is done, he thought.

Within an hour they'd hauled the mung bean lady in for questioning. She'd hit the top of the list after Lizzie's alert. She was the first of several more vendors near the murder scene to interview. He and his partner would take turns asking for information until they figured out how to play this one.

Guetierrez, the renowned charmer, took the lead. "Now Miss Matilda Rasland, your booth, only a couple down from the victim's, touted the use of mung beans to cure people?"

"It's Matelda, young man. Not Matilda."

Milano studied her while the two talked. Kind of snooty and arrogant, and tall with a spine fortified by mental titanium. He tilted his head and took a closer look. Thin-boned, frail for someone proclaiming a miracle product. Guetierrez continued with the questions and she huffed back the answers.

"Well you don't have to hold your nose when you speak of my creation. It works and that's what counts."

Milano hung back and considered her over-all look. The felt cloche hat appeared glue to her hair and looked like it had been through the washer. Guetierrez badgered her with questions. They weren't the problem. It was his attitude. What was the guy up to?

He scrunched his upper lip under his teeth and kept quiet. He watched the woman, too, for reaction as much as appearance. For someone barely middle-aged time had been harsh. It either bleached out her color, or she thought insipid yellow-green strengthened her product image. Milano mused about the color of the beans, since he'd never eaten or seen any. Maybe they were purple, for all he knew.

Miss Rasland didn't go in for tact. "And I don't shove some mung beans into the bottle and claim it's a cure. I created the finest mung bean seed coat extract and combined it with green tea leaf extract." He heard her response to his partner's question and took a peek at his reaction. Good job. Not even a half-grin.

She spouted her slogan, "Health Ahead of its Time."

Guetierrez probed deeper. "When did you last see the man? Why did you hate him? Did he do something to you to spike your ire?"

"You're the only one spiking my ire, young man. You're supposed to wait for an answer before you fling out the next question. I never saw him and didn't hate him."

Milano considered her with care. They were running out of steam. Looking at her took you into a sepia-toned picture. Strange. The clothes appeared up-style when separated from their color. A vine-design quilted hip jacked that matched her solid pants. And the cloche when taken with the rest of it might add panache for anyone else. Instead it served as a lid for her hair sticking out of it in straw shocks.

Guetierrez plowed on. "So it cures cancer?"

She sniffed. "My literature doesn't mention cancer."

Milano pulled a bottle from the brown paper bag they'd collected when they brought her in. His partner grabbed it and read the blurb. He stared her right in the eyes. "Worse, it says it reduces chronic inflammation."

"Don't say it with a sneer. It's a good thing. High chronic inflammation reduces the length of telomeres and when that happens, you die young."

Milano rose and braced his hands on the table. Leaning forward, he said, "Kind of like Howell died young?" Guetierrez waited a second than threw the follow-through punch. "Were you afraid his telomere product would outsell your stuff?"

"Stuff? You call my highly developed scientific research 'stuff'? How dare you." Her voice escalated as she leapt from her chair.

Milano grabbed her wrist in time. Who knows how strong her anger would have impacted her swing. His partner grinned. He'd attempted to arouse her ire. It had worked. What a team. The only result of her anger proved to be more fury. No confession.

No confession. No evidence. No proof. No arrest.

The partners shared looks as she left in a huff. Guetierrez said, "She's tall enough. Mean enough. Self-absorbed enough to want him dead."

Milano waited as he scowled. And added his own thoughts. "But I don't like her for it." They both shook their heads, then said "Nah," at the same time. Milano asked Nederhoff to delve deeper into her background, and sent Jerry to interview other vendors near the booth. But they felt it was a dead end.

Milano went back to his office. His partner gravitated to his spot in the doorway. "Who's next?"

"It'd help if we had someone, wouldn't it?"

Guetierrez dropped his head as he turned. "The killer would be good."

CHAPTER TWENTY-ONE

"You're sure this is a good idea?"

"Delia, quit fussing. We *must* find the killer." Lizzie straightened a few papers on the podium, though she'd prepared no speech. The herbalists they'd called to help find the solution arrived to report in.

Each one had spent years in research. How different could this be? Okay, learning the benefits of parsley—detecting who would kill. Not the same. But in the field you worked with what you had. Her team today—plant lovers. How could they find this killer?

Her sister sat in the chair nearest Lizzie. How nice. She's here to provide support. But as the chosen few filtered in, Delia whispered, "You'd better know what you're doing."

"No complaints from you yesterday. Why now?"

"Fear?"

Lizzie made a wry face, then looked over the group.

"As you all know, we gathered here this morning to find a killer. It's time to report progress.

The frilly Lois and her close friend Sheila glanced at each other. The elderly man, George, and his friend, Edie, also signaled acceptance as they straightened in pride and attention. Now the group was on board.

"Edie, you were to calm the conference attendees. What happened?"

"I think it helped. Herbalists are all nice people. They managed to settle themselves down. About the murder? I didn't learn a thing."

Lizzie looked at George.

"I wowed the vendors with all the buyers I brought through yesterday. Cheered them right up."

Julia shouted out. "You should have asked for a commission."

He grumbled, "Should have. And I missed the herbal talks all day."

She sallied, "But George, you've heard them all over the years. You could practically give them. We know you come now just to look at the pretty new faces."

George cackled. "Yeah, ain't that the truth." Then he faced Lizzie. "I'm sorry. I didn't see no one suspicious at all."

"We need your ideas. A discussion of more far-reaching possibilities than the police have considered. They work diligently to find the murderer of Alexander Howell. We could narrow the search by figuring out the why."

She held up her hands as the noise level rose in chattered talk throughout the room.

"They determined Howell died from a blow to the head. The security cameras were malfunctioning so they have no description of the killer. He was killed after the vendor hall closed on Tuesday and before it opened Wednesday— but most likely just past midnight. His product has been analyzed and no one could have a serious injury from an overdose or misuse."

When she paused, George's friend Russ stood. "What can we do?"

"Let's be organized. We need to find attendees and vendors in the hall as it closed. What did they see? Also, if it was a vendor who killed him, what would be the gain? Third, if an herbalist attending the conference did it, again, what would be the benefit? Fourth, was it deliberate?"

Lois interjected, "Could it have been someone from the outside?"

Lizzie added, "Maybe we should start there. If we can eliminate that possibility, it would help."

Russ said, "It's a great concept. Enter in secret. Commit the kill. Leave the area. The conference is a perfect setting. It throws suspicion on all of us. With so many prospects, why look elsewhere?"

Sheila agreed. "The death might have nothing to do with herbs. Or an adversary in the field could use the opportunity to eliminate competition."

A hand shot up in the back of the group. "How easy is it to get in?"

Delia, answered on behalf of the conference committee. "Unfortunately, too easy. Outside people frequent the resort for dining, for use of the beach. We try to restrict entrance to the speeches and programs. But for the large talks, attendees come through in groups and the door guard might not notice a stray person mixed in."

"What about the vendor hall?"

"Not as easy," Natalie Turner, as conference chair, spoke with firmness. "But if someone light-fingered attended a talk they could snag a name tag. It's not like this is Fort Knox. Usually, we have trouble filling the seats."

Worried about despair in the group, Lizzie scrambled mentally for a bright note in their plans. None popped up. Just then, the door banged open and Persephone rushed in like a whirlwind and strode to the front. "So sorry. So sorry. My alarm didn't go off."

Several friends snickered. A brave one announced, more to the crowd than to Persephone, "Maybe you should stop throwing it across the room."

The woman in question laughed. Most knew anger and pettiness bounced off her. "Okay. I imbibed a little at our spontaneous party last night. The alarm can be so, well, alarming. Why do we have to meet at eight in the morning?"

Before anyone answered, she added, "And who was that strange man lurking by the door out there? I've seen him before, just can't place him."

Lizzie perked up. No, it couldn't be Abby's stalker, could it? Abby said not a word but looked at her wide-eyed. Both Lizzie and Delia raced to the door, and flung it open. Several of the closest herbalist checked out the corridor and shuffled back in, shaking their heads. "Empty."

They all stared at the new entrant. She looked around. "What?"

"Can you at least describe the man?"

She stuttered. "Well, I was rushing to get here. I didn't see much. He was tall and lean. Medium everything else. Clean. Not grungy."

Lizzie winced at the vague description. The Abby patrol needed to be put on full alert. And Milano would get an earful when she saw him. She thought he planned to protect her young friend.

Persephone nudged her way into the seat next to Delia's. "What did I miss? Why are we meeting?"

Arising from her knees where she'd been whispering assurances to Abby, Lizzie moved to the podium again and gave a short version of their discussion. So far we have not eliminated the idea of someone coming in from the outside.

However, let's move on and leave this concept to the police. Delia can check with them later and discover on progress there. Meanwhile, let's pursue what benefit would a conference herbalist gain by Howell's death? Any thoughts?"

Natalie responded. "We know his research into telomerase had world-wide ramifications. His is not the only product offering longer and healthier life. Many scientists work effortlessly to find the answer." She looked around to see apt attention. "We don't know how close Howell's elixirs came to a medical breakthrough."

Sheila kept her head lowered and mumbled, "So a competitor in fear of Howell's success is a strong possibility."

"I'm afraid so, Sheila," Lizzie said, "But I question why that night and why here. Though the location could throw suspicion on all of us, it also means numerous people could have seen it happen or see the killer leave the hall."

George piped up. "We could assume for a minute the killer hadn't planned much ahead. And probably did it in anger. A not so spur of the moment meeting, but a definite spontaneous kill. Otherwise they would have brought a weapon."

Abby added, "That could be a competitor, or an herbalist angry at Howell's affront to natural and pure herbology."

Lizzie reminded them of the tampered security cameras. That required some forethought and not instantaneous anger. She vowed to find out more, but continued with the meeting. "Do any of you remember a fellow herbalist or vendor speaking against telomerase or Howell's product?"

They looked at each other and shrugged. Nothing. She was ready to pursue a different approach when Abby said, "That man I introduced you to out on the patio? We discussed Telomerase Might. He acted friendly enough. His name is Jacob, and we did talk about other things, like herbal things."

Lizzie urged her own when her voice struggled for further words.

Abby cleared her throat and mumbled Uh, he called the umm, dead man, a quack."

Lois jumped in. "I know we try to vet all our vendors, but even if he was a fraud, why kill him?"

"Good point, Lois, but I think a casual conversation with the man couldn't hurt." She nodded to Abby. "We'll look for him later."

Another hand shot up from the group. "Maybe it was a vendor who wasn't selling a competing product, but someone angry he was racking up sales. Money that might have filtered over to the others?"

Abby interjected. "I walked through those aisles quite a bit on opening day. I didn't see him sell a thing."

Lizzie said, "Russ or George, could you talk with vendors near Howell's booth and see what they noticed? And take a friend. Never question anyone alone."

Oliver, who'd snuck in at the last minute, grinned. "Yeah, make sure you're not alone when you talk with Matelda. She might rope you into a tete-a-tete behind her booth."

They all laughed, until the doors slammed open again and Detective's Milano and Guetierrez trod down the aisle toward Lizzie. "So much for our secret meeting. Anyone else coming?"

Detective Milano caught Abby's eye and smiled. Then he turned to Lizzie. "Snideness does not become you Miss Ort. We came to get Miss Natalie Turner." He swiveled around until he saw her. She stood when she heard her name. All the others gasped.

Both detectives acted surprised, but Milano must have realized their concern. "No, we're not arresting her. Excuse me, Miss Turner, but you didn't respond to our phone message we wanted to meet with you urgently. Michael was kind enough to direct us here to get you."

Lizzie growled under her breath. *Traitor. That man will hear from me.*

CHAPTER TWENTY-TWO

Lizzie opened their door later in the evening to a subdued Abby. One she'd not seen before. As frightened as she'd been during the stalker report, she never looked so dejected. Though not the maternal type, Lizzie pulled her into the room with a hug. She set her on the sofa in the suite and knelt down. Not letting go, she held the woman at arm's length to study her face. "Tell me. What happened?"

Abby shivered in the warm room. "I'm not sure anything did." Then she hung her head. "But I'm afraid to go home."

Standing abruptly, Lizzie strode across to the refrigerator. *Where's the soft and tender Delia when I need her? I don't do nurturing. She snorted. Fat chance the government would have wanted her as a spy if she did.* She grabbed a bottle of juice in one hand and poured it into a glass as she struggled to open a mini-bottle of rum with the other. *Do I chug it myself or mix it into her drink?*

She turned back to Abby, after dumping the contents of the bottle into the juice. This was as motherly as she got. One way or the other it might do the trick. Mellow is good, right?

Her friend had added a stiffened chin to her repertoire, to accompany the shivering, but it hadn't quashed the shakes. *Maybe I should have made tea instead.* If the rum and juice didn't work, she'd make tea and drench it with more rum.

She didn't know how to mother but she did know interrogation. "Tell me where you have been this evening."

Abby swallowed, then blurted, "I was walking through the vendor hall. I wanted to place the next day's agenda at each booth."

"Wasn't that Miranda's job?"

"Yes, but she wimped out after finding the body." She stuttered, "I'm sorry. I wasn't polite. I don't blame her for being afraid. I never saw the, umm, body."

"That's okay, dear, we'll do polite some other day. So you dropped off the schedules and something bothered you. Were the vendors all still there?"

"Some were. It was late. I only saw two people strolling the aisles and a few vendors sticking it out till the final minute."

Lizzie looked her in the eye to calm her. "Then what?"

Abby couldn't hold the stare. She hung her head. "This is the silly part. I whipped around the corner to the next aisle and crashed into Oliver. You know Oliver?"

"He's an herbalist with a vendor booth just down from the victim's. He's a huge and strong black man who kids about the elf-warrior meaning of his name. Did he do something to scare you?"

"Yes. No. I had just finished leaving the last agenda and wanted to go home. He startled me. He's so big, you know. And my heart tripped. Don't know if it was him, or the draped-over Howell booth that did it."

"He is a gentle man. Though I suppose his proximity to the victim's area added suspicion."

"Oliver was kind. He walked me to the building exit. The only other person I saw was Jacob. The guy I introduced you to on opening day. You remember him?"

"The German we mentioned in the meeting? Now there's a quiet man who bothered me for no known reason. Sorry, I never saw him today. I should have looked him up."

Abby emptied her glass and settled back. "I'm glad I'm not the only one who can't quite be comfortable with him. And he seeks my attention."

With the shivering ceased, Lizzie relaxed too. "Was it this Jacob who frightened you?"

"Not really. But I didn't want to see him. He tried to walk me home the other night. Thank heavens that nice Detective Milano came by and escorted me himself."

Lizzie clamped her lip. This was not the time for matchmaking. She didn't want her silly little inward grin to seep out. "Then Jacob doesn't know where you live?"

"Right. And I didn't want him to follow me tonight. So I came here."

"Intelligent and logical. You did the correct thing. Why be frightened?"

"I told you I don't know. The shivering started when I caromed into Oliver and wouldn't stop. That's what scared me. It was my reaction."

Lizzie pulled her up and into a hug. This time it was a delight. She laughed out loud. "Abby. We are our own worst enemies. It's a cliché for a reason, because it's true. And it happens to all of us."

Abby smiled. Even though it was sheepish, it brightened her face. Lizzie turned but kept her arm around the woman's shoulders. "I take it you didn't drive today?"

"No. And I know I promised the detective I would. But I'd planned to walk home in the daylight."

"I'm sure he wanted you surrounded with friends at all times, missy. Not just at night."

"I got roped into this job at the last minute. Miranda and I talked for a while. Boy, is she smitten with that Detective Guetierrez. By the time we finished and I grabbed the schedules, it was late and hardly anyone was around."

As Lizzie feared. The protection brigade was crumbling. Nothing on the surface proved the need so people got lax, entangled in their own lives in this short stretch at the resort.

She walked Abby home. Time to eliminate suspects. Or find a killer. *If I could figure the connection to Abby it might speed up progress. Should I call Milano and see if he has a lead?* He acted concerned about Abby, yet, here she stood, alone. To be fair, he had many angles to pursue. She halted part way back to the resort. The police had enough time. Now she would do this herself.

She tried Natalie on her cell as she walked to Oliver's room. The woman knew most people at the conference. Her opinion of the man would provide what approach to take. No answer. Before she reached his building, she tried Miranda, who was young but knowledgeable. Maybe she knew the man. When the girl answered the phone, Lizzie sat in a chair in the social lounge inside his building to talk.

Miranda did know him. According to her, he was firm and brave. She asked her own questions. Lizzie revealed as little as possible. No sense in scaring this young woman, too. Miranda delivered a few scathing remarks about anyone who might suspect Oliver.

"Why, ah'm thinkin he's is the most stalwart and true person I know. His ethics run every aspect of his life and his business."

"Settle down, girl. I felt the same about the man but I was sure you knew him well and could support my decision. If the police decide to vet all of the vendors near the victim's booth. May I tell them you will back the man?"

"Absolutely."

Resolved to form her own conclusions, Lizzie knocked on Oliver's door. It opened in an exuberant swing to match the man within.

"Why hello, ma'am. How can I help you?"

Nice. He didn't ask why I was calling at eight-forty-five at night. "I have a few questions for you. Do you mind? Abby mentioned running into you tonight. She appeared upset."

"Yes, ma'am. She did."

"Do you have any idea why?"

"No. But I walked her to the door. I would have escorted her further but she said she was fine. I needed to return to my booth."

He gestured for her to sit. The pristine room echoed his appearance. Though a large man, he dressed well. His temporary living quarters reflected his elegance. The bone-handled brush and comb on the dresser. The necklace of onyx and gold hanging on the mirror. No fast food leftovers.

"Please. How may I help you?"

"Could you tell me more about the herbal product you sell?"

He walked to the desk and pulled a bag from the drawer. "These herbs are my main product. To treat respiratory ailments. The mix contains much fennel. There are variations. Some bags have dill added in equal measure for those who cough."

She looked at him. "Why do you sell these? I don't think it's for the money."

A booming laugh preceded his comment. "No. I was sick once. The herbs cured me. I believe it was a sign God wanted me to help others. My products will do that."

A scant fifteen minutes later she erased his name from her mental list and moved on to the next guy. It was a man Oliver expressed concern about. She'd never met Harold Polymer. Nine o'clock at night wasn't too late to check on someone. People's guards are down late due to weariness. She used this to her advantage. Thank heavens she'd copied Natalie's room assignment list onto her phone that day after the scuffle with Howell. Harold Polymer was in for a treat. A crash course in interrogation by one of the best. Too bad he was on the receiving end.

He was a hefty fellow, with a square face, puffed up with age and junk food detriment.

"What do you want?" He growled, the saggy jowl saved by another square, his chin in a perpetual scowl that elongated his mouth and thinned his lips.

He'd opened the door just enough to study her. *Private. Or fearful?* She determined to find out. He always wore those glasses that darkened in the sun and he sat in the back of his booth where they hid his eyes. She'd wondered about the purpose then. Square shaped lenses of course, as if he wouldn't want to soften his face any. She stepped forward, extending her hand in greeting to accompany her smile. Her left elbow bumped the door in supposed clumsiness, thus opening it further.

Polymer lacked grace but not enough to slam the door on her arm. The man let her in without question. Her age did that sometimes. She liked to think it was her physical stature, but didn't care as long as she was in. He provided a limp handshake. Her eyes took in the room and his height in one glance. He was tall enough to knock Howell on the head. Not exactly strong proof there. She needed much more.

"My name is Elizabeth Ort. I'm part of the conference organization team. How are you?"

"I heard you speak. Don't usually have time for such but the vendor hall was still closed that early in the day. What is it?"

Difficult to hedge into things when he was so insistent. She'd opted for the tried and true. "Would you tell me a little of the product you sell. Sprig of Janus, right?"

The man could smile—what a surprise. And he attempted to tuck his shirt in surreptitiously. It hung out of his khakis in a wrinkled state. Either his packing skills needed improvement or he always looked disheveled and he didn't notice the effect. Did this guy think he projected a professional image? Or maybe he believes herbalist prefer the casual look. His head sprouted fine tufts of hair like he'd been electrocuted. Should they seek a warrant to search his hotel room to look for a comb?

Finding one, on the other hand, might be difficult. With any hope, his science evoked neater resolve. His bottled gold, that being her name for it once she heard the cost, held top spot in his life interests. No doubt about it. He hadn't even asked why she wanted information on his product. Did the man know Janus was the Roman God of Portals and Beginnings and Endings? Maybe he had a good marketing department.

He ushered her into a chair and sat down himself. "It's a miracle cure for sure. Do you need some?"

Fat chance. I could probably take him in one move despite his height. Instead she said, "I'd want to know much more about it."

"The chemistry is so complex there's no way you would understand it, but trust me, this product will save your life."

"Good to know if I'm going to fall off a building. How does it work—parachutes?"

The smile disappeared and the pasty jowls tightened. "You joke? Why this product controls pain like none other you've tried."

"Hmm. Continue."

"My Sprig of Janus hits the same opioid receptor in the brain as morphine. Sprig of Janus helps bind to the serotonin receptor and decreases pain. And it all comes from a native plant in the southeast Asian nations."

She never expected he'd give out so much information. But she tried for more. "Is it addicting, like morphine?"

He jumped up. "No. They've used it in Thailand for thousands of years."

I'll hit him now. "How well did you know Alexander Howell?"

"Who?" He scowled. "You mean the dead guy? I never met him. "Didn't have time. My elixir cures. I heard his stuff only claims to extend life. Somehow."

"Wasn't he competition, though?"

"You're kidding! Believe me. I sell to a different crowd."

"Do you develop your own product?"

"With my team back home. But I know it's pure. And reliable. I use it myself. Works wonders."

The bell rang in her head as she bid farewell. The ashen face. The sunglasses. Howard Polymer was a former addict. His product substituted for morphine. Unless Howell died of an overdose, Polymer was in the clear.

CHAPTER TWENTY-THREE

"I guess it's not a good time to pester Milano about the phone number I gave him in Chicago." Lizzie speculated to Delia.

"That's for sure. I thought you called the number yourself, the day you found it in Howell's room."

Lizzie led her sister through the aisles of the vendor hall. She wanted to make a list of all participants near Howell's spot. Detective Milano probably interviewed them already but it couldn't hurt to check. That Rasland lady epitomized weird. After making a note, she answered Delia, "I only called Howell's receptionist at the main office. I said I could reach no one at the number. When I rattled it off she confirmed it was Howell's personal research lab. I'm still waiting for Milano to reveal what they found."

"Yeah, the man has no sense of urgency. Why it was all of a couple of days ago," Delia said.

Lizzie walked further down the same aisle, "Sister, snideness doesn't become you. We only have two days left to the conference. All our suspects will be gone. We've got to break open this case." She halted and jerked Delia's arm. "Stop. look. That's the man Abby talked about, that Jacob guy. The one who we argued with over herbs usefulness in lengthening telomeres."

Following Lizzie's gaze, her sister asked, "The one with the wire-rimmed glasses?" At Lizzie's nod, she added, "I'm on it." Delia stepped into place behind some people, and minced her way through the crowds until she arrived a few feet from where the man stood. Lizzie came behind at a sedate pace, stopping here and there to chat with vendors she knew. Abby's interest in the man urged her to listen and watch. His eyes moved rapidly everywhere though he didn't speak. He watched Harry, the muscle builder, peddling his new organic protein shake.

Delia had stepped back and waited for her. Now she spoke nonsense to appear occupied. Lizzie looked over her shoulder and saw him observing Justina, the mousy vendor five down from Howell's old location. The woman sat with her bowed head, hiding in the back of her booth. Was he casing the place, looking for an easy steal? Hunting down more competitors? Whoa, where did her vicious thinking come from? He looked a gentle soul. Quiet. Peaceful. Too peaceful. Or is he calculating?

Her sister heard her whisper the word out loud. "Calculating what? Now he's watching fellow herbalists meandering through the aisles."

Lizzie had no answer, but said, "It's strange he never seems to know or greet herbalists. I saw him yesterday before a program began. Most people talked animatedly to each other but he remained aloof. I didn't think about it much. Then."

Delia tipped her head sideways, awaiting a clue from Lizzie for what to do next. Lizzie contemplated options, and shrugged. I would have cornered him before but had no specific questions. I can't accuse him of stalking on instinct alone.

Jacob turned, glared at the two women. He couldn't have heard them, yet he pushed his way through the herbalists lingering by the vendor booths. Some frowned at him but moved. Delia raced after him but Oliver and a friend lurched in front of her. Lizzie saw it and ran the opposite direction in hopes of cutting him off at the end of the next aisle. Sweet Julie, grabbed her arm. "What's happening? Are you okay?"

"Julie, I'm fine. But in a hurry. We'll talk later." Lizzie wrenched free and stumbled to the main corridor. No Jacob anywhere. Delia arrived at the same time. They shook their heads simultaneously in puzzlement and disgust. Lizzie sighed. "Am I getting too old for this?"

Delia grasped her hand and ushered her out into the patio. She settled her at one of the tables in the corner. "It's okay. This isn't your venue. You're more dark streets and fiends. Not friendly herbalists."

She succeeded in making Lizzie laugh. "You're right, sister. I'm still in my prime and it's just the surroundings that have changed."

Though they were not secluded, Lizzie realized no one paid them any attention. They could talk. An urgent question bounced around in her brain. Maybe Delia could help pull out an answer. "Do you have an idea why he ran? Was it because of us?"

Delia also checked the people traffic before she spoke. "He did take off the instant after seeing us. But was it because he saw us? And why would we be a threat?"

Lizzie stood. "Good question. If, indeed he is Howell's killer, he's stayed under the radar so far. Why give himself away? And why now?"

"We're answering questions with questions. Not much forward progress."

"Ah, but it is progress. He can't know we are helping the police. So it must be something besides us. Let's check out the area he was, and the booths near where we stood at the time. There's got to be a clue somewhere."

"Should we call the police, instead?"

Lizzie's upper lip curled in disdain, and with only a cursory glance at Delia, she took off. Her sister followed, dragging her feet. *I should be more sympathetic. My sister isn't cut out for this life, yet she won't quit. God bless her.*

Lizzie had a plan. A short term one, but a plan none the less. She liked the orderliness of it all. It palpated with urgency and hope. She reached the door to the vendor hall and peered in. Now, where was Jacob standing when he tore out of here? She assessed the spot they'd been, then moved from there to his last location. Okay, it wasn't an all-out run, but he'd sped up. For all she knew, he could have remembered the time and raced to meet someone. He glared right at them, though. She decided to stay and question the vendors.

The Herbs for Inflammation lady had been the closest. She waited her turn and quietly asked the woman if she'd seen a man in the last hour with wire rim glasses. Her face looked blank. Then Lizzie described him. "He was lean and maybe five foot, nine inches tall."

The woman's face brightened. "Yah, I saw him. Very intense face. Didn't talk much. He didn't even touch any of my bottles to read them. Just looked."

Lizzie said thanks and stepped back, puzzled. This didn't seem to be a crucial element of the mystery. What was the man up to? Of course, this is just four down from where the victim's booth had been. The police had dismantled everything by the end of the first day. Now, a large easel displaying the scheduled talks for the week, and a wide variety of blooming herbs filled the space. She asked each of the neighboring booth owners about this Jacob. Nothing.

She studied the area where she and Delia stopped to talk. The herbalists exuded innocence and good will, as well as the products. One featured herbal tonics for many ailments, another an array of digestive bitters. No clues there, though the bitters might be a necessity if they didn't solve this murder soon. Lizzie shrugged in dismay while she asked around about Jacob. No one remembered him.

As she turned from the last booth and final disappointment, Glenn, an old timer at the conference, and a dear friend of Natalie's mother, touched her elbow. "Delia sent me to find you. She said you were looking for Jacob. Or clues. I met him with Abby. He's a German. Last name, uhh, the pea guy. It will come." His face lit up. "Mendel. No, Meindl. That's it. Jacob Meindl. I saw him stride out of here like his feet were on fire. Didn't know to follow him. Sorry."

They walked to the patio. Glenn stopped and found a table but Lizzie wanted to continue her search for information. "Thanks. I forgot to ask Abby for his last name. You've been a help." Distracted with further concerns about this strange adversary, she bumped smack dab into Detective Milano.

"Why, hello sir. Looking for an herbal pick me up? There's quite a few products I could point out to you. I was eyeing the bitters myself but maybe you need help with your liver. Or over there, the perfect bottle of pills for heart palpitations." His attitude surprised her. She'd attempted to irk him. Or make him smile. But his wide open eyes and pursed lips made her wonder if he thought she was guilty of something.

I know my face doesn't reveal guilt. I was schooled in the innocent look and honed it over the years. Why a clenched jaw? She felt the light touch of Delia's fingers on her arm from behind. Once glance at her face and she knew why his resembled churned butter. *Delia, dear, why must you appear so culpable. We didn't do anything. Only hunting a killer.*

She patted her sister's hand. "He's on our side, dear. We're after the same thing. Justice for poor Mr. Howell."

Now, the detective's eyebrows reached for his hairline. *Maybe I overdid it a little. Rule number one—distract.* "Why detective, I'm so glad we've met up. I have a question for you. Do you have time for a cup of coffee, or a pastry? This resort has some of the tastiest. My treat." She hooked arms with Delia and the detective before he could respond and marched to the refreshment area.

Delia excused herself. "You're on your own. I have a committee meeting—the main speaker just lodged a complaint. Has the finest digs you can imagine and he's not happy."

Once the detective settled into a chair, Lizzie said, "I'll be right back."

This time he was too quick for her. He gripped her arm like instant glue and pulled out a chair for her while still seated. "Thank you, but I had an early start, and plenty of coffee already."

Defeat disguised with her smile was still defeat. The smile only lessoned his satisfaction. She saw it in his eyes. With any luck she could turn the tide swiftly in her direction. "Officer, you're very serious today. What can I help with? Is Natalie, I mean Miss Turner, okay?"

"Your friend is fine. And you can take that look off your face. I'm not pinning a charge on her. She was occupied late into the evening on the night in question. Numerous phone calls from distraught attendees kept her up most of the night, but too busy to haunt the vendors hall."

Lizzie said, "I'm relieved you've moved on. You're sure now?"

"Yes,, she's a little pipsqueak of a woman and I doubt if she could pull a banner pole down, let alone strike a heavy blow with it."

"So that brings us to . . .?"

"Funny, I was going to ask you the same thing? I hear you've been organizing troops and interrogating suspects."

Her outraged, "What?" would have deterred most men. Not this guy. He just sat looking at her, waiting. So she filled the silent space. "Have you heard anything from his lab in Chicago?"

"Yeah, I heard you called there before the local police arrived. Why not just announce they had five minutes to clean out anything suspicious that might get them caught?"

"I gave nothing away, sir. Merely called the office and asked for Alexander Howell, proprietor. I gave her the number on the sheet of paper I gave you. Said he gave it to me and did I have it correct. She seemed surprised he'd given me the number to his personal lab."

"I would guess so. Since he was already dead a day when you found it."

"I did mention he'd confided in me about the secrecy of his research. And maybe mentioned he wanted to hire me. I asked for an employment application, and well, any pertinent information she could provide. Why let her know I knew he was dead? It might instigate a crying jag or something ghastly like that."

"Indeed. Always sensitive, that's you, Lizzie."

She ignored the sarcasm and admitted the woman in question wailed anyway since she'd just found out he was dead. Milano wasn't dazzled by her creativity, but he didn't shout, either. *Good sign. Take what you can get, Lizzie. Let's keep going until he cries uncle.*

"So what did the police find?"

"Nada. They confiscated his computer and flash drives and their IT team is matching files up with ours. Interesting that he had no computer files in his home or official lab. Those places were trashed, ransacked. The Chicago police suspect local kids looking for drugs when they realized he was gone. Who knows what they did with the computer. Though the receptionist said he protected it with his life."

"She didn't happen to mention why he needed to carry around his own phone number?"

"She did."

Lizzie could wait out the best of them. Milano hesitated only a moment. He was too experienced to fill the silence. He acknowledged they were on the same team, so why make her pull it out of him?

The detective answered, "He'd just changed the number, again. She said he was getting paranoid."

"Maybe not. Well, I have to run, detective. Nice chatting with you."

"Nice try. Why don't we discuss which poor suspects you interrogated so I don't have to scare them again."

She ground her teeth for a second. Then favored him with simple answers and no guile. "That Howard Polymer. He's innocent. His product proposes to do a lot of things. I think it serves as a substitute for morphine addicts. Perfectly legal in Florida, so far."

The detective whipped out his tiny notebook, just like they did on TV and jotted a few notes on it. She didn't speak her thoughts. Then she added three other names of innocents she'd talked with. She even provided the names when he asked. She mentioned Oliver so the detective didn't waste time interviewing an upright, goodhearted man. At least that was her view. He'd do what he wanted.

They sat in silence. Looked at each other.

"The conference closes in two days."

He nodded.

They rose simultaneously. Discouragement permeated the air; she inhaled it with every breath and it stuck in her throat.

CHAPTER TWENTY-FOUR

Detective Corporal William Milano agreed to a joint questioning of Jacob Meindl. On the way, he reached to guide Lizzie over the curb to the Jasmine, Building Two of the resort. With graciousness, she accepted his help. It didn't take him long to realize she had as much agility as he did in these matters. Strange he thought of her as considerate, while other times as deadly. Thank heavens for their peace treaty. He felt like he'd negotiated with the queen, but the alliance might be worth it.

Within minutes they found Jacob Meindl's floor. Milano stepped into an alcove and pulled Lizzie with him by the gentlest touch on her arm. Reunited like old buddies. Not likely. But he wanted to make sure they concurred on the issue.

"We both think his actions in the vendor hall were suspicious. Beyond that, what do you hope to gain from talking with him tonight?"

"In an ideal world, I would love to have the man say, "I killed him in a fit of rage because . . .""

He raised his eyebrows. "You want to refine your thoughts before we get there?"

"What do you mean?"

"Tell me you'll be a little open minded? Look for nuances?"

She grinned. "Of course. I don't live in an ideal world. Do you? We have a murder on our hands. Kind of takes away from perfection, don't you think?"

His shoulders relaxed. "Ain't that the truth!" He clarified, "You will let me lead, right?"

"Sure. Wouldn't it be better though, if I asked about seeing him in the vendor hall earlier? I could be gracious and apologize for causing him to rush off."

Milano's steady gaze didn't leave her face. Could he trust her? Her idea was good. He'd try it. With a curt nod, he moved forward. At Meindl's door he knocked, then smiled at her. This feels familiar. Reminds me of the time when Guetierrez and I stood outside one of these doors."

"But Delia and I were on the inside. So long ago."

He smirked, "Just a few days."

The he added, "But, oh so many in the course of an investigation." And added, "I'm glad you changed your mind and brought your concern about Meindl to me. We'll confront him here for now. See what's what."

The door opened with an abrupt jerk inward. Jacob Zebadiah Meindl glanced at each of them without speaking. Then he clicked his heels together and said, "A welcoming party? Way too late. The conference is over shortly. Must be something else. What can I do for you?"

Milano watched the man. Did his salute of sorts hide fear? Or irritation? Too soon to tell.

Lizzie spoke. "May we come in? I came to apologize."

Milano saw, even then, the man hesitated. When he motioned them in, Milano looked around and noticed nothing out of place. No obvious reason to stall. He didn't see anything personal at all in the room. It looked unoccupied. *Strange. But not an uncommon way to hide something.* He waited, unable to search. He'd promised Lizzie she could begin, though he itched to interrogate the man.

She smiled. "Jacob, you remember me, Lizzie Ort? I'm a friend of Abby's. She speaks well of you."

Milano frowned. Did Abby actually like this guy? He reined in his personal concerns and saw the man's eye's react to the name, Abby, but his mouth stayed closed, in a tight line. He appreciated the way she addressed him as Jacob, all friendly like. I'll play it formal, though.

The man still hadn't asked about Lizzie's apology. Seemed strange to him, but then she struck, as fast as a death adder snake. "I wanted to know what caused you to run away from my sister, Delia, and me?"

A cool, but blank expression settled on his face. "Run away? Why would I run from you?"

"I don't know. That's why I'm here. I saw you in the vendor hall and you took off. I feared I startled you."

He acted puzzled. "Oh, by the vendors. This afternoon? Where was I?"

Milano bit his tongue and let it play a little longer. This may just get them somewhere. He watched Lizzie to see if she registered surprise at Meindl's response.

She didn't. She stated. "In front of the Herbs for Inflammation booth."

"I wonder why I was there? I have no inflammation. And don't know anyone who does. Not that I'd ask them such a thing. Are you sure that's where I was?"

She nodded. And waited. Milano gave her credit. She knew how to play the game. He, himself, was sure the guy was blathering on trying to cover up something. But then it was his perceptiveness getting him paid those big cop bucks.

Meindl's answer returned him to the current scene. He heard the man say, "Was I stopped? I observe a lot. I learn from each of the vendors and the herbalists. There's so much to know. Maybe I was just walking down the aisle with a gradual sweep of the area."

"You were racing. Away from the booth. But it appeared like you took off right after seeing me. I'm sorry if I frightened you in any way. That's why I'm here. To say so, and to wonder what I might have done. Or how I can fix it."

Wow. Those words flew off her tongue like silk. Milano was impressed. He studied her eyes again. Then her mouth. Looked like she swallowed bile. They needed to talk. He'd love to know more about her. Later.

Right now his interest sparked on seeing this perplexing man's reactions. If he was a killer, he lacked professionalism. If he'd bashed Howell's head and it became his first murder, he didn't tremble with apprehension. That was a couple of days ago. Enough time for someone to get over their shock and act naturally? He'd never tried it himself so he wouldn't know from personal experience.

As if in a fog their target said, "Why, I wasn't frightened. If I hurried from the hall it could have been the time I rushed back to my room. I'd forgotten my blood pressure medication. I'm not used to carrying it around with me and I left it by the bed, again."

"Causing so much of a concern you ran out?"

"I'm sure I just sped my step a little."

I've waited long enough. It's my turn. "We have a witness that described your race from the room. You moved so fast no one could find you."

Still exhibiting no panic, Meindl said, "I didn't know anyone needed me or I would have stopped, I'm sure."

Remembering that Howell's killer had the foresight to dismantle the security system before confronting him, I kept my calm and attacked, verbally still, but stronger this time. "Where were you when Alexander Howell was killed?"

Meindl spun his whole body to face Milano. "And who are you?"

"I'm Detective Corporal William Milano from the Sheriff's Office. Investigating Howell's murder."

"And you've come to me?"

The man's reaction showed just enough anger to puzzle me, but I knew it could mask anything from trepidation to terror. I charged forward. "Answer the question."

"I was in bed. Alone."

Lizzie produced a light smirk, then settled back.

"We never released a time of death. How can you be sure?"

Meindl straightened his shoulders. "They found his body in the early morning. Everyone knows the time. So he must have died during the night."

Lizzie balked when Milano asked for Meindl's driver's license and Social Security number, and then said goodnight. But he gave her points for following his lead.

It was near midnight when they sat down to discuss what they learned.

An intense wrinkling of the lines on her face revealed the depth of Lizzie's thinking. What she came out with was startling. "I see now why you work at night."

"What do you mean?"

"I moved at night. For me the dark served as a cloak for stealth."

He returned her look, but just nodded.

She continued her explanation. "For you, the police, those seeking a criminal, it is all a time element. You can't afford to quit at five. Those you seek won't stop because they have no set work day. You don't stop, either."

He sipped the tea she made him. They sat in the kitchen nook of her suite. Delia, had turned in hours ago. He spoke, then lowered his voice and motioned his cup toward Delia's room. "Won't we wake her?"

"Oh heavens no. She has a switch. When her head hits the pillow it shuts everything down till morning."

He gave her a steady look. "You're not like that, are you?"

"She twirled her mug methodically, in half circles. "No, but then I never was. I was recruited young and unable to sleep well ever since. I guess working through the night for me also helped my success rate. Too many bad guys. So little time."

"Is Jacob Meindl a bad guy?"

"I think so. No proof. Yet. Maybe my ancient ways aren't altogether lost. Those good old days, when I sweet-tongued more than one operative. I found it difficult now to play the elderly concerned lady."

He laughed, then squelched it in deference to Delia. "Sorry. I saw you trying to swallow your words as if they were cod liver oil."

She reminisced out loud a bit, recalling times that weren't much different as she aged. "I'd refined my skills so well. Probably why they didn't retire me till I injured my ankle."

Lizzie stopped. Then looked at William. "Enough digression. Jacob's innocent act in front of you didn't trick me, as much as I played along. Did it fool you? That is what's critical here."

"No, but I don't even have a legal reason to go back and question him again. Unless I think of a new cause. And remember, men can be deceptive for many reasons other than murder."

Lizzie perked up at his words, despite the caveat. She obviously sensed some of what was not said. He added, "On the surface, he played the intrigued beginning herbalist anxious to learn more. Still, I don't trust him. His answers appeared glib."

Lizzie's head bobbed up and down while he finished. "He didn't exhibit the deep interest he professed, based on your description of him sliding through the aisles and programs without engaging anyone."

She waited, eyes narrowing.

"I promise I will check him out thoroughly and let you know anything I find, okay?"

The eyes stayed slits. He added, "I guess it won't hurt to tell you. After intensive screening of what footage we could see from the security cameras, we saw a shadowy form after closing hours in the corridor outside the vendor hall."

He held up a hand to stop her sputter. It could have been Howell, or even the killer. All we can say is, from the height and build, it could have been Meindl. Or quite a few others."

She acknowledged his willingness to share but didn't smile. Instead she pried. But this time he figured they were in it together. "I plan to interrogate Wesley Martell, the main speaker. I find it suspicious he's stayed under the radar and hasn't even asked the police what's happening. I overheard someone say he couldn't stand the man."

"Ugh! That self-righteous bigot."

"He's a bigot?"

"He hates grass-roots herbalism. He wants to commercialize everything. I admit it's not a strong enough reason to arrest the man for murder."

He shrugged. "True, but I can question if he knows anything to contribute to our investigation."

"One possible problem. Remember Delia left us earlier to deal with a complaint about a person's room? That was Wesley Martell. I'm sure they must have just changed his location."

"Not suspicious in itself. We were to be notified if anyone left or checked out early."

"Sometimes it gets complicated. These top people are hounded by other participants. They conceal their room numbers from everyone."

"I'm sure they'll let the police know."

"You can find him?"

"Lizzie. May I still call you Lizzie?"

"Of course, William."

"I'm a cop. That's one of the things I do. We find people. But I'll admit tracking down this particular killer has stretched our resources, our mental parameters, and . . ." He yawned. "Our working hours."

Lizzie opened the door. "If you don't find him soon, I'll look for you on the lost and found beat."

CHAPTER TWENTY-FIVE

"Burt! What do you mean he checked out?"

Burt wiggled back and forth like a puppy in need for the outdoors, but his voice stayed firm. "Sorry, detective. You asked for Wesley Martel." He pointed to a notebook just beginning to curl on the edges. "And when I looked him up right here, it says. 'Tell anyone who asks, he checked out.'"

It was seven in the morning. Milano was way too short on sleep. His voice held firm instead of shrieking high like a banshee, which it felt like doing all on it's own. *He* held firm. "Burt, I'm not just anybody, I'm the police, on a murder investigation. Which you are hampering."

The man's wiggle halted, maybe in fear. Detective William Milano didn't care. What he wanted was to talk with this man. Now. He stared. He waited. Burt stumbled backwards through the private door behind him. "I'll get the manager, right away."

Milano raised his eyes to heaven and mouthed, "Thank you, God," when he saw the day manager push through the door. He didn't know what the man was doing working in the early dawn, but it would definitely make his job easier. Nothing against night managers. Some were the nicest people. But he needed someone with knowledge and pull. Whatever it took to pin down Martell.

The man barked. "What can I do for you. His face worked it's way through a frown at Burt to a smile at Milano in a blink."

"I need to speak to Wesley Martell. Now. Is he still here or has he checked out?"

The huge man winced. No smile now. "It's a little more

complicated than that. He left the resort but is still scheduled to give another program at the conference."

Milano scowled.

The manager rushed to explain. "Don't panic yet. He handed his talk requirements to the committee yesterday. He'd made some changes and needed a different kind of projector. I was right there when he did it. I'm sure he'll return."

"So he's gone, but not."

The manager winced, but pursed his lips and didn't answer.

I guess I wouldn't answer that one either. This is a nightmare. He asked with polite enunciation, holding all disdain in check. "When's his talk?"

"Martell is scheduled to speak at the end of the conference."

Milano tired of the dialogue. He whipped out his badge to remind the man what the word "detective" meant. "Too late. I need to speak with him this morning. If you know he's around, I'm sure you know where he is. Exactly."

The manager dragged a second, smaller notebook, from beneath the counter. He flipped to yesterday's date and snapped out, "He moved to the Willow Reed Resort, still on Gulf but further down. Here's the room number." He jotted it down on a company notepad and ripped it off in a rush.

Totally perplexed now, Milano asked, "Why on earth would he do that?"

The manager leaned forward, looked both ways to make sure no one was near enough to overhear. The detective hadn't seen a soul since he arrived. Who did the guy think would hear them? He whispered, "He's having an affair and his mistress is staying with him. He made it sound like he was unhappy with our suite, but come on, it's the executive suite. He didn't want anyone seeing her and reporting back to his wife."

Milano swore to himself. *I'm never, ever going to have an affair. It complicates life too much. Right now, it's complicating mine.* A sweet, kind girlfriend would be nice. Abby's face came to mind. *Of course, with the hours I'm working, I'll never even have a romance.*

Grant Guetierrez accompanied Milano to the Willow Reed Resort. He wasn't sure if he needed him in an official capacity, but Grant might keep him from ripping the man apart before he could speak. Which might be most likely since it was not yet eight in the morning. He handed two photos of Meindl to his partner. "Keep these handy. When I say 'photo' flash them at this guy and watch his face for recognition."

Grant grabbed them, took a peek, and asked, "Where'd you get these?"

Lizzie took them yesterday. I knew the woman could probably shoot a gun from the hip but she must have shot these photos from the hip, too. I never even saw her pull out a cell phone or camera."

"Hah! She probably has one of those high tech ones that look like a button or something."

"Doesn't matter to me. As long as we have them. Can you believe she had the photos delivered to my desk before I got there this morning?"

"I wonder if she ever sleeps."

He cleared his throat and made no comment, other than the photos might come in handy. A clerk at the front desk of the Willow Reed gave them directions or they'd still be wandering around the humongous place. He'd lived in the area most of his life but had never gotten this close to the executive suite in one of these most luxurious resorts in town. Milano pulled out his badge with one hand while he banged on the door with the other. The door knocker alone would pay for his new stereo. Unbelievable!

"Maybe I should bang on the door with the butt of my gun and see if it makes more noise than that swanky, useless knocker. He turned to Gutz, than thought, Grant. Thank God he didn't voice it out loud. Calling the guy by a real name was tough after the nickname all year. He said, "What does it take to get this guy out of bed?"

Guetierrez squinted his eyes and looked at him like he was nuts. "Like I'm supposed to know? He probably needs to untangle the mistress from around his body."

Milano nodded like that made sense. *How would I know what it's like?*

The door swung open on silent hinges and the man in the white robe, barely covering his massive body, barked, "What in the hell do you want? Are we on fire?"

The man was staying in a two-bedroom penthouse with a huge living area behind him and he couldn't afford a bathrobe that fit?

He shoved his badge right up to Martell's face in case he didn't have time to grab his glasses. "I'm Detective William Milano and this is Detective Grant Guetierrez. We have some questions for you."

The man ushered them in. *I doubt if gracious is in his vocabulary but I'll take "in" any way I can.* Sheesh, so this is what an "airy suite and a 500 square-foot balcony" looks like. There's no way the conference paid for this. Which means this guy is no herbalist. Time to charge. Let's find if there's a connection with Meindl.

"We have a photo we'd like you to look at." Guetierrez was there on cue with both shots of their suspect. "Do you know this man? His name is Jacob Zebadiah Meindl."

The man snorted. "What'd he do? Is he the killer?"

"We're just checking out some suspicious activity," Guetierrez said.

"Never met him. And the name sure doesn't ring a bell. He's not one of the regular old-timers. I'd recognize the name if he was."

Guetierrez's eyes perused the room but Milano stared straight at the burly guy and didn't blink.

"There are dozens of new herbalists at the conference this year," he whined. I don't know them. Been kinda busy, if you know what I mean." His head swung over his right shoulder to check out the bedroom doorway. He acted relieved when it remained empty, and said, "The conference folks advertized extensively. People like the location, kind of unique in the herbal conference world. A lot of newbies."

Milano changed course. He waved his arm around to include the room and the view. "You don't act like an herbalist. Do you mind my asking what you do for a living?"

Martell chuckled. "I suppose I don't look the part any more. But I even had the long hair and leather tie back in the day. Then I developed a product from herbs that hit the market and never stopped running. Great rejuvenating lotion."

He slung his briefcase up on the settee. He flung it open and pulled out a couple of plastic tubes. "Here, have some on me. Just smooth it on your skin at night."

Guetierrez grabbed one. "Sure. Thanks."

Milano glanced at his, then said. "So you weren't in competition with the Telomerase Might?

"God forbid. Though I'm hearing more and more about this magic elixir. Not his. Some of the big labs are even looking into it."

"Heard anything at the conference we should check into? Anything?"

"Nah. Though I admit this time around I wasn't paying much attention." He winked. "You know what I mean?"

Guetierrez motioned once more to the photos in preparation to stashing them away so he could look at the lotion label. "You sure about this guy? He held the photos straight upright at nose level so Martell had no choice but to stare at them, or him.

Martell squinted and looked closer. "You know, that could be the guy I saw standing outside the main lecture hall. Twice in fact. I gave the opening talk and then a smaller one the next day, reserved for some of the specialists. I noticed him standing there each time because he wasn't inside, with the rest of the attendees, just lurking outside."

"You're sure?"

"No. He could have attended opening lecture since it was a full house. But I'm sure he wasn't there for the second one. It was mostly the dedicated old timers."

"It was a couple of those old time herbalists who steered us here. Said you acted erratic since you arrived."

The suspect's eyes swiveled toward the bedroom suite. Though no one was in sight, he still whispered. "I didn't want anyone to see Eloise. I was going crazy keeping her happy but away from the others at the conference."

"So that's when you moved in here?" Guetierrez asked.

"No. She freaked when the vendor was killed. It took me two days just to arrange this. I'll have to pay for it myself and I'd appreciate it if you keep this all from my wife."

"We're not here to rat on you. Just trying to find a killer."

Eloise strolled into the living area. Milano had to kick his partner to unglue his eyes from the woman. He couldn't tell if she'd done it on purpose but when she saw them she made no move to scurry back to the bedroom.

"Come here, sweeting," Martell said, waving her further into the room. "Take a look at these pictures. Did you see this guy around when we were staying at the Neptune's Oasis Resort?"

She pranced forward in her see-through robe and four-inch-high stiletto slippers. Guetierrez stared at her sashaying hips. Milano whacked him on the arm and motioned for the photos. His partner fumbled in his pocket and dropped them. Milano finally grabbed them and showed them to Eloise. *Wow! Did that woman smell good. Too strong though. He preferred Abby's light floral scent. Always made him feel like he was in a serene garden.*

Eloise reached toward the photos and tapped the man's face with her fuchsia red fingernail. "Don't look like anyone I saw. But then Marty here never let me near the guys. Didya, honey?"

Milano knew when to retreat, and pushed Guetierrez out the door, thanking Martell and Eloise for their help. They walked down the hall. He stuffed his new lotion into a pocket vehemently. "I feel like we're back at the beginning."

Guetierrez chuckled. "Aw come on. You must have gotten something out of this interview, didn't cha honey."

He kept laughing as he marched down the long, lush hall out to the car.

CHAPTER TWENTY-SIX

A fist slammed through the herbal display in the smaller conference room. More fists flew every which way. Lizzie stepped over two men in sport coats tangling on the floor. An elbow struck her ankle but she kept her stride. No time for delay. She rushed to the head of the room.

Delia intersected her half way there. She anchored Lizzie's arm with a downward thrust that forced her sister's hand to remain in the pocket. Lizzie's furrowed brow turned to her. It carried about a dozen question marks. One look into Delia's eyes and she knew that Delia knew.

"Lizzie, my dear, you can not pull out a pistol and shoot it."

"I might as well. This place resembles the Wild West. Just one shot into the air?"

Delia looked up at the ornate ceiling. Her attention stayed there until Lizzie raised her eyes. "Okay, so it's Italian plasterwork."

She jerked her hand out and wiggled her fingers, indicating the hand was empty. No gun. She marched forward with Delia at her heels. "Someday, remind me to ask how you know a pistol from a shotgun."

Delia's head reared back. "You wound me. I've studied some guns. Enough to learn what that gun is in your case at home."

Lizzie's step faltered for a second but she held back her surprise. Instead, they both wound their way through the crowd to the podium. Lizzie shouted to her, "Why didn't you just ask?"

Jerking her head sideways, Delia had no time to respond as she moved with great deftness to the front.

Lizzie turned her mind to the immediate problem. Fear ran rampant among the herbal attendees, at least the ones in this room. Even some vendors wormed their way in. The morning was so fresh the sales hall wasn't open yet. What had brought them all together?

The herbalists were vitriolic about the cops not finding the killer; the vendors even more so. It appeared they all accused each other. Lizzie looked around. Not even an island of calm in the storm. Now what?

She wrenched the microphone from the stand and flicked it on. She put on her Christian smile. *I can do this without hitting anyone. Use your words, Lizzie. Use your words.* She surveyed the melee. *Oh dear Lord, what words?* With her deepest, official, voice she barked. "Everyone on the ground." She then slammed the microphone onto the podium causing a sound like a gunshot. Darned if half of them fell to their hands and knees, chins raised to see what was happening. The rest slowed their motion into a still life. Unfortunately, one person's fist kept moving enough to knock over her friend, Glenn. Elderly and on the rail thin side, he had no hope. His body dominoed into the next guy.

An imposing Oliver raced in the open door, saw the ruckus, zeroed in on the immediate problem and reached for Glenn. He straightened him up one-handed before any more damage occurred. His other hand grabbed the offending neighbor and shook his head at him. The man lowered his eyes and his arms went limp. Lizzie saw it as a classic case of surrender. "Thank you, Oliver," she shouted.

Everyone turned to face Lizzie.

Oops. Now what?

Oliver came to the rescue, again. Maybe it was his magnificent, almost majestic stature, but as soon as he spoke, many stopped to listen. "These nice ladies want to help find the killer."

He glanced around again, stopping at a number of the troublesome people. The he continued, "If you all act violent, you'll all look guilty."

I had to use the microphone to grab their attention. His voice communicates like a lullaby. Enamored, she let him talk. He advised them what to do to protect themselves. To keep in groups, not wander around alone at night. "Above all, remember if you are here to promote health, most everyone else will, too."

He looked around and his eyes steadied on as many as he could, one second at a time. The pause worked wonders. Then he continued. "But this is a vacation as well as a serious conference. These are your friends. Some of you have known each other for years. Treat all with the kindness they deserve."

The herbalists looked around at their friends. Some grinned sheepishly. The men slapped each other on their backs. One of the oldest females, Edie, had tears in her eyes as she hugged her friend. Other women rallied round and did the same. Lois and Sheila, who helped Lizzie calm some of the herbalist earlier in the week, had stayed close in the middle of the foray but hadn't joined in. Lizzie watched as they made an effort to quiet those around them. *God bless them. What a fine group of people. I see their love for each other. I can not imagine one of them as the killer. He cannot be here in this room. So where is he?*

Several offenders attempted to right themselves and nearly knocked Delia over. She danced sideways just in time and gave Lizzie a thumbs up. *Probably afraid I was going to pull out my gun. Not today. Not now, anyway. But it's time to prevent another killing. Let's get to the crux of the problem this morning.*

Even George, the kindly old herbalist, had become cantankerous, but settled after Oliver spoke. George whispered an apology to the man next to him. The one with the swelling lip. Lizzie looked around and determined to never be in charge of crowd control. You couldn't know how people would respond. Oliver had stilled a riot.

Lizzie piggybacked on Oliver's efforts and raised her arms upward, speaking into the microphone. "Everyone, remember why we are here. To heal. Let's all say it. We're here to heal."

The experienced conference attendees were familiar enough with this rallying cause to shout with her. "We're here to heal. We're here to heal." As they slowly circled around and repeated the chant, others picked up on it. The noise level was loud again but this time on a cheerful note. *However, I'm not any closer to finding the killer. Well, maybe a bit. No one tried to run out during the melee. Did that mean no one here deliberately started the rioting? Or just that no one feared recognition?* She lowered her arms and studied the much happier crowd. My instincts tell me the man who knocked Howell on the head isn't here. *We need to move on.*

She motioned Delia to the front of the room. Time to shuffle this group into the hands of the Conference Committee and return to her self-appointed role of detective. She stepped to the side, grabbing one of the vendors not participating in the spontaneous pep rally. With her stern demeanor in force, he stopped his ranting. She said, "Why are you so angry?"

He thought for a second. "I guess I'm not so much angry as scared. We probably all are. Many of us didn't know how to say so." He hung his head. "Or weren't willing to admit it."

The man next to him, a vendor who sold herbs for athletes, said, "The why doesn't matter. We still have a killer on the loose. What should we do? Just stand in our booths and wait to be struck down?"

Lizzie practically dragged the man to the front by the microphone. She grabbed it and snapped it a few times to gain attention. "Now we've all settled a little, this man has something to say." She motioned to him and he shook his head vehemently. "Okay," she whispered to him. I'll talk. What's your name?" He spoke in her ear, then she turned back to the mike. "Paul here is a vendor. He is concerned, as are the rest of you. The point is, someone was killed. Do we all move around in fear? Will this help the problem?"

Glenn and George gravitated together, maybe in commiseration for their terrible morning. They stopped a few whispers around them. The crowd all nodded to each other. Their fear had been voiced.

Lizzie addressed it. "Who will be the next one killed? If that's your worry, consider the odds of another one of us being knocked over the head in their booth late at night. It's astronomical. But for you to feel safe, how can we protect ourselves?"

The meek vendor in the front row said, with a question mark in her voice, "We leave the hall when it closes? If we must stay, make sure several of us are together?"

Lizzie responded with a booming, "Yes."

Those in the back were still not on board.

The voices of two men by the door, new attendees as far as Lizzie could tell, rose in anger and a fist struck. Oliver had moseyed back there. She noticed with his long legs it took no time at all. Before the second fist swung, her newest best buddy grabbed both of them and knocked their heads together. *So much for the soothing sound of a lullaby.* Oliver gave them a stern what for and walked them out the door.

Lizzie raised her voice and continued, "But more important, this was not a random killing. The only thing to put you in danger would be for you to know something, and the killer knows you know, and you've kept it to yourself. What have you learned from this?"

Sheila's hand shot up. "If you've seen or heard anything at all, tell Detective William Milano, right away."

"Oh dear God. Abby." She looked around with fevered urgency.

Delia nudged her. "What are you mumbling about?"

"The Abby protection brigade is all here. But no Abby. Our best hope is she's still at home."

Delia studied the quieting crowd. "She could be with Detective Milano."

"He went to talk with Wesley Martell. I'm sure he wouldn't have taken Abby with him."

They both gave up on locating the missing Abby in the crowd. Delia said, "Why don't you call him? Oliver and I can handle this group if you need help to find her."

Lizzie stepped to the side of the room in the small display alcove. As she reached for her phone she prayed, *God, I hope you're with her because it looks like we all fell down on the job.*

She vowed to do more. She'd get some writing samples of the suspects on her meager list and scan them to her phone. Once her friend, the handwriting expert, reviewed them, it might narrow the field. Handwriting reveals so much about a person's character that studying it was like peeling off the surface layer of skin to see beneath. It was time to peel.

She'd call Abby's cell phone once more.

Just then, the missing woman ran in, breathless. She saw Delia up front motion toward Lizzie in the alcove and hurried over. Lizzie sighed in relief when Abby came in, and returned the phone to her pocket.

"I heard the herbalists decided on this last minute meeting. She held up her hand to stop Lizzie mid-stutter. "I remembered what you said and planned to take the car. It wouldn't start. But I called my friend Jimmy who hadn't left for work, yet, so he came right over. Strange. He said the thing-a-ma-jig fuse had gotten loose somehow. He just shook his head, put it back, and I was good to go."

Lizzie interrupted. "Why didn't you answer your phone?"

"It didn't ring?"

Delia joined them. "What?" She turned to Lizzie. "You called the *house* phone, didn't you?"

Lizzie sidestepped the implication she hadn't used her brain. I must not have the cell number."

Abby watched the sisters verbally battle it out. Curious to know how the meeting came about, Lizzie turned and asked her.

"I heard word of mouth," Abby said. "Sheila told me. Said she was calling all those she could think of last night."

Lizzie was relieved. Sounded innocent and impromptu.

As Abby saw everyone leaving, she frowned at a cut lip or two going by. "What happened?"

"Just a misunderstanding."

Delia shook her head in disgust, harrumphed, and walked away. As she passed Lizzie, she whispered. "It's time, girl. Let her in the loop."

"I'm afraid it's more like a rubber band, stretched beyond it's limit, ready to thwack me in the head."

CHAPTER TWENTY-SEVEN

"You did *what?*"

Lizzie stepped back more in surprise than alarm. Who could fear such a gentle woman, though those fangs sprang up when she heard what Lizzie and Detective Milano had done the night before. "Now, now, Abby . . ."

Abby's eyes pierced through her, straight and true. Might as well have been a laser beam. Thank God she'd dealt with worse people than this young lady. Chewed on a few of them, too. *I give her credit though. She's not giving in. Who taught her to make sure the other guy talked first? But I like her. I can fix this.*

Lizzie looped her arm through the girl's. "Let's sit over at one of these tables and bask in the sun. You may enjoy the delight every day, but I'll be back home soon, freezing to death in a foggy wind."

Abby followed, though the drag on Lizzie's arm registered her reluctance. She sat with pursed lips. She waived the waitress away with a flick of her hand, never breaking eye contact with Lizzie, who wanted fortification and didn't hesitate to ask. This place had the freshest cinnamon roles this side of heaven. "One Cinny Bun and coffee, please."

Abby waited. Lizzie waited. In another minute, the young woman's mouth would be sore from pouting. *Then I'll strike. Bad use of words, she realized. You don't strike with a sword; you sooth with honey. I got it!*

"You just can't believe how upset that nice Detective Milano was when I told him you thought Jacob might be a threat to you. Then I explained he ran off when we saw him in the vendor hall."

Eyes widened at that. At least she'd broken through. "Why, he wanted to pursue Jacob Meindl right away and have him arrested for scaring you." *God forgive me. It's only a little exaggeration.*

The waitress arrived, wreathed in smiles revealing no clue she realized the depth of anger she interrupted. "Here you go ma'am." She turned to Abby. "Are you sure I can't get you anything, miss?"

Abby bent.

"A coffee, please." She then looked at Lizzie. "Tell me all."

"It was just coincidental I ran smack dab into Detective Milano when I lost that Meindl guy."

This perked Abby up. Who knew what would garner her attention. "You chased Jacob Meindl from the vendor hall?"

"Well no, dear. Delia and I dashed *after* him. There's a distinct difference."

Abby plopped down her coffee cup so fast it splashed part way across the table. "*Delia* was running?"

Hmm. Maybe she gave this girl more credit for brains than she should. She obviously had difficulty following the gist of the story. "Yes, dear. We wanted to catch him, question him. He was running. We ran. Delia went one way and I took the other. My sister's not so quick on her feet, you know. And Julie delayed me. The man got away."

Abby wiped drops off her cup and sipped what was left of the coffee. She frowned. "Lizzie, why were you chasing Jacob Meindl?"

"I'm beginning to feel like Laurel and Hardy. Please focus, Abby."

"You said 'please'."

Now Lizzie frowned. "Yeah."

"You know that word?"

"I took it out and brushed the rust off just for you. Now concentrate."

Abby bit her tongue and didn't say another word.

Lizzie related the whole incident with Jacob in the vendor hall. And ended with a wistful expression indicating her hope the interview with Jacob would gain them a lead in the case, and despair that it had not. Abby held true and didn't interrupt. When she finally wound down, Abby tweaked her head sideways in a silent question of "Can I talk now?"

The waitress sidled by and hesitated long enough for Lizzie to order another coffee for each of them. Lizzie nodded to Abby to go ahead and speak.

"What I don't understand, is why did you think it important to follow Jacob just because he left the hall in a hurry? Don't you have any suspects in the case yet? Chasing innocent herbalists doesn't seem your style. And certainly not becoming of the police."

Lizzie didn't even twitch. "Abby, the whole point is, we weren't sure he was innocent any more. I know you're a lovely lady but he is hanging around you a lot. William was . . ."

"William? You call him William, now?"

Lizzie recognized a little more irateness than curiosity in that question but let it ride. Besides, it proved her premise that there was a match going on here, even though neither one of the matchees showed knowledge of it. Yet. Instead, she answered the question with calm efficiency. "He asked me to use William when we joined together in this investigation."

"That's official?"

"Of course not. It's just understood. I bet he'll call to update me on his morning appointment with Wesley Martell any minute." She glanced at her watch and frowned. "He should have been here by now."

"You said something about William before my rude interruption."

"Yes, it was rude. I've lost my train of thought."

"About 'I'm a lovely woman, but . . .'"

Lizzie shifted her position in the chair to look out at the beach. Another beauteous day. The water sparkled like jewelry for those daring enough to pursue the gems through the chilled water. And here they sat, exchanging views on a murder investigation. Well, maybe they were discussing romance, in a round-about way. That lightened her mood. After all, she'd come to this conference to help make the shift from dealing with murder and mayhem to retirement mode. She winced. *Working out for you, Lizzie girl? Maybe I should sit here in the sun and have a delightful conversation with Abby about the fine elements of romance.*

Abby's whole being sat still. Her head jutted forward, as if eager to meet her half way.

Lizzie broke under the pressure. "I'm thinking. I'm thinking."

Yet her mind slipped right back to where it'd been. *I've never had a romance. Never time. Never the right people. I've chased plenty of men, but racing through the blackened streets of Calcutta isn't quite the same. Not with my Browning in hand. Come to think of it, I've had more years with a gun than any one person.*

Abby looked expectant, bent further toward her. Staring, like she tried to see into Lizzie's brain.

"Sorry dear. That was a combination of reminiscing and wondering what to say to you. I'm trying to learn cooperation can be better than working alone. I wanted to tell you William became distraught when I told him about Jacob following you. And Oliver scaring you. It reminded me of lost opportunities for romance. I do hope you aren't holding this little murder investigation against William. He is trying, you know."

Abby's hands jerking up, creating fists, and slamming down onto the table gave away one clue as to her feelings. Even though her fists landed in a gentle plop rather than a bang, so as not to draw attention. Her stuttering attempt to form words was a second clue.

Lizzie wasn't sure how far she had to backtrack on this one. She went with years of experience in negotiating. Vague. Keep it vague. "What concerns you, dear?"

Abby said, "What romance? And *little* murder investigation? Why, I'm at the top of his suspect list."

"That's ridiculous. He determined you were innocent long before you met with him that day. And when I told him someone may be following you, he decided he must protect you. Haven't you seen more of William since then?"

"Yes, but I never dreamt he was protecting me. I thought he liked my company," she wailed.

I guess this is why I have no success in matchmaking. Stuck foot in mouth. Try to pull it out. It's time to get back to business. Murder business. I'm better at that.

"Why he asks about you." Another white lie, but worth it to cement their relationship. *Okay, I'm still looking for some glue, but showing he has interest in her can't hurt. Did I ever lie this much when I was an operative for the government?*

"What does he ask?"

"He wants to know how you are. Have you had any more close calls? More threats? More frights? You don't like talking with him about these things, Abby, but he needs to know, as difficult as it is to confide in people sometimes. I've held my tongue in the past but it was a lapse in judgment."

Abby gasped, then bit her lip.

"I hope you're not making the same mistake. It could prove dangerous."

Abby blinked this time. Could it mean she was listening? "Dear, you may need protection for a while. I thought your Detective Milano wanted to deal with your security, but if he hasn't . . ."

The man in question stepped up to the table. "Good. Delia said I'd find you here. Have you told her about her friend, yet?" His eyes shifted to Abby.

Abby's eyebrows furled together over her nose. Lizzie saw them and thought, That girl's gonna have permanent wrinkles there. What is her problem?

The girl had no difficulty speaking, though. Chin lifted beyond a comfortable location, she sputtered, "What brings *you* here?"

He pulled out a chair, the metal scrapping across the patio bricks in his haste. "I thought it time we all talked."

Lizzie nodded.

Abby said, "What friend?"

Unaware of the snare, Milano kept talking. Lizzie hoped she could just watch. Looks like it might be fun.

"My officer said that when he arrived at your house this morning he heard a noise so he circled around from the back."

Abby sat with her mouth open. Coffee cold and forgotten. Lizzie lined up her lips and not a a sound escaped. She didn't want to cause a falter in this scene.

The detective continued, "When the officer saw nothing out front, he went to search the back yard. Ten minutes later, he heard people talking by the car in the driveway. He found Abby chatting with a man that looked like a mechanic. At least, he was replacing a fuse. My officer stayed hidden, as directed."

He stopped then and realized he hadn't let anyone else speak. He looked at Lizzie, got no response, and swiveled his head toward Abby. "Well?"

Abby stared at him. Lizzie was sure she searched for the unicorn horn, or three evil eyes on his forehead, anything to seal this as a fairy tale. Or a nightmare. She kept her own lips firmly in line, in a wise move developed in the field.

Abby's hand reached out and grabbed his arm before he could wave it in the air to summon a waitress. "Your officer? What officer? *My* back yard?"

Lizzie's fingers inched across the table and shifted Abby's coffee cup away from her other hand, which fluttered as if unattached from her body. Or at least disconnected from her brain. *This was love and romance? Maybe I was lucky to have it pass by.*

Abby's fingers still clutched Milano's forearm. Kind of looked like a death grip. It would be better if I stepped back and provided some distance—at least give the impression. The man was on his own. He needed to be able to handle Abby without upsetting her. *If* this was to be a love match. She stared at Abby's fingers. The death grip gave her certain qualms. Didn't resemble a loving caress at all.

The detective spoke. To Abby. Lizzie wondered if they'd notice if she left. But then she'd miss out. She stayed.

"I've, I mean we, have been worried about you. Detective Guetierrez and I just came back from interviewing the main speaker at your Health Naturally Conference. His activity caused suspicion and we'd hoped he was involved in Alexander Howell's death. He wasn't. So now we're back to having no obvious suspect."

"Why does that make you worry about me." Abby's breathless

voice asked so much more than what the words said. Would Milano pick up on it? He answered the stated question, instead. Lizzie hung her head. But she listened. He spoke in detail. At least he opened up to the girl. Must have decided that keeping her in the dark was a bad professional step. Or he thought it would help him in romancing her. Maybe there was hope. She perked up, looking for clues.

Abby's posture straightened. Her fingers uncurled but remained on Milano's arm as he talked. Shock may have been holding her in place, or the desire to anchor herself to reality.

A list of reasons Milano wanted Abby safe spewed forth, as if he needed her to understand. The police eliminated most of the vendors and herbalists whose product or area of interest was remotely related to Howell's. The man's trashed lab in Chicago held no clues. The local police had declared it vandalism, probably by a gang searching for drugs. Someone wrecked the lab the day after Howell was killed. Could have been the same person who killed him, but it meant a tight schedule. The airline awaited a list of names before providing any information. He finished his litany with, "We even checked and double-checked the Rasland woman. Couldn't find a thing."

Milano used his free hand to pat Abby's fingers where they still lay. Calm now. Then he waved it up to order a coffee from a passing waitress. The brief pause allowed him to glance at his notes. Then he continued, nodding at Lizzie. "The personal lab, which we found later, held no sign of entry and no formula for this elixir from Howell."

He studied Abby's face. "We have two vendors in custody until we can uncover missing pieces of their backgrounds. But, what stands out now, are the strange occurrences around you. You think they may be inconsequential. No one else has felt followed, had a car practically crash into them, had this Jacob Meindl hanging around."

He thanked the waitress who'd arrived with his coffee and he drank for a moment. "Martell mentioned it might have been Meindl who lingered outside each of his lectures. Lizzie pointed out odd behavior. None of it proves anything."

Abby said, Is that why 'your man' is hanging around my house?"

Lizzie leaned back as far as her chair would allow. Crunch time.

"His job is more to 'hang' around you. To make sure you're safe. He's a friend of mine. He offered to help when I'm otherwise occupied. You may see Detective Guetierrez around, too. When I'm not."

A smart man, Milano didn't stick around for questions or retributions. He rose, said he had to leave, and did so. Abby sat there. Her expression crossed between anger and wonderment.

Lizzie decided to depart. She saw the latest Abby protection volunteer lingering one table over and signaled acknowledgement.

For Abby, she nodded goodbye, and handed out compassion masked by a smile.

CHAPTER TWENTY-EIGHT

A blood-curdling scream torpedoed Detective Milano through the sandy ground along the edge of the woods near Abby's house. When he walked the distance with her a couple of days ago, it took five minutes. Today, in the gloomy fog following the rain, it felt like hours, plenty of time for his heart to stop. Then kick-start again.

The soft sand devoured his feet like quicksand, with small hard-packed islands to trip up the wary. He ignored the soil trickling into his shoes. No time for another path. *Move.* The drag on his feet delayed his race to find Abby as he heard her scream one more time, trailing to a quiet squeak, and then a whimper. His body lurched forward, hampering his search for the unsuspecting as he ran. Should he shout out? Or would that cause more harm? What was the threat?

He reached the cottage and saw Abby, erupting out on her front porch. She lunged down the stairs. Hesitated. One hand on the rail, she looked scared. Uncertain. Like she didn't know which way to run. Milano tore through the small stand of trees and shrubs to reach her. He knew the second she saw him. She screamed and turned back toward the front door.

"Abby, it's me. Detective Milano."

The girl slumped onto the steps so fast he feared she'd been shot. Now he yelled out. "Are you hurt? Where is he?"

Abby whimpered.

He reached her in two more strides, gun help down to one side. He wrapped her with the other arm into his chest and held tight. His head swiveled around and observed the area, seeking anything moving or unusual.

He whispered to her. "Is there someone still in the house?"

Her voice came out muffled and he realized he had her in a tight embrace. She shoved off him with belated strength. Had she pushed him away out of distaste?

"I can't breathe. I looked around quickly once I found the note. Didn't see anyone. No more notes. Escaped out here."

She stood. He backed away.

"What did the note say to frighten you so?"

She stared inside the front door as he opened it. Her expression changed and she moved forward inch by inch. "It's not what it said, as much as how it was said."

"Shall we go in and look at it? I don't want to leave you out here alone. Stay behind me and we'll search each room and then inspect the note. Okay?"

She stiffened her spine and lengthened her neck as if preparing for battle. He warned, "Keep back."

Milano saw the note as soon as he entered the living room. No one could miss it.

"Did you touch it?"

She shivered and shook her head 'no', while her eyes focused on the note. He reached for her arm, still keeping her to the rear, and checked each room. When the house was clear, he moved back to the living room and returned his gun to the holster strung over his shoulder.

Footsteps thundering up the porch steps had him swinging around and aiming the gun at the door before Abby could react to the sound. He heard Guetierrez shout, "Abby, why's your door open?"

Guetierrez halted at the revolver pointing at his chest. A second later he breathed loudly as Milano put the gun away.

"Good way to get killed, man. Next time just tell the killer who you are and that you're coming in."

His partner halted, but said, "I came to drive Abby to the lecture room. They want her to return and substitute for some woman who came down with the flu."

"Why weren't you with her? Weren't you supposed to stick with her until I could get here?"

"Well yeah, but Jerry delayed me at the office."

Milano noticed Abby drag her feet toward the cardboard note propped on the coffee table, as if it called her. He reached for her arm and held her close while he finished speaking to his partner. "Did you see anything outside when you were coming over? Anyone or a car leave the area just now?"

"No." He thought more and then said, "And no vehicle. Unless you count the steady stream on Gulf Boulevard."

Milano wasn't surprised. Abby had been gone all morning. A friend had escorted her over to the conference early. The cardboard could have been left any time. He and Guetierrez interrogated her about what she saw and why she might be threatened.

"I didn't do anything to deserve this. I attended a program on hypoglycemic and demulcent herbs." Both men looked at each other with blank stares. She explained. "They're the herbs to help regulate your blood sugar levels." The men shot questioning looks at each other. She gave up. Her voice rose with irritation. "I didn't mention Howell. Or his death. Or a stalker."

Many people had been lined up to be with Abby where ever she went, but no one gave *her* the schedule. He didn't know if it was stubbornness or inability to accept her situation out of faintheartedness.

She rose and circled around toward the kitchen, staying clear of the living room. Guetierrez had gone out to the car and returned with some gloves. After slipping them on, he picked up the four-foot square cardboard. Touching it only by one corner, he turned it over.

"There's nothing on the back. Looks like it came from a large packing carton."

For once Milano was grateful the man was around. He was afraid to let go of Abby's arm. He did for a second and returned to the edge of the room with a chair from the kitchen. Here, Abby. Sit and take a breath. Looks like everything is fine."

She stuttered, pointed to the cardboard. Huge block letters dripped with something suspiciously like blood. It read, "Leave the conference now."

She said, "Doesn't *look* fine."

Lizzie rushed in shouting, "Abby, where are you? What's happened?"

Milano shook his head. "It's like an overbooked airport terminal here." He continued, less irate. "She received a note that scared her."

He pointed, but Lizzie had already seen it. Her face wrinkled into a puzzled expression and she sputtered, "But she hasn't done anything. We're the ones poking around."

Milano let it go, knowing he had to check later on what exactly Lizzie was investigating. Instead, he squatted down in front of Abby. "Have you been looking for the killer?"

"God no! I want nothing to do with him. Do you think it's the killer that's stalking me?"

Lizzie shrugged and left the answer to him. "Yes, I do. We just can't figure why." He shifted upright and looked around. Guetierrez had taken a sample of the red liquid and secured it into an evidence holder.

Milano changed his approach. "Were the doors locked?"

She bowed her head and mumbled, "I thought so, but then I did rush out this morning. I had a rough night. I kept hearing noises outside, but when I went to look I couldn't find anything."

He shuddered at the thought of her going out in the dark alone. There were no street lights nearby. He firmed his lips to keep in any chiding, and nodded for her to continue.

"I tossed and turned, then fell asleep at dawn. When I realized how late it was I hurried to get to the first talk." She raised her head and her eyes shone. "Miss Edie's my favorite speaker. I was ready just as Glenn came by to walk with me. We went to the conference together, by the path."

Milano assumed there was a good chance she hadn't locked the door if she was in a hurry. Guetierrez called a couple of tech people. Lizzie had helped him bag the cardboard and then gone to the kitchen to make tea for Abby. While there, he heard her phone someone at the conference and explain they'd have to find another substitute for their panel.

He agreed. Abby would have to stay close until they found this guy. Like Lizzie, he was puzzled though. Why Abby?

Lizzie returned while the water warmed up. She bent over in front of Abby. One question. What do you remember from the second you walked into the room? Before you noticed the sign, or note, as you call that monstrosity?"

Crossing her arms, Abby wrinkled her brow. Her eyes widened as she looked up at Lizzie. "The room smelled different. Just a whiff of something. Not citrusy. More like bergamot or clary sage. Then I saw the note."

Milano was impressed. Maybe they could pursue those later, whatever they were, but he had to deal with Lizzie. He motioned his head sideways to signal Guetierrez to keep his eye on Abby, and followed the woman to the kitchen when he heard the kettle whistle.

"Do you have a permit for the gun in your pocket?" The sheepish look on her face was enough of an answer. "I'm letting that go. For now."

"I have one. Just not here. For this specific gun."

He raised both eyebrows, revealing what he thought about subterfuge. He settled into a chair at the table while she continued preparing the tea. "What brought you rushing over here with a gun? What made you fear Abby was in danger?"

She turned on the timer to let the tea steep for a few minutes. The stronger the better. Abby hid her shock well but he could see it in her pale face and twitching hands. They could use the time to talk.

Lizzie came over to him. "Nothing new happened. I noticed Abby wasn't around. Asked Natalie Turner what they were whispering about, and heard the speaker had the flu."

"So you went to get your gun?"

She sniffed and finished steeping the tea. "Glad to see you still have your sense of humor."

She added some honey to give Abby a perk-me-up. "It was just a couple of days ago I was in here fixing her tea. Seems like forever."

He noticed Abby watching the forensic team get to work. She didn't move an inch. He worried about what the fear might be doing to her.

Lizzie glanced at the girl, too. "When I found they were looking for Abby I realized she was gone. I didn't know if someone was with her, but figured it safe to rush over here and see why she'd disappeared."

"You were going to use the gun on her?"

"No snide remarks, please. But if needed, I'd use it. Of course, not on Abby. "I admit I've been carrying it since Howell was killed. Made me feel more comfortable."

He understood, though he'd never keep one of those guns in a pocket. "Must be driving you nuts to have it there."

She stopped in the hall, and looked at him over her shoulder. "You'd be surprised where I had to stash my gun at times. We didn't walk around with holsters, you know."

He'd never given it a thought. Being a cop was hard enough. Seeing Abby sitting still in the chair where he placed her, he figured it could only get more difficult.

Lizzie said, "I've been thinking a lot about why I felt the need, amongst these normally gentle people, to even carry it. But habits, once engrained, stay part of you."

He added. "Her stalker is dangerous. Don't let those habits die just yet."

She passed him on the way to the living room and said, "You will protect her, won't you?"

By then they'd reached Abby. He walked past her to the front window as his phone rang. "What's up partner? You disappeared."

He barely understood the caller's muffled response, so he walked away from the officers behind him.

"Yes, I know your work was done here. No criticism intended. Where are you?"

"You're where?" He spun to look at Lizzie. And spoke loud enough for her to hear the rest. "There was a Volkswagen Bug reported stolen from the conference area and you thought it might be connected?" He pursed his lips and watched Lizzie fumble the mug of tea, spilling a few drops. "A rainbow-colored Bug?"

He smiled. "That's okay, Gutz. I found it abandoned near Abby's house. Yeah. No kidding. Strange world. We'll have it returned right away." He shook his head, staring at Lizzie. "No. Don't need the keys. I'm sure we'll find a way to start it."

Lizzie must have decided to turn the conversation back to Abby. No soft couching. She said, "I don't think the stalker is trying to kill Abby. Or he would have."

Abby jerked out of her stupor.

He reacted, barking at Lizzie. "Great job, woman. She wasn't scared enough."

Instead, Abby said, "But that's kind of good news, right?"

CHAPTER TWENTY-NINE

Help! Lizzie looked skyward for inspiration and saw Detective Milano doing the same. Maybe he was praying to God, too. But then, *his* face was purple. He was either blowing off steam or suffering from gas.

She told Abby they'd return in a minute, motioned for her to drink the tea, and accompanied the detective outside. He watched her hot wire the car in seconds, shaking his head the whole time. Getting out, she said, "I just borrowed it."

"Like a rental?"

"Kinda."

He stood further away and studied the neon glow of the rainbow painted on the side, the top and even the bumpers. "Glad you didn't borrow it for a get-away car."

"Funny. I was in a hurry. Something told me Abby needed help. The car jumped right out at me when I ran out."

"I can imagine. Surprised it didn't knock you over."

He motioned an officer to the car and gave him instructions to drive it to the conference parking lot and find Detective Guetierrez. He pulled Lizzie to the side and said he'd be rechecking suspects today. "I made a list of everyone who should get a second look-see. Here."

He handed her the names. "If you have any new ideas, I'm open."

She nodded at some, expressed puzzlement at others. Pointing to Wesley Martell, she questioned the detective. "I thought you accepted his explanation last time. Did something change?"

"Not really, but I've had several people who are in my confidence on this, tell me his excuse wasn't plausible."

Her raised eyebrows alone prompted him to continue. "Even the chair person, Miss Turner. When I asked her opinion, she said, "No way."

He shrugged as she reared back in surprise, and added, "I'll try anything again if it leads us to the killer. Meanwhile, I'll return in time to pick up Abby from the conference."

His plan coincided with hers. Never let the woman alone until this was over. Lizzie raced back inside to stand next to Abby, who reached out and grabbed her arm. *God didn't answer my plea. Wouldn't be upset about the car, would he?* No hope now. She'd have to wing it on her own.

"Abby, sweetie, it *is* good news. But we still need to keep you close. If you've dealt with all the policemen's questions, what would you like to do this afternoon? I'll go with you." She swirled her skirts to hide the gun in her pocket. Buggers. Maybe she should hitch on a holster. Might cause a hassle with some of the more peaceful herbalists, though. Pockets it was.

Ignoring the question, Abby didn't even blink. She watched as the forensic team finished up, acting more like she never heard Lizzie. Delia arrived as soon as her sister sent the SOS. Delia insisted on cleaning up the place and attempted to shoo the tech guys out the door. Lizzie would have laughed if Abby didn't look white as a jasmine with a little bit of hibiscus pink around the eyes. Like tears turning stale from lack of release.

Lizzie couldn't stand the agonized look and clapped her hands in joy. She had a brilliant idea. The forensic team jumped as a unit. Abby just stared at her. Undaunted, Lizzie said, "We could go to Butterfly World. Those exotic creatures will lighten the soul. Or the zoo. Monkeys always make one laugh."

Abby looked around and then straight at Lizzie. "I'm going back to the conference. That's why I registered. To attend. To learn. Right? Isn't that why you're here?"

Milano shook his head at Lizzie. She saw he made sure to stand behind Abby's back so she couldn't see his consternation. Looks like he wasn't about to get involved. Then his face brightened. He motioned for Delia to step in and mouthed, "Keep her busy." He pulled Lizzie aside. "I've got to get back to the office. I have an idea for someone to stay with her at the conference all afternoon. Let me work on it."

Lizzie agreed to occupy Abby until he contacted her. "But then we have to talk. Time to take action."

The detective looked at the room, at Abby. His jaw firmed with a brisk nod and his stride echoed determination with each step. He motioned for the forensic guys to finish up and then left. Lizzie watched them scramble. Good thing they'd completed their work. Delia was on a mission to complete the clean-up. Get Abby's life back to normal, more or less.

She followed Abby, as she'd risen from her chair and floated out the door. Looks like the detective's just about had it. *Time for the closing act. If we don't get this done soon we'll all lose it. Even me. That thought jolted her. She contemplated it for a minute. Not possible, or at least it never was. Could she be normal? Like your average human being?*

Delia was right behind and motioned them both into a sedate black rental limousine.

Lizzie's eyes widened as she turned to Delia. She didn't even need to ask. "So I borrowed the first car I could. Sounded like you all required help."

Lizzie's eyes couldn't open any more. *Delia wouldn't. Would she? Nah. She doesn't know how to hot wire.* "You borrowed it?"

Her sister turned to her from the front seat. Lizzie'd been so shocked she didn't even fight over who was driving. Delia said, "Yes, I borrowed it from the rental place. Paid a fortune too. But it was out front ready to go and I needed wheels quick."

That was her Delia. Behind the scenes until you needed her. And then she materialized with help.

They arrived at the conference just in time to catch the last few seats in the back row of a program on lemon verbena. She couldn't imagine anyone having enough to say about the herb beyond the slight acerbic but pleasant taste it added to tea. Familiar with it since it was used as an ancient anti-inflammatory and sedative, she didn't care to learn the full science of it today.

She was lost at the second paragraph when the lovely young woman talked about the slope lag time and oxyradical antioxidant capacity of the herb. And the speaker, with her ponytail, didn't look old enough to pronounce such words. Thank God her cell phone buzzed. She motioned for Abby to stay put, struggled to grab it from her deep pocket, and strolled out the door. As soon as she reached it she raced away to talk without being heard inside. "What's up."

Milano was just abrupt. "I've got someone to latch onto Abby like a leach until I can get back to her. Her name's Laurie Nederhoff. She's an officer. She works the front desk and wows us with her research. Today she'll look and act like a civilian unless the cop in her is needed."

Lizzie heard his fear for Abby. Before she could say they should combine efforts and thoughts, he added, "As soon as she gets there can you come to the office? We need a game plan."

Returning to her seat she surveyed the crowd for the enemy. If he lurked between the wrinkled old man who spouted essential oil trivia at every turn, and the ditzy lady with the ornamental hat, she couldn't find him. *Doesn't feel right. I know. It's the first time I seek evil amongst my friends. Is this my life now?*

Laurie surprised her and Abby as they left the program. She barely recognized the strapping young cop turned frilly lady with the blond wavy hair. The ecru stretch jacket with frayed trim hid her holster quite well, while looking like it came directly from designer heaven. She needed one of those. Never dreamt she'd be asking clothing advice at an herb conference. From a cop. Maybe later.

The woman carried a schedule of events. She turned to Lizzie as if they were old friends and said, "Sorry I couldn't join you till so late in the conference, but I'm dying to hear the rest of these talks."

"Laurie." Uh-oh she forgot to ask if she'd be using her real name. Laurie encouraged her with a discreet nod to continue. "Glad you made it."

Abby didn't recognize her from her own short visit with Detective Milano. Not surprising, since Officer Nederhoff appeared up-scale but not like a professional law officer. Lizzie introduced her to Abby and Laurie took over.

"The talk on the phytochemical and pharmacological profile of dandelions sounds fascinating."

Abby enthused. "I agree. I'm heading over to the talk now. Do you want to come with me?"

Laurie hooked their arms together like they were old friends and they walked away chatting. Laurie tilted her head in a secret goodbye to Lizzie.

Wow. Who woulda thought? Not that the subjects weren't intriguing but she had difficulty concentrating right now. Alpha Lizzie controlled the brain until they found the killer. Maybe she and Milano could make serious progress today. Grateful for the reprieve, Lizzie took off in another rental car. She'd be keeping this one for the duration. Thank heavens you could rent them at the resort. Or she would have had to borrow a Bug. Some things were not fond memories. Besides, you never knew when you'd need speed, or God forbid, anonymity.

She flounced into his office like she carried only a third of her years and no worries. The new hair style with the modern messy bun helped. Still didn't look twenty-five, but details counted. She understood camouflage. Her age, her purpose, and her feelings. Which bordered on scared.

She lit into Detective Milano as she flitted through the door as if she had a handle on her life and knew where she was going. And he blocked her path. Spewing forth her concerns she opened volley right away. "Abby is a good person, deep, overall, to and for anyone. She doesn't deserve this fear forced upon her."

"Hey, take the gloves off. We're on the same side. And whoever this guy is, he damn well better not hurt Abby."

That deflated my sails. No breezing through this now. Instead, she confessed. "I don't know about you but I can't seem to find a given direction, yet. We're running out of time."

His glum looked reflected the feeling in the pit of her stomach. She said, "I've always had to dig deeper. I know how to. But this time, I don't even know where to dig."

The detective started to laugh but sobered before it reached his vocal cords. She could see he understood, and maybe felt the same way. He said, "I've denied this until the incident with Abby a few hours ago. None of those on this morning's list proved any more viable. I've been reading people for a long time. These just didn't do it."

He nodded once, passing the ball to her. "You haven't found anyone else?"

"Not one person remembers seeing lingerers in the vendor hall the night Howell died. Several trusted people interviewed vendors and fellow herbalists."

She bounced it back to him. "What happened with Martell?"

"He admitted it was his first and last affair. He was grateful I only mentioned it to a few trustworthy associates. Said he couldn't stand his own self-deprecation, let alone living with other's disapproval."

"We're back to Abby, aren't we?"

His eyes echoed her despair. "She's our only connection. And we don't know why."

"Let's find out. The only thing she remembered was talking to Jacob Meindl about telomerase. And he was getting a bit clingy. Should we start there?"

She saw his not-so-casual lean towards the desk. "She's quite attractive. People like her. With a smile to warm your insides. Meindl couldn't have been the only one tagging after her. I have two officers looking for other so-called suitors. She'll hate me for pestering her friends, but we need new leads. Now."

Lizzie agreed. "But she doesn't flirt, and wouldn't even know how to reel anyone in."

His despair thundered into the room as anger in his loud voice, narrowed eyes and gasp of pain. "Where does that leave us?"

"Abby must have seen or heard something that threatens the killer.

"But she can't remember. Again, where does it leave us?"

She assumed it to be a rhetorical question. Then shoved back her chair so hard it fell over and she shouted, "You *want* to use her as bait!"

"No. I *want* her protected."

Lizzie pursed her lips, and thought. She consciously shifted her shoulders back and straightened her spine. "We have to look at every suspect again. And review all the information."

His body slumped in defeat as he gathered together the dozen or so files organized on the floor around him. He added them to the two on his desk and said, "Help yourself. This has been my bedtime reading for the last week."

She gulped, not realizing just how much the police had accumulated.

Shuffling through the top few, he said, "Some of these are real horror stories."

She jerked to attention. His words spawned hope, until he spoke again.

"Several of your exhibitors rank off-the-wall in boredom quotient. Not to mention borderline crazy."

Hope went the way of a fast-deflating balloon. Her body collapsed also. He'd never know. Her shell remained upright and in tact. But the spirit waned.

He left, saying, "Take a look. I have a meeting with Detective Guetierrez. Maybe he'll have something useful to report."

She noticed the door stayed open as he walked out. What'd he think? That she'd steal his guns? Or worse, his folder allotment for the month? She thought the notes would call to her, telling her which one housed the lurking killer. She could handle him if he leapt out of the pages. What she couldn't deal with was the lack of any sign. Not a squeak came from the files.

Grabbing the top one, she read. An hour later, the detective returned. She made one more note, than looked up with hope. "Anything?"

He collapsed into his chair. "Nothing. Fingerprints this time, though." That hopeful bug reared its head before she knew it, only to be squashed when he said. "Whoever the guy is, he's not a known criminal."

Her face scrunched up, creating wrinkles she could feel. They caused grooves in her skin that would require tons of putty, or whatever stuff other women used. She never had time for it. And right now, the grooves didn't matter. Saving Abby did.

She rose, placing her hands palms down in front of her on this side of his desk. She stared at him until he looked her full in the face. "I want Abby safe."

He stood up. "It's taken care of. For now."

She turned to go, her voice drifting behind her. "I hope so."

CHAPTER THIRTY

"Detective Corporal William Milano, you *kidnapped* me," Abby exclaimed as she nestled in the luxurious seats of one of her favorite restaurants.

"It's William, and I did not."

"I'm surprised I'm not sitting here in handcuffs."

He winced when a waitress walked by in time to hear. But she didn't care. "What's going on?"

William wriggled around, looking not quite so comfortable. It wasn't the chair. Must be his conscious. Abby relented and lowered the rant level of her indignation. "Does Lizzie know you kidnapped me?"

He scowled and said with deliberation. "Stop using that word before they arrest me."

She giggled. "It would be funny."

He tilted his head and waited for her to settle down, then answered. "Lizzie knows you're with me. We agreed it was a good idea. She'll meet with you as soon as we go back."

Abby sobered. "What am I doing here eating dinner with you?"

"You don't like Mary and Tony's Beach Grill? It's quiet, off Gulf Boulevard to avoid some of the noise. And near the conference so you won't be gone long. I thought you'd like it." He looked at her with such earnestness she couldn't continue with the fake attitude.

She sniffed in delight. "Of course I like it. It's a fantastic restaurant. Famous for a number of foods. But you practically pulled me from the conference lobby and shoved me into your car. Your police car."

This time his face puckered into a pure grimace, but she was embarrassed.

He calmed, and staring into her eyes, said, "We're here because I thought we both needed a break. An hour away from the stresses of the last few days." He placed his hands in his lap and she saw the sheepish look with that little quirk of the eyebrows he had as he finished speaking. "I've thought of asking you out, just not quite like this. In a rush, with no warning."

"You think I need a warning before you invite me out?"

He laughed. "Okay. I'll quit talking now before I need a shovel."

Her eyes twinkled, but she restrained her tongue. "What I have to know—I mean what's most important here . . ."

He leaned forward, worry etching his brow. "What?"

"How did you get us in without a reservation?"

"I have a friend on the staff."

Just then Paula, their server, came by. At least it said Paula on the name tag. Her generous smile and "Well, hello there, William. I haven't seen you in a while," was directed straight at the detective. *Probably that friend. So much for feeling special and calling him William.*

He mumbled a greeting and asked for the fried calamari for an appetizer. He looked at Abby. "Want to share, or order your own?"

"I'd love to share."

They chose the wine, then dissected the menu to make their choices. She passed on the spectacular nut-encrusted tuna. It was a favorite, but today required something new, an exciting change, she thought, as she looked at the detective. William. The fact he wanted her to use his first name thrilled her. She smothered the gleam inside to exhibit only a slight smile. No fun in letting him off the hook without a little squirming.

She ordered coconut shrimp and he decided on the blackened mahi-mahi with mashed cauliflower. They were allowed to order from the early bird menu even though it was shortly after the cut-off. *Waitress: Paula, old friend. Right!*

"Did you know this is one of the restaurants that serves many local-sourced foods?"

She sipped her wine as soon as it came, then nodded her head up and down a little as she swallowed and let it trickle down her throat. Hot day for a kidnapping.

"That's right. You've lived here all your life. You could probably steer me to the best food ever. Gutz and I grab a burger at a bar when we get the chance to eat.

She lowered her eyes and her voice and answered, "I reserve the Number One rating for my kitchen/dining room. I'm told I'm a great chef."

Despite all the worries over a stalker, and a dead man, who still lay in the morgue, unclaimed by anyone, she floated as if above it all. His smile erupted like the world had settled when she implied she'd invite him over. All was well. Maybe he *did* want a future relationship. Boldness distressed her. But it worked!

Abby sobered when the vivacious waitress brought the appetizer. Of course, he'd know a lot of waitresses. Even though he claimed he only frequented bars. Let it go. Give him bubbly personified if he likes it.

Instead, she laughed, as if he told a joke when he mentioned where he and his partner ate. "Why do you call him Gutz?"

"The 'Gutz' began with irritation on my part and habit by the time he stopped aggravating me every day. His laid-back attitude grated, more so when I'm rushed. It still does, but I'm trying to reform. When it's informal, he wants me to try 'Grant.'"

"What wrong with that?"

"All the other things he does to exasperate me. Talking about Gutz, Grant, or whoever, is not relaxing. Switch of topics. I'd love to take you to some great beachside restaurants later. They're fabulous under the stars."

She sighed at the sun just beginning to lower in the sky.

William jumped in to explain. She saw he'd noticed right away. He was a cop, after all. "I have to get back to work tonight." His words and mood stopped as if he hit a wall.

He didn't return to the 'later' part of the sentence, and she knew it was because so much was precarious right now. 'Precarious' was her calm version of stalker and maniacal nightmares. Precarious. It was a good word. It meant things were uncertain, on edge a little. The trick was not to fall off the edge. Or at least not into the killer's hands. She'd thought and thought about who she saw and what she said at the conference. Nothing. Just the nightmares.

Attempting to hide her concerns, she shuffled the silverware around. The man must be remarkably astute.

He said, "Abby. I would love nothing more than for you to discover a lead tonight. When he pulled out an essential oil bottle her surprise overwhelmed her. Before she could ponder it, he said, "One question. He opened the cap. Is this the bergamot you smelled in your home when you found the warning?"

Leaning forward, she sniffed once. Then waved her hand in front of her face for a moment. "Oh yeah, that's it."

"Okay, we're one step further. However, it may be difficult to impossible to find the man who uses this."

"It's more than likely one ingredient in his cologne."

"Even tougher. But we're here to relax. Maybe later, this, or something else will just come to you. For now, you are safe. There are policemen at the conference trying to keep an eye on things. They know to watch for anything out of place."

She wrinkled her napkin in despair. "But with so many rooms? So much area to cover?"

He attempted to assuage her worry. "The resort pumped up security. And repaired the cameras. Someone is viewing them every minute. Relax."

"How do the sheriff's men search for a killer?"

"They don't. They look for inconsistencies. For people running. For out of the ordinary."

"He could be gone by now, right?"

"Maybe. But, if so, who wants you to leave? And why."

Her agitation grew—cracks appeared in her calm layer of frivolity. Her fear leaked out in unconnected hiccups between her words. He must have seen what it was doing to her since he suggested they relax and enjoy their dinner.

She tried. She did. The wine helped some. The asparagus was

cooked to perfection and dreamy lemony taste of the sauteed vegetables soothed her palate and her soul.

He watched her savor the shrimp. "I'll bring you back sometime for the lobster and shrimp specials."

"I'm quite fine with something like Beverly's La Croisette's up by Seventy-Fifth Avenue. Scrumptious breakfasts and lunches."

He ate large bites of his fish, then looked right into her eyes. "We could go together soon." He went back to devouring his food. It looked delicately prepared, with a plentiful mound of vegetables. When he kept eating, he said, "Sorry, I'm starved."

It was a strange counterpoint, when he asked, "Have you ever tried Sloppy Joe's in Treasure Island? Now that's a place with tons of good food on a platter."

Men. Maybe quantity always equaled quality. But together, they talked about crazy nothings and enjoyed each other's wit. She plied for personal information to round out knowledge gained so far only by reactions to difficult events. Did he want the same?

Abby's heart lifted. Maybe it was the excellent wine. Or the company. She wouldn't delve deeper. Then the mellow glow shattered like a broken light bulb.

He said, "We think you need to get out of the area. Lizzie's making plans."

"She's planning to get rid of me? Traitor."

"Just for a while."

"What? I live here." She glared. he didn't react. She glared more. When he emitted no response, she emphasized each word. "I—am—not—leaving."

Detective Milano stiffened. Not William anymore. He sure wasn't acting like a William. He'd gotten the message but weakened her stance when he expressed his concern. "I'm not sure they can protect you if you stay."

"I won't leave. That's what he wants."

"We're hoping that's all he wants."

"Why? I don't know what he thinks I know. I didn't sleep at all last night just trying to remember anything—anything." She slumped back in her chair, the rest of the coconut shrimp forgotten. "What more could he want?"

The detective leaned forward, only placing one finger on the table. She watched it mesmerized. He tapped once. "He's getting desperate." He tapped twice. "He's gotten more brazen, entering your home." He tapped again.

Before he could talk, she whispered shrilly. "Okay, okay. But I won't leave. And I can't move in with someone. If I'm in danger, whoever I'm with will be in danger."

He relaxed in his chair. "Now you're thinking."

"So I'll move into a hotel room until you find him."

"Sounds good to me. Lizzie can stay with you."

Her eyes widened. "Lizzie's gotta be at least eighty. I don't want her in danger."

The detective backtracked for a minute, looking chagrined. She didn't know what he could have been thinking. "Please stop. Lizzie's very wise. And maybe even devious. But how will that help if I am in danger? I'm not sure, but, there's got to be a better solution."

"Abby, Lizzie is trained in self-defense and no offense to you, but she's stronger than you."

"Sure, but that's not saying much. " And I can't shoot."

He shuddered. "Thank God."

She hunched into herself. "And I can't throw a punch."

Before she could get any more maudlin, he said, "We'll think of something. Meanwhile, why don't you finish that shrimp while I mop up the rest of my meal. I haven't eaten all day."

She nodded and grabbed one of the huge butterfly shrimp with her fingers and pulled a large bite off with her teeth."

He smiled, as she'd hoped he would. "I've always wanted to do that." I lose half the shrimp when I use my fork."

All of a sudden not wanting the evening to end, Abby asked, "Do I have time to order a drink?"

He glanced at his watch and said, "Sure. I'll pass though, since I'm heading back to the office. What would you like?"

"I'll try to stump the bartender. Maybe I should ask for a Hangman's Blood."

William dropped his fork. "A what?"

"It's a drink mentioned in a novel 'A High Wind in Jamaica.' It's from 1929, but they still make it."

The fork stuttered in its rise as William attempted to act normal. She wondered if he worried about her being a heavy drinker. Then he asked, "What's in it?"

She smiled. "A combination of rum, gin, brandy, and porter."

"Have you ever had one?"

"No, but I thought it might surprise the bartender."

William shook his head, and kept doing it. Then he laughed. "What happens when you have to drink it?"

"I'd probably get ill."

Finishing his meal, William settled back and patted his stomach, obviously replete. He signaled the waitress. Paula rushed over. He whispered to Abby, "Think of something else, quick."

"Hi Paula, who mixes the drinks tonight?"

"Why, I do."

"Could you fix me a Barracuda Cocktail please," Abby asked. "The kind with cream."

"Sure. Right up. Anything for you, William?"

"No. Duty calls."

Abby felt relaxed and happy. For the first time in days. Having this time with William was more than a great idea. It gave her a second wind. No way would she cower in a hotel room. She just wouldn't tell William just yet.

Paula delivered the drink with flourish, and waited for Abby to taste it. She did, and turned to the waitress. This is fantastic. Perfect. What's in it?"

"I used Baileys Irish Cream, Canadian Club whiskey, and a couple of ounces of cream. Added ice and a cherry garnish. I'm so glad it's what you wanted."

Abby and William both looked puzzled.

Abby sipped some more and said, "You sound like you've never made one before."

Paula smirked. "House rules. If you don't know it. Look it up on the internet. I use it for research all the time. You can find *anything* on the internet."

William drank some of his water while he watched the interchange. "That's it!"

They both said, "What? What?"

He jumped up, hugged the waitress, and gave her a big tip. "That may be the lead I'm looking for." He intertwined his fingers with Abby and pulled her out the door.

"My drink!"

"I'll buy you another one. Later. I need to get Venezia onto the internet."

She flopped into the car. "What?" She'd repeated 'what' a lot today. What did it portend?

CHAPTER THIRTY-ONE

"Ive got it!" Detective Milano shouted into his phone as he drove out of the restaurant parking lot.

"I've got it!" His partner Detective Guetierrez said as soon as he answered.

"What do you mean you've got it. I called you." Milano told the man as he neared Neptune's Oasis Resort to drop off Abby into the hands of Lizzie. Old or not. He trusted her.

His partner kept talking. "The financials just came in on Washburn, Jefferson, and the other security people. I think we got a hit."

"Great. My idea might take longer but where is yours leading?"

"Washburn's been burning up tons of money this week. I think he was bribed to fix the camera recordings."

Milano stopped the car but didn't get out. He listened to Grant but, when Abby opened her door he grabbed her arm and motioned for her to wait. "Hold it for a second."

"Hold up the investigation?" came over the line in an astonished voice.

Milano sighed. "Not you Gutz, uh, Grant. Partner. Whatever. Fantastic work. Find Washburn. Now. I'm heading back to the office to get Venezia onto a deeper avenue of research about the questionable enzyme thing."

He waited for a minute while his partner finished speaking. Then ended with an "I'll catch up with you if you need it, or if you find the guy, call me."

Abby said, "You know who did it?"

Switching from a tight grip on her arm to a gentle squeeze of her fingers, Milano said, "Sorry. We're not that far yet. But if this man fixed the security recordings so no one could recognize anyone, then he may lead us to whoever killed Howell."

She sputtered, but before she coordinated what she wanted to say, he said, "Let me make another call real quick."

The phone must have been answered immediately.

He said, "Juan Jose Venezia why are you still working this late?" Milano chuckled at the response, then said, "I'm sorry the twins are teething but glad you're there. Can you pull up your research on telomerase? Extend it to find other companies working on solutions."

He waited, nodded, then spoke. "Right, and concentrate on those who already have a product on the market. Maybe a relatively new one. Any link. Doesn't have to be an exhibitor here. Maybe an attendee, or a relative. Anything. Get back to me on my cell with whatever you find. Any time."

He was all detective now, in super fast mode. But he could tell Abby was keeping up. He asked her, "You know where I'm heading with this? Tell me how much time we have. When does this conference end?"

"Tomorrow."

Hoping for at least one more day, he curtailed expression of concern. "How early?"

"A few people leave tonight. The rest will be gone by late tomorrow afternoon."

"We've already flagged the early ones. Not too many. We interviewed them all. Not much there."

Abby attempted to scrunch around in the passenger seat to face him. It looked uncomfortable, so he said, "Let's go sit over at one of those tables. I need to wait for Lizzie, anyway. He withdrew his hand one finger at a time, and walked around to help her out. He'd called Lizzie and given her their location before he got to the resort.

He pulled out a chair for her. Placing his mouth by her ear so only she could hear, he whispered, "If I get a call from Guetierrez, I'll have to run. If Lizzie isn't here, you race right into Burt's office and don't leave till someone comes for you."

He knew he'd startled her when she jerked her head around to look him square in the face. Her angry expression bled out into white fear before she spoke. What squeaked past was a subdued, "I will."

He figured this was as good a time as any to tell her they stepped up security. Sliding in her home amongst the conference and resort site where men stood guard, he hoped to assuage her angst and sense of violation. It didn't seem to help. As much as he worked with victims in cases like this, he'd never had to comfort anyone where he felt as connected as he did with Abby.

He patted her hand and continued explaining. "Since we don't know why you were singled out, we must keep you close and guard your home, too."

She asked for details. He didn't have many. "One man is there guarding things, and another will replace him. "Your home is protected so don't worry. Still, I want to find you a secret, safe, location for you. And I'm sure you'll be back soon."

Not knowing what more to say, he faced the beach, and marveled at how the resort was laid out to see at least a section of the ocean from any lounge area. High above the water line, safe from the tides, bodies soaked up the sun, seeking cancer with their tans. Thongs on spicy women enticed the men, while tight briefs called to the women who dared to look.

Abby looked, but her scowl reined in his jealousy. Not the time and place. He studied her as she observed them, peeking to see what caught her attention. Male and female alike sported the greased up look, ready to be barbecued, somewhat like the pig with an apple in his mouth.

In this case, the offerings of the day guzzled fruity water and electrolytes as if they'd raced through the sand rather than lying in indolence.

He reached for her upper arms and turned her to look at him. The puzzled frown on his face reflected in hers before he expressed his concern. Her countenance brightened when he said, "This doesn't seem like you. Like it's the wrong style gown that doesn't fit."

Her smile widened. "This isn't me. It's a resort. I'm not often fearful. Like now. Pointing to those on the beach, she said, "It's probably not even them. It's an escape from who they normally are, what they endure or love doing daily. A break from the routine."

As delighted as he was to know Abby was someone else quite different than those lying out in front of him, it disheartened him. Without the surface veneer, she embodied under-layers he'd yet to discover. He sensed a lovely and endearing core beneath. But her comment prompted him to wonder if the man, or person, they were after, who murdered and threatened, also lived a separate life daily from the one they were compiling to help search for him. Wouldn't it make him even more difficult to find?

Lizzie's boisterous arrival broke the spell. She took one look at Abby's face and plunked down into a chair. Her raised eyebrows told Milano all he needed to know. She would defer to him—for now. He brought her quickly up to speed. She, in turn, told him of the consensus from the organizers of the conference.

"We didn't know a high percentage of the attendees. Some of the exhibitors were new, so we concentrated on those, as well as any of the old ones revealing a connection to Howell's research."

He circled his hand around to motion her to continue. She gave him a list and said, "None were crass enough to advertise the fountain of youth as such." She mumbled an aside to Abby, "Made it more difficult, let me tell you." She told Milano they reviewed all of the suspects again, with his officers. He asked, "How did the mung bean lady fare?"

Abby's chin ducked down and reared her neck backward. A wordless exclamation of "What the heck?" She swiveled her head between the two of them until Lizzie commented, "Forget it. She's fine. Crazy. But fine. And her research is quite scientific and fact-based. Just so you know."

He glanced at the list in front of him, and did some mumbling himself. "Not sure I want to live forever if it means eating mung beans every day."

Abby said, "I thought for a minute there we were having a serious discussion. Did I end up on the wrong train? Wrong track? Going the wrong way?"

Milano smiled at her. "You know, anything said here can not be mentioned anywhere?"

"That's okay. I don't have a clue what just went on here. Except no one appears evil enough to have killed Alexander Howell, and we have no idea who's stalking me."

The detective looked sheepish for a moment, but his cell ringing interrupted what might have been an apology.

Guetierrez shouted into the phone, "We're banging on his door now." He repeated the address then nodded to Lizzie. "Can Abby stay with you in your room until I return? This may be a long night."

"I'll escort Abby to our suite now. We won't tell anyone. If I need to leave for a bit, Delia will be with her."

Abby bristled. "I'm not a cat or a baby. I'll be fine." But she agreed to go with Lizzie.

Torn between duty, concern, and hope this may all end tonight, he moved to kiss Abby goodbye and realized the advance may seem out of place. A pat on her hand, again, was all he could excuse. This time she looked like she was going to take that hand and gut punch him with it. Escape appeared the better part of valor. He raced off without waiting for more.

* * *

Lizzie rose and wrapped her arm around Abby's shoulders when she stumbled out of her seat. "Come on Abs, let's go play some cards. I haven't played in ages. I wonder if I still know how to cheat?"

Abby laughed.

Smiling at her, Lizzie continued to walk. "What, you haven't been called Abs before?"

Keeping up with her long stride gave Abby a workout, and kept her in motion. Lizzie's plot all along.

"Of course I've been called Abs. Too many times to remember. But I have never been warned going into a card game my opponent is going to cheat. I'm not sure if it takes the fun away, or provides more challenge."

They marched through the shaded pavilion and across the courtyard that revealed the ocean in all its glory. Waves hit the beach in a rhythmic one-two punch with a third assault always possible but never arriving on demand. The cadence is broken but not uninteresting.

Lizzie stopped so they could both absorb the power. The foaming crescendo of waves drowned out obnoxious human-induced sounds, cell phones and cars. "It's marvelous. The natural clash of water hitting land wipes out the noise of all that new machinery that runs our lives."

She continued walking toward her room. "What a delightful privilege to luxuriate in this whenever you want. A definite advantage over the snowy north."

Abby's voice oozed sarcasm. "Yeah, when you're not being rushed inside all the time." She added, "I used to enjoy the softness of the evening light and the air when the sun's warmth sneaks off in the night, only to meander back at dawn. So much. I didn't realize what I had until it's all been swept away."

Lizzie smiled. "Oh, swept aside, temporarily, maybe, but not away. And it looks like Detective William Milano got caught in your broom."

Abby blushed.

Delighted to have a guest, Delia offered drinks and snacks. Abby acted too gracious to refuse. Ever grateful her sister's charm warmed people no matter the circumstances, Lizzie dug out the resort-provided playing cards and shuffled away. When Abby won the opening hand, she outright asked, "Are you hustling me?"

Lizzie played the affronted card shark to the hilt, bringing laughter to the group. She knew her concentration was off, thus making it so easy for Abby to win. Time was running out. She hadn't heard back from her handwriting expert friend and it disturbed her. Any lead would help right now. She excused herself and escaped to the bedroom to dial her one more time. Her audible exhalation when Kat Everitt answered drew attention from the others, but she smiled and turned her back to badger her hometown friend. "Where have you been? Did you look at the handwriting samples I e-mailed you? Any ideas?"

She halted instantly at the volley of words rushing through the phone. "Okay, I'm sorry. It's kind of dangerous here. One at a time."

Silence ensued. Then she responded, polite but abrupt. "I'm glad you had a vacation. And sorry a snowstorm delayed you, but . . ."

She listened. Then spoke with astonishment. "Of the four samples I sent you. Only one stood out. That definite?"

She completed the call with a thank you. "I know, I know. Handwriting analysis reveals only propensities, and a person's nature. But he's the one I disliked from the beginning. Gotta run."

While Abby studied the cards, Lizzie prepared to leave. Delia noticed the anger etched on my face, and watched me don the new summer jacket with large pockets I purchased today. She didn't need to see me move the gun into my right pocket as I turned. She was my sister. She knew.

"Girls, I have to run out for a bit. Delia, you'll be in for the evening, right? Delia nodded with a look in her eyes to confirm she understood the real question. Abby, you stay here and remain safe till I get back."

Abby's look of apprehension stopped her for a second. "Everything okay?"

Lizzie forced the smile, practiced over years of stealth. "It will be."

CHAPTER THIRTY-TWO

Never protected someone before. Bad at it. I hope Delia and Abby stay safe. But this, I'm good at. Ending evil.

Lizzie walked throughout the resort, arms pumping like an old lady on an evening constitutional. No one noticed her. She was the invisible elderly. She could play that when needed, though it wasn't her favorite role. For now, it provided anonymity. This worked.

She swiveled her eyes while appearing to look forward, and saw groups of people out for the evening, ambling toward the beach, or sporting their finer wear, strolling to one of the fancier restaurants. Sometimes it appeared the only difference in style was the upgrade from flip flops to loafers and heels. Resorts were casual. She sought someone specific amidst the camouflage of happiness. So far she didn't see him.

Too many people stood in, or walked through, the parking lots. It would have helped if the landscape plans included more sidewalks. *I'm probably the only one who cares.* Most think sand. Sun. She looked around as she exercised, studying details. Okay, there weren't *any* sidewalks. Everyone wandered through the parked cars. What were they thinking when they designed this? How could she break into a car with all these people around?

Hearing the handwriting expert confirm her suspicions about Jacob Meindl forced her into motion. No waiting around for the cops, as nice as they were. The detectives approached this with approved strategies, she went straight to the heart. Find the killer. Secure. Then prove.

Natalie in her role as conference chair, had procured all the samples of handwriting she'd requested earlier. She tried to be fair and add other villainous types.

This man's handwriting didn't shout "evil," but then handwriting never did shout. Kat said his handwriting changing speeds continually, signified concealment. Additional whisperings from her friend that the man could be deceitful and unstable was enough for her to pursue him. And then, his lower case n's indicated temper. There was more, but it was enough for her. At least enough for capture. Afterwards, she'd see.

It hadn't taken much for Lizzie to memorize the few vehicles associated with these guys from the registration lists when Natalie wasn't looking earlier that day. She'd made sure to note Meindl's. It triggered interest in itself. Strange he had a vehicle, since he flew in. Some guests would rent cars to sight-see. He didn't seem the type. And who would rent a truck to drive around and see the beauty of this area?

She'd circled the whole resort twice. No one had seen her circuit so none wondered how her breathing came as silent as a still breeze. When she reached the smallest rooms on the ground level of the Jasmine Building, she marveled at the audacity of those who would hope to glamorize a concrete building with the name of something beautiful. She slowed as she turned the corner, her thoughts a step behind. She wouldn't know much about prettifying by conferring a fanciful name. Just look at the names Lizzie and Delia. Maybe their mom didn't play that particular game. 'Lizzie' fared well enough for her over the years. It would do.

Jacob's room was down the corridor on the left, if he was still there. She'd already been here with Detective Milano. But Jacob's attitude then made her grit her teeth. She swung back around, deciding to check the lots for his rental truck. Did he think no one would suspect it was his?

Miranda walked by, studying the notes on her pad, almost in front of her nose. *I'm surprised she doesn't trip.* "Hi, Lizzie, nice night, isn't it?"

The young woman didn't stop to hear an answer, but at least she acknowledged people. Unlike some. So much for being invisible. And then Lizzie stumbled. *Damn. Okay, God. I get it. Quit thinking unkind thoughts. Tough to do. I'm out to kill someone. Well, disable, I'm out to disable him.*

Lizzie straightened her back, brushed off her palm that took the brunt of the fall, and moved into a casual stroll. Kind of a cool off phase to her walk. The evening breeze was about the only thing cooling down. She needed to rev up the pace. This guy wasn't going to stick around forever.

"Hey, Lizzie. Ready for the last day of the conference?"

Oops, she missed seeing Julie. Her brain cells must still be lagging behind. "Hey to you, too. On to anything exciting for the evening?"

Please, get on to whatever. Away from here.

"They're having fireworks on the beach in a bit. Thought I'd stake out a spot. It's the most popular event of the conference."

"Uh, what about that fantastic speech? The one on ancient herbs?"

At least Julie didn't laugh uproariously, but her body did buckle a little with her chuckle.

"You know you're the best speaker, ever, Lizzie. The room was packed."

"Okay. On your way. Don't let me hold up finding your prime location."

Lizzie saw the truck and circled that area of the lot, perfecting the casual stroll. Her eyes never revealed she'd checked out the license plate, confirmed it was Meindl's and noticed the locked doors. Did it mean he was in his room?

It could just as easily indicate he wanted people to think he was around while he stalked Abby. Thank God she stayed concealed in the suite with Delia. She turned the last corner and there—the answer to the puzzle of how to approach his room. Miranda, again, sitting alone in the courtyard, going through her notes. A decoy.

"Miranda, sweetie, I need a big favor. No questions. But it's crucial and time is running out. Will you help me?"

God bless the girl, she slapped her folder shut, stood, and said, "Tell me what y'all want?"

Her friends, Natalie and Abby, and the Detectives Milano and Guetierrez swore that only those on a need-to-know basis knew who found the body. Miranda said she didn't want to talk about it, with anyone. She'd begged Delia and Lizzie to keep her secret before leaving the room where she'd been sequestered. She didn't want people to repeatedly ask her about how the body looked. Delia, Lizzie, and the others had kept their promise. So the odds were the killer had no interest or knowledge of Miranda. That helped quiet her conscience about involving the girl today.

Gently tugging her into the corridor, Lizzie told Miranda to turn her back while she picked the lock on the linen closet. Reaching inside, she tied a towel around the girl's waist and hoped it would look official enough at quick glance. Then she handed her a pile of towels and said, "Hurry, I need you to knock on a man's door and say, 'Mr. Meindl, these are your towels.' Loud so he can hear through the door."

Miranda practiced till they reached the door. "You're towels are here sahr."

God bless her soul. I forgot she was from Texas.

Her game plan jerked to a halt for a minute. Miranda only twanged when she was under stress. No question why she felt anxiety after finding a bloody body. But she noticed the accent the second she'd asked the young lady for help. She'd been pleasant enough. But where was the stress sitting in the late day sun reviewing notes?

Had Lizzie's thoughts turned Miranda into a suspect? Because of an intermittent accent? Now she felt crazy. Even Detective Milano said it appeared the killer was tall, lean and strong? It couldn't be Miranda. *The young woman probably associates me with the killing. I am the first person she saw after running out of there. Stay on target, Lizzie girl. No time for dithering. But, was it a dither? Or a warning instinct?*

She kept to the plan. And remembered to step out of view in case Meindl was in the room. With luck, the man won't notice the accent or won't wonder why she's employed in Florida. It is a multicultural state. Everybody knew that.

Miranda swept into the role like a leading lady on stage. She repeated her phrase several times, louder on each one. The last time she varied it a little and knocked with vigor. If the guy was in his room, alive, he'd heard her.

Now came the hard part. Did she let Miranda see her pick the door lock? That way, if Miranda stayed around and they stumbled on the man coming out of the shower, it would appear as if the cleaning lady used her key thinking no one was in. On the other hand, she didn't want Miranda to be anywhere near the killer. *Jeesh, working alone and undercover. Much easier.*

"Here's how we're going to do it. We go in, you first. If you see anyone, you drop the towels on the bed and back out. Immediately."

The game plan should work. Who would shoot a towel-bearing lady? And if anything, Miranda's southern charm oozed from her warm nature. He'd be able to feel it, and her innocence right away.

This was why she worked alone. Now she worried about danger to Miranda. But the fact the woman stayed at the conference after finding the body revealed a steel core beneath the Texan fluff. She hoped she wasn't justifying using her, now?

Miranda's answer pulled her back to the moment. "Ah'm supposed to go out *backwards*?"

"It looks more courteous."

The young woman shook her head, then straightened that spine, and said, "Ah'm in. Let's do it."

The drapes were drawn. No one responded to Miranda's final declaration of towels. Lizzie released the young woman from her role, gently pushed her out the door, and suggested she drop the pile on one of the tables outside, pick up her notebook and leave the area. She felt bad enough bringing the girl into it at all.

Instincts carried Lizzie through the search. Her training sped up the effort. She looked over, under, and in. She knew to look for anything from fake shaving cream cans to inside hollowed out books. She sought a flash drive with the formula on it. A laptop or tablet. A smart phone. Anything with a Cloud connection. Alexander Howell must have died for a reason. If the death was an accident, the altercation was not. She did not believe the killer left empty handed.

This room may not prove it, but everything within her pointed to Jacob Meindl. *Could this be the first time I'm wrong? Was I retired because my instincts splintered—no longer infallible?* In this moment it didn't matter. She'd continue her pursuit. But the room revealed nothing.

Finding Miranda in a casual lean against the outer railing of the walkway spooked her. Not something easily done. Her worries about the woman returned. Why is mousy Miranda out here? Why has she morphed from a shy girl into a compelling woman? Or worse? Why was she around so much all of a sudden?

Oh God, guide me. Provide me a gentle way to probe. She may be just an innocent girl bound into the twisted intricacy of murder.

"Miranda, what on earth are you doing here?"

The woman turned and smiled at her, putting Lizzie on edge. It wasn't a mousy smile.

"I was standing guard," Miranda said. But the accent returned as she stumbled over her motives.

Lizzie let it go. She didn't have time. The fireworks would begin any minute. It would be her best opportunity to search the truck. She urged Miranda on her way, saying she'd found nothing and shrugged her empty arms to prove it. Suggested the nocturnal display over the ocean could be entertaining. And waved her on her way.

Frustration accompanied Lizzie through the parking lot. Adrenaline picking up by the minute. Fear seeped in. And would you believe, many folks didn't care about fireworks? Some still lingered in the area. Thank God she didn't have to blow up the truck. An explosion might draw a few people. *Silly. You don't want their attention. Just their disappearance.*

Once inside the truck, she felt safer. Yet anxiety escalated. Like time ran through the hourglass faster than normal. Fear worked its way around—until she found Howell's computer. She finagled through the stupid password choices right there in the tiny back seat where she'd found the laptop, all snuggled under the mat.

Jeesh, Howell practically discovered the fountain of youth but he wasn't creative enough to come up with something other than his initials and date of birth. The formula was there, and proof the computer belonged to the dead man. It didn't prove Meindl killed Howell, but the blood might help.

She leapt from the vehicle. Time to find reinforcements. A couple of brief calls later she reached Milano. "Had to leave the room. Can't connect with Abby or Delia on cell or room phone. Sent Michael up to check—waiting to hear."

Her breathlessness caught his attention more than her words. When she stopped for a second she asked, "Where are you?"

He snapped out a reply like he was driving and answering at the same time. "I'm heading toward Jacob Meindl's room. Washburn from security gave him up. He's our man."

"He's not in his room."

Before he could ask, she spoke. "Doesn't matter how I know. No, he's not dead in there either."

His answer was loud. Unrepeatable, even for her.

She whispered, "Find him before he gets to Abby, please—he's definitely the killer. I have proof of sorts."

CHAPTER THIRTY-THREE

Can't believe Delia sprained her ankle. Refused my help to the hospital. What a mess! Abby Weiss walked past the jasmine and inhaled the sweet scent. She let her mind wander. Better than focusing on her fear. The jasmine aroma was mild and pleasing. The darkened skies reminded her how late it'd become while she and Delia sat and played cards. She quickened her step as she admired how the landscapers kept the plants back from the walkways to prevent bruising of the delicate flowers. Even though the conference would always evoke sadness with the death of Alexander Howell, she loved this resort. Until now. When it threatened her peace—maybe her life.

Delia wanted her to stay in the suite until Lizzie returned. The poor woman couldn't walk without a crutch and her reddened face and shaky arms reflected her unspoken misery. Abby managed to help her up and onto the bed to keep her foot elevated. But the swelling and Delia's high level of pain indicated more was wrong. Delia called her friend Carmen for the ride to the hospital, She'd driven to the conference so had an available car, unlike Abby's, which was parked at home.

Abby wanted to call the resort but Delia refused. "It wasn't their fault I tripped over the footstool. I just wasn't looking." And she absolutely refused to call Lizzie. She blasted out, "Never. Not now." That sure surprised Abby. Delia wouldn't say more.

When the injured woman sat ensconced in the back seat of Carmen's car, Abby'd returned to the suite. Walking around the rooms, alone and hesitant, her adrenaline drained. And she felt out of place. As nice as the suite was, the jitters erupted as she sat in the main sitting room. She'd thought about just buying essentials from the delightful gift shop on the lower level. But, she wanted her own home. In her mind, it was security. She'd lived there all her life.

She raced down the steep path on the shortcut. *No one knows I was in Lizzie's room. No one to follow me.* As nighttime settled in, everything became obscured. The air around her felt more dense. But despite the trees hidden helter-skelter in her path, she negotiated her way without mishap.

She agonized over the killer. Her stalker. And the nature of her relationship with Milano.

Her heart was another matter. Was it connected in some way to a man who's personality morphed from the warm William to the stoic Corporal Detective William Milano? How would that work, she wondered. For now, she just wanted to go home. He'd said his men monitored activity there. Once she reached it, she'd be safe. Her haven—under police guard—but a haven, still.

The few minutes it took to walk through the woods stretched into a timeless dread. Her legs ran faster. Against her better judgment, which said to slow down around the trees. Just then she burst through into the open field next to her house. Small area, but useful. Her vision opened up. Enough to see her home. And the one officer out front.

His gun was drawn and facing her. She stumbled over her own feet as she stopped dead.

She raised her hands. He strode closer. Relief washed his face, and hers, as he recognized her. Thank heavens he was one of the officers she'd met earlier.

In a simultaneous move, they each took a deep breath. "Officer Ferris. It's Abby. I, uh, I live here," she stuttered.

He said, "You can lower your hands now."

Abby swiveled her head and stared at each of her arms as if she didn't recognize it. Her hands fell straight down like they'd been held there by a puppet string that broke. Her purpose there changed when she saw how her fear congealed even at her own home.

"I came to pack some personal things so I can stay elsewhere for a bit."

"Great idea."

When she moved forward, her steps minced like her feet were uncertain how to walk, but she soon managed to organize her legs into a normal rhythm that steadied her heart and her resolve.

"Do you need help?"

"No. I'm fine."

The officer walked beside her. "Okay. But don't plan on leaving through the woods. Neither of us wants another near heart attack."

Her feeble laugh strengthened and she ramped up the charm. "I'm so sorry. We won't take a vote on which one was most scared. I'll pack a few things, then come out to you and we'll discuss my getaway."

"Just come to the front door and call out to me."

"Better plan."

She entered her home by the front door. Instant reprieve. All her muscles eased. "Maybe she could stay here."

She turned and saw Officer Ferris as she closed the door. *Maybe not. I'll pack my things. I left my herbal notebook at Lizzie's. Nothing else. Just a few personal necessities from here and I'll go.*

At the suite she'd wanted her own pajamas. Her own clothes. Her own Dr. Ken's Natural toothpaste and favorite toothbrush. And the comfort those brought, like a security blanket she desperately needed right now. That's why she decided to sneak home.

And here she was. And her home no longer felt safe. How could it, with a policeman in front and a stalker out there somewhere? Walking down the hallway to her bedroom she heard a noise. Was it in the front foyer? Or outside? *Didn't I lock the door? I know I did.* Yet . . .she crouched low, as if that would protect her, and slipped into the kitchen and out the back door.

Tiptoeing around the side of the house, she didn't see the officer. Maybe he was patrolling much further from the house this time. He took his duty to protect her with sober deliberation, but could have been the one to make the noise. Or any wildlife in the area. She giggled, despite her troubles. Picturing a dangerous squirrel.

She inhaled deep and let it out one puff at a time, then checked the front door. Unlocked. *Well, what did she expect. She never locked her door. A habit. I lived here all my life. Mom never locked her doors, either.*

She entered again. Locked the door this time. The foyer looked the same as always. She gathered her things in the bedroom, swept her crucial items from the bathroom sink with little care into a smaller case that fit in her duffel. No lingering looks back. She marched straight through to the kitchen. *I'm getting a cup of tea before I leave. I'll pack a few of my favorite blends to take to the resort while the water boils.*

Strange, that scent was bergamot, though she had no such tea amid her choices. It pestered at her memory as she bustled about. This was normal. Her routine brought comfort. It didn't alleviate her concerns. Just softened her tense muscles a little. The tea would finish the job and she'd be on her way. The kettle whistled only one note before she switched it off.

CHAPTER THIRTY-FOUR

Lizzie panicked. But she did it as she sprinted back to the killer's truck. It was closest. And she hot wired it faster than running to the room for her car key. Abby: missing. Delia: missing. Jacob Meindl: missing. Life: not good. She carried proof of theft from the victim. It could be more. Blood. On the laptop. *Dear God, let it be Howell's.*

Her mind raced with the accelerator, picking up speed despite the late evening crush of traffic. Shoulder. Open. Go. Squeeze back to right lane. Okay. That man only looks like he had a heart attack.

This time she wouldn't go it alone. She called Milano again. So she probably broke three rules. Driving over the limit. Like a maniac. With a phone at her ear.

I'll have to learn how to use one of those blue things. But for now, she drove. Maybe a cop would see and follow her right to Abby's. Instinct headed her there. She didn't know where else to look.

"Where are you?" she shouted into the phone the second Milano answered. No time for niceties.

"Guetierrez and I are on our way to Abby's. The policeman we posted there isn't responding." She overheard him speak to himself, "Gutz for God's sake don't hit that ditch." He spoke back into the phone. "Gutz's driving a car ahead of me. If he dies in a crash before we get there, I'll kill him. Gotta go."

"Wait. Did you hear from Michael?"

"Michael says there's no one in the room. No signs of disturbance. No note." No where else to look right now. So we chose her home. We're here. I'll let you know."

Lizzie raced further down the road. Almost there herself. Move. Slide to left lane and turn. Light's only orange. Punch it.

The drive took longer than running through the woods. But darkness blurred the trees into shadow shapes that could hamper her. Wheels on asphalt—much smoother. Her phone rang. Oh God, what did they find? When she heard her sister's voice she sighed with relief. "Delia, where are you? Where's Abby?"

She slowed her mad dash just a little. No sense joining Gutz in a ditch. "You what? How long will you be at the hospital? Is Abby with you?"

She listened, her muscles constricting as she heard the story. "Sorry, Delia. She's not in the room. Guess you should have tied her up. I'm at Abby's. Later."

She managed to hang up as she dropped the phone. And stopped the car before she reached Abby's house. Lizzie scrambled from the car, gun in hand and sped foreword.

* * *

Reaching in the pantry for her travel mug, Abby startled the man standing behind the door. In one second, her muscles tensed again. She froze. He held a knife. Facing her, he said, "Back out of here into the kitchen. Slow."

Abby did what he said. But when he grabbed her arm, her mouth opened in fear. Her body jerked into action. He grappled one-handed with her flailing arms. She couldn't make her voice emit more than a squeak. As soon as he heard, he swung her around, and mashed his free hand across her mouth before her scream built up.

That did it. Her resolve returned. Admittedly, in slow dribs and drabs, but she felt it. Filling her being. Strengthening her body. She remembered this morning's quote from Joshua in the Bible. Something about being firm and steadfast. She recalled it all now. The rest was, "Do not fear nor be dismayed, for the Lord, your God, is with you wherever you go."

She repeated the verse like a mantra, over and over in her mind. She managed to push out a "What?" before he pushed harder on her mouth. She'd seen his face long enough to recognize Jacob. He wasn't clinging like a hopeful lover any longer. But what did he want? He wouldn't let her ask.

She tried. She only blurted "Why?" before he shook his head back and forth. He waved the knife in front of her face as a means of reinforcement. Seeing it so close sealed her lips. It also made her cross her eyes. He thwarted her attempt to inch back from it by grabbing her arm.

He just stood there. With a knife. Her knife, she realized as it veered closer to her face, again.

He's going to kill me with my own knife! If I don't do something I'll be dead. She risked biting his hand. Hard. He yanked it off her mouth. She didn't want Officer Ferris killed if he came to her rescue. Still, she needed reinforcements. She shrieked for help.

A man rushed in at her scream. But it was William. Grant raced in behind him.

Jacob moved behind her, grabbed a hank of her hair, and pulled her head up. The knife was at her throat. "Stop."

The men halted mid stride. Arms down in sublimation. She glanced at their hands. They each held a gun. She saw the fear in Williams eyes as he stared into hers.

"Drop the guns or she dies."

Both men hesitated. Abby watched William revert to detective mood in a blink. He said, "Jacob Meindl, you don't want to do this. What has she done to you to deserve this?"

Jacob said. "I had no choice. I needed to protect myself. She got in the way."

Abby wondered if she was visible. They both talked around her like it was someone else with a knife at the throat. So tight if she breathed deep it would cut her. She stopped breathing altogether for a few seconds. Who needs to breathe all the time anyway. Overrated compared to dying from a sliced artery.

But then she couldn't hold it any longer. When Jacob finished his excuses as to why she couldn't live, she inhaled. The knife drew blood.

She felt the blood trickle down the side of her neck.

Detectives Milano and Guetierrez bent down in slow motion and placed their guns on the floor.

Only moving her eyes she looked at each one. If there was a plan she'd missed the prep meeting. And they gave nothing away.

Uh-oh. Now what?

CHAPTER THIRTY-FIVE

Turning the last corner on foot Lizzie halted. Two police cars, lights flashing. One driver door still open. *Oh dear God, what happened. Please help me.*

Lizzie released the safety on her gun. She looked into each car. No blood. No guns or weapons. She squatted behind the open door. Searched the field in the dark. Then the flower beds around the house.

One side and the back of the house were out of sight. What would she find there?

Time to reconnoiter. The shrubs would be the most difficult. They grew out of control in front of all the side windows. It was a good thing she was so tall. She could use every inch. The doc told her just last month she'd lost a half-inch. She wished it back now as she crawled to the front window and stretched to peer in from the side.

Jungle duty didn't scratch as much as these damn branches. Sorry God, 'darn' branches. She didn't see a thing. No shadows either. Odds were no one was in this front room. Can't turn around. Backing out without knowing what's behind her took some skill. Then she inched the same way to each window. Only the kitchen left.

Where was everyone? She saw the officer on the ground at the edge of the house. Praying it wasn't Detective Milano, she ran to his side. Didn't take the time to kneel. Not Milano. Or Guetierrez. This officer—unknown. His pulse was firm, though he was out cold. She found the wooden board near his head but didn't touch it.

Have to get inside. Shimmied around the corner. Saw nothing in the back yard. An attack dog would be better than this 'nothing.'

Lizzie scurried to the other side of the house. The blinds were closed on both windows. Probably bedrooms. Placing her ear to each window, she listened. Nothing. Again, nothing.

When she returned to the back door, she heard talking in the kitchen. Finally. Abby's voice. Brief. Then a man's. Not Milano. Certainly not that slight accent of golden boy Guetierrez. The killer?

A peek inside the window showed the two cops. No weapons. No movement. Couldn't see what they stared at. Wouldn't take the chance. Lizzie sidestepped the back porch. Wooden. Too noisy. They all were. Even the fake wood ones. Abby's shone with the patina that only comes with old age. Bound to creek.

Near the back door. Another window. The pantry. She'd been in there. Had Abby left it open like before? She peered in. Only the screen. Thank you, God. Small window, but she could fit.

The pantry door opened inward, but was closed except for a slight gap. The kind to occur when the door requires a shove to push it the last few inches. Once she got inside she'd have to jerk it open fast.

Could she do it without detection? She jerked her shoes off, then raced back to the officer. Hoping no one would see or hear her. Yes, he had a knife. She borrowed it. And found a stronger pulse. Left him. No time.

The grass felt silky on her feet. Abby kept a good lawn. Now to help her. The screen tore like silk, too. What a break. Taking strand by strand she ripped it out enough to fit. Risky. The gun went under her chin. She threaded the knife through two tears she made in her sleeve. With gun and knife as her artillery she levered herself in. Decades of experience coated her moves with silence.

Any squeak was her enemy. Lizzie tip-toed across the pantry. Careful. On the lookout for any bag or box that could snag her clothes. Thank God she wasn't wearing her earth-girl skirt. Slim pants saved her today.

The door to the kitchen—still open a crack. Jacob holding Abby. Had to be Jacob. His back to her. She couldn't see more. Was afraid to take another step and spook him. What would save Abby? The two detectives stood paralyzed. Milano's eyes reflected Abby's face. And what looked like a knife to her throat. Oh God. *Help me. Help her.* Then Abby moved. She jerked her head sideways despite the knife. It allowed her head to dip enough to bite his arm. He cried out but didn't drop the knife.

"I'll slice your throat right now if you bite me again. You're dead anyway. You know too much."

Abby shouted at Meindl. "What do I know? Nothing. That's what. Nothing! And you were the one stalking me, weren't you?"

"What of it? I wanted you alone. Now you're coming with me."

"Why would I go with you? You just said you'll kill me."

Lizzie itched to get closer. She could barely see Meindl as he pulled the knife tighter to Abby's throat and jerked her a step backward with the left arm around her waist. She yanked it down. He moved enough to allow her to elbow him in the gut. The knife dropped.

Milano and Guetierrez each stepped forward. But before they made it half-way there, Jacob grabbed Abby's throat with both hands and moved to drag her out the kitchen door.

Abby gagged. Her breathing hitched. With only a whisper. Her mouth couldn't suck in air. His hands strangled her even more as he tugged her backwards toward the kitchen door.

Guetierrez circled around. Milano went the other way. They didn't take the time to pick up their guns. Why bother. Everyone was too close for a clean shot to Jacob's head. Lizzie didn't think.She flung open the door. It stopped all motion in an instant. Even Jacob halted.

She waffled for a second. Confront him the old way, or the new, righteous way? Is there a righteous way to attack someone? Lizzie didn't threaten. Moved to subdue him. Pistol whipped the side of his head in just the correct location to fell him instantly. Out cold.

Abby struggled to breathe. When Guetierrez saw Milano catch her, he bent down and cuffed Jacob while he was still out. Milano just held her, soothed her throat with light flutters of movement to encourage her to pull in air. Gentle pats for gentle breaths.

Abby recovered and hugged him and cried. Suddenly she whirled around. Ran to Lizzie. Hugged her and cried more. Detective Milano shuffled back far enough to retrieve the guns while never letting his eyes off Abby.

Lizzie patted her shoulder. "It's over now girl. All over. Wipe away those tears." Guetierrez whipped out a clean white handkerchief and offered it to Abby in a bow and a twirl like a gentleman of old. She grabbed for it and blew her nose, breaking the spell and provoking laughter. They all looked down at Jacob. Not moving.

Guetierrez decided to check his pulse. "Good job Miss Ort. Stopped him on the spot but he's got a strong pulse."

A slight nod of her head offered acceptance of his compliment. Her words provided the high praise. "You may call me Lizzie."

Abby looked down at him, shuddered, and went back to Milano's arms. They settled around her like a warm blanket.

"Hey! I'm the only one not getting hugged," said Guetierrez in a miffed voice. "And I gave Abby the handkerchief."

Lizzie put her arm around his shoulders and turned him to the kitchen door. "Your officer's on the ground past the corner. He should be fine but see what you can do for him. Maybe call an ambulance. He got conked pretty good on the noggin."

"Officer Ferris?" Milano said. "We wondered what happened to him but heard Abby scream and didn't take the time to look. Thanks."

Worry about the officer brought Abby around. She followed Guetierrez out the door. Milano pulled her back. "He'll handle it. Relax."

She snuggled. Then he said, "We'll get an ambulance for you, too. You're still bleeding."

She bounced away. "Not happening. I'm fine."

He stared at her, hoping to change her mind. Lizzie knew better and just watched.

Abby stood silent for a minute, then the questions rolled out. "How did you all know to come just then? Why did he want to kill me? Did he kill Howell?"

Milano explained, ignoring the fight about the ambulance. "Guetierrez tracked down a man named Washburn, a security guy from the resort. Jacob Meindl paid him to fix the cameras for the crucial time period when Howell was killed so nothing could be seen clearly. We're assuming that's what happened, though he didn't tell Washburn what he planned. He never gave Washburn his name but the security technician recognized Meindl's photo. We headed to Meindl's place but a call from Lizzie tipped us he wasn't there, and of the urgency in finding you. Came here right away in hopes you'd be here."

Gladdened that he initiated the discussion, Lizzie used the moment to ponder how to phrase what she did. No point in going to jail if she could avoid it.

They both turned to her. "I couldn't reach you or Delia on the phone."

Abby frowned and glanced around. "I must have left my purse and phone in the suite at the resort, after I spooked and left in a hurry. I *did* plan to return there."

Lizzie continued. "Delia finally called from the hospital." She let a humph escape as she finished. "The sprain's not too bad. They're keeping her overnight because of her age. She thought you'd still be in the suite."

Milano turned to Lizzie, "How did you know Jacob Meindl wasn't in his room?"

"The maid was cleaning the rooms as I came by to find him. I didn't have any tape to keep the door from latching so I just bribed her to let me in when she finished. Thank the Lord I had money on me."

The lies rolled off her tongue. *I'm too good at this. It has to stop.*

He looked at her bulging pocket holding the gun once again. "So you keep more than guns in those pockets. I wondered."

"One gun." She smirked at him. "Useful too."

Abby smiled like sunshine. "Thank you, by the way."

Lizzie slid in the part about finding the laptop in Jacob's car.

Milano didn't let it go by. "The maid help you get in there, too?"

"No. It was unlocked," she answered with a sincere face. *No point in explaining how it got to be unlocked.*

He responded. "Though we're all thrilled we've stopped Abby's stalker, we can't charge him with murder? Is he the killer?"

"Howell's laptop is still in Meindl's car. Right around the corner. Maybe it will help." The ambulance sirens announced it's arrival. The diversion delayed Lizzie's comment about the blood. Better save for later.

She went to search Meindl's pockets but Milano stopped her. "What do you need?"

"You might want the keys to his truck."

His eyebrows shot forward, but he must be getting used to her ways because he didn't ask how she got it there. Just reached in and withdrew Meindl's key.

The first ambulance left with Officer Ferris. Guetierrez jumped into the second one with Meindl. Abby watched it pull away. And trembled. "That could have been me. With no lights flashing."

CHAPTER THIRTY-SIX

Milano's options are zero. Abby shivered despite the heat. He needed his police car and the truck back at the sheriffs office. And to deal with Abby. His men compiled what evidence they could find inside. Lizzie saw his decision forming as he shook his head sideways back and forth. In reluctant slow motion he handed her the truck keys. "Could you drive it to the station? You've already touched it. Might as well be you. I sure as heck won't let you drive *my* car."

She attempted to hide her chuckle as she reached out. The sound stopped abruptly in her throat. He looked up. "What's wrong?"

"You should get the laptop out and secure it right away. I didn't touch but one spot. There's blood on the edges. If we're lucky it might be Howell's."

Abby stood by in silence. She may not have realized the significance of that. Milano did. He dropped back into detective mode in an instant. Straightened his spine. Ran to his car and pulled out his kit.

They all walked to the truck. She pointed to the back seat. "I'm afraid it was under the mat there." She motioned for Milano to open the door. "I checked it earlier to see if it was Howell's laptop. Stayed away from the blood. I was worried about Abby so set it on the piece of plastic and took off."

His solemn nod and grimace was an acceptance and a hope. She wondered again, would they be lucky? This could be over with one test. She showed him where she'd touched it. His gloved fingers worked with deft efficiency. Grabbing the spot he placed the laptop in the evidence bag. His eyes revealed the same wavering expectation.

He left to talk with the two officers who'd arrived, and Lizzie and Abby walked next to him. He said, "There's not much to do here. We all saw what happened and there's little evidence to collect, if anything."

"Officer, will you bring in the board on the ground over there? Secure it. It was used to attack Officer Ferris, who was patrolling the property."

He turned to Abby. I'm sorry you were left alone to deal with that maniac. He softened his anger. Lizzie knew it was not at Abby, but at the situation. The girl did not respond. Her face reflected the trauma she'd lived through. Her demeanor suggested more.

Abby took a deep breath and exhaled. She raised her bent head and whispered, "I'm sorry. I shouldn't have come here. I wasn't supposed to."

Milano's stature rose in Lizzie's esteem. He didn't hesitate. "Abby, you did nothing wrong. None of this was your fault. At your worst, you were cordial to someone you thought was a fellow herbalist. Don't change."

Abby managed a weak smile.

Lizzie studied her. She looked exhausted. In a whispered aside to Detective Milano, Lizzie asked, "Do you think she should stay here tonight? It's late and she's dead on her feet. Abby withdrew even more. *Bad choice of words, Lizzie. Remember, think before you speak.*

Milano saved her from further response by barking, "Of course she can't stay here alone. We'll hold off her time reviewing the incident with the police until morning." He looked around as if lost. Trying to find a way to let her go, protect her, and comfort her, I bet. And still keep his professionalism.

She could see he chose protection and set the rest aside for now. "Can she stay with you at the resort tonight?"

She put her arm around Abby's shoulders. "Do you want to come? I'd love to have you. Delia will be in the hospital so there'll be plenty of room and you can just sleep."

Abby agreed. "Let me get my bag. It should still be in the kitchen where I dropped it when I went to make tea."

Detective Milano accompanied her inside. Lizzie called Natalie and asked for a ride for Abby. She arrived only a few minutes later as Abby came outside. "Hi girl. Here I am. Your personal chauffeur."

"I promise you they will lock up thoroughly before they leave," Detective Milano said, touching her hand with more than a guarantee. "I have work to do. I need to meet Miss Ort at the sheriff's department and write a report on this."

Abby smiled her thanks and trudged to the sedan as if her bag held all the books in the world. The detective grabbed the bag and put it in the car.

Natalie lifted her head to study Lizzie who handed her the key to the suite and said, "Be gentle. She may not be ready to talk about it."

Natalie's expressive eyebrows shot to the hairline. "About what. Want to tell me what's going on?"

Lizzie whispered. "Short version. Abby was attacked earlier. We have the guy. And maybe the vendor's killer. Update later."

Reaching for the car keys in her voluminous purse, Natalie shot back. "You betcha. Every detail."

Lizzie never understood why so many women keep their car keys loose in their pocketbooks. The woman just got out of the car. Didn't she think she'd need them again? Then Lizzie noticed her stretch pants had no pockets. How impractical can you get?

Detective Milano tipped two fingers to his forehead in a salute to Lizzie and climbed into his car. She hopped into the truck and followed right on his bumper. *Finally, some answers. She couldn't wait. Being covert CIA was a lot easier than solving crimes. This mystery never ends.*

By the time they arrived at the sheriff's office and dispatched the computer to the lab, Milano heard Meindl was conscious. They waited till he was released from the hospital. Once in his own office the man maintained his detective persona, sitting behind the desk and offering her a chair. Calling her by her formal name, he discussed how an officer would interview her, and later Abby Weiss, for their testimony as to what transpired. "Detective Guetierrez should be arriving soon with the suspect, Jacob Meindl, and we'll begin our interrogation."

Lizzie's ears perked up. She wanted in on it. Her skill set

contained valuable questioning techniques. The man must be attuned to her wave length by now because he spoke before she could formulate her request.

"No. Absolutely not. You cannot be in on the interrogation."

"Can I look through the window and hear it?"

He faltered. "One-way mirrors are obsolete. We replaced them with cameras."

She sniffed. "So can I view the interrogation whichever way is possible?"

Officer Rutenberg walked in to conduct her interview. "Where would you like me to do this, boss?"

"The room next door is fine." He looked at her. Nodded. "Finish this first. The officer will bring you in when you're done."

Her statement flew past. She could answer questions like that in less time than it took for a hit of McCallan whiskey to slide down her throat. Too bad she didn't have any handy. Ah, the good ole days. But today she valued the speed, since she didn't want to miss Meindl's interrogation. Not that she didn't trust Detective Milano, still. . . .

Jacob Meindl sat in a chair, looking somewhat like a man at his execution.

"Here you go, ma'am," Detective Guetierrez said as he pulled out the chair. "You watch the recording from there." Lizzie settled in her private viewing room in the comfy chair provided. As he left, Guetierrez said, "Detective Milano will open with the questions."

The men worked their way backward from Abby to the murder. Milano took the lead. "Why did you follow and attack Abby Weiss?"

Meindl answered with no fluctuation in his voice, as if a robot on drugs. "I was afraid Abby might remember the discussion we had on telomerase and telomeres, and even worse, on Alexander Howell."

"And this bothered you why?"

The man gained some life and he paused to answer. Lizzie itched to get in there and talk with the guy. She squeezed her fingers to the tabletop and let the detectives do their job. Meindl's response revealed his desire to hide some of the facts.

"I just wanted to talk with her. Convince her not to say anything."

The twitch in Milano's eye was so prominent Lizzie could see it on the live recording. He said, "How were you going to accomplish that? Kill her?"

They were getting nowhere. She wanted in.

Then Detective Milano surged up from his casual stance against the wall. "We've got Howell's blood in your car, on his computer. It had to land there when he was hammered on the head."

Meindl jerked but no words came from his open mouth. She saw his startled eyes drain of emotion as realization struck.

Milano continued. "You killed him. Why?"

The suspect dropped his head, but blurted out. "When I arrived a day early at the conference I read the entire vendor brochure. I learned Howell had a product similar to mine. My start up company would wow the scientific world. But I needed to be the first."

I wanted our meeting to be in secret, hoping for a grand combination of research to blow the field wide open on a fountain of youth drug. If it didn't work I planned to frighten him. So I bribed Washburn to blur the cameras when I saw he stayed after hours. I knocked on the door behind Howell's booth. He let me in. We talked."

Neither detective spoke. They waited.

"Howell lost his temper. I got angry. He wouldn't agree to anything. All of a sudden I had the banner pole in my hand. I guess the banner fell right off."

Milano motioned for him to continue.

"He screamed. I hit him to shut him up. When he fell, his arm landed on a small box and the computer laptop fell out near his head. I grabbed it, searched for any papers, replaced the banner, and ran back through the same door."

He stopped talking, waited. Then continued. "I thought if I could steal all his research, erase it from his files, I'd be fine." He cocked his head. "So I flew to Chicago the next morning."

"Yeah, we know," Milano said. "We finally tracked you using the Clearwater International Airport to Rockford, Illinois." He hesitated. "Thought you'd trick us?"

"Well, it didn't work, did it?" Meindl snarled.

The detective attempted to cool him down a little and asked a simple, genuine question. "What did you expect to gain?"

"The formula, of course. I ransacked his home. Then his lab. I found nothing. The guy had it all in his head. Or hidden on the computer."

"Why'd you stick around?" Guetierrez asked.

"I was afraid if I left you would think it suspicious and come after me."

Milano broke in. "Weren't you worried about Washburn?"

"Who's he?"

"The security technician you bribed?"

"Duh, no. He never knew my name."

Milano shook his head. Whispered something to Guetierrez and walked out. He wanted to speak with Lizzie. He said, "Our men searched his room. Fingerprinted everything. Documented everything. Will they find any trace of you?"

She grimaced and jerked her head back. "No."

"What about this 'maid' who helped you out?"

Guetierrez had called another officer in to guard the suspect and joined Lizzie and Milano. The room was shrinking. He asked, "What's taking so long?"

Milano shrugged. "I needed a break. Thought I'd ask Miss Ort about her search of Meindl's room before we continued. We've been rushing things here. Poor organization. Just wanted to fill in some gaps. keep from saying something I shouldn't." He looked back at Lizzie. Waiting.

She decided to give it all to him. There was still a slight fear Miranda was more than she appeared. A connection between her and Meindl was far-fetched but she thought the police should know. "I had Miranda Pennywinkle pose as a maid. She was near when I needed someone. After I unlocked the door, she went in to make sure the place was clear. She didn't touch anything and as soon as we knew the room was empty she left. I told her to drop the towels on a table in the lounge and leave the area."

Milano understood her better now. He sensed the unspoken, and just stared at her and waited for her to continue.

"She was outside his door when I came out. Said she was standing guard."

Guetierrez interrupted. "You're talking about that mousy Miranda? The one with the beautiful periwinkle eyes?"

Milano rolled his eyes and shoved Guetierrez back to the interrogation room. He spoke over his retreating shoulder to Lizzie. "I'll look into it, but she checked out earlier. As uncomplicated and sincere as she seems."

Uncomplicated? Maybe, but some men could be fooled by periwinkle eyes. Could Detective Milano?

CHAPTER THIRTY-SEVEN

Lizzie and Abby absorbed the inherent beauty of a brilliant red and orange sunset, standing in the sand at the ocean's edge. Even the water devoured the golden hues and flung them back across the surface.

Detective Milano phoned early to set up the interview with Abby. He cleared up Lizzie's worries about Miranda when he called. The young woman was, indeed, a shy but loyal friend who wanted to help Lizzie. *How wonderful to be developing innocent friends. She'd waited a long time.*

Officer Rutenberg had kindly conducted Abby's interview that afternoon in the sisters' suite at the resort. Delia, who returned in fine vigor that morning, was out attending wrap-up committee meetings. Lizzie graciously agreed to stay in the bedroom with the door closed. Didn't the officer know, even in a luxurious resort, the inner doors were thin? Her bedside glass tipped just right on the surface, didn't hurt. In hast, she'd dumped the remaining water in the flower pot on the dresser. *Oops. fake. Well, it needed washing.*

Abby learned the answer to her final question. "How did he get in the pantry?" Meindl had covered his foray into the house in detail and the officer explained the man had seen her walk out of the kitchen. He was hiding on the other side of the building, having just knocked out Officer Ferris. "As soon as you left toward the front, he moved in the back door and hid in the pantry.

From there Abby answered all the questions. She remained calm yet steadfast.

Lizzie and Delia would fly home in an hour. The conference

ended with everyone knowing the killer had been caught and they were safe. Most had left that morning. After the officer left and Delia returned, she packed while Lizzie said her goodbyes.

They strolled toward the water's edge. Abby reached for Lizzie's hand as they stood on the beach. "You'll come back?"

Surprised at the handhold, and even more so at the fact she didn't want to let go immediately, Lizzie said, "Whenever you need me. You'll come to visit Pennsylvania?"

"Yes." With a wistful sigh, she added, "Maybe I'll bring a friend."

Abby's hand brushed against Lizzie's empty pocket. "So Lizzie. You didn't need a gun after all."

"Actually, it's been very helpful in my efforts to move into a lighter realm of self-worth and humanitarian work."

"How can a gun do that?"

"Well, you noticed I didn't shoot anyone?"

"Right. You cracked the gun into the side of his head."

"True. But I didn't fire it. It's a softer form of violence. A big step for me."

"You should have told Jacob when he woke up with a concussion and a baseball-sized lump on his head. I'm sure it would have made him feel better."

A little chagrined, Lizzie laughed. "But it was still less invasive. Shooting him through the head would have caused a mess and probably, irreparable damage."

"Why through the head?"

"Anywhere else was too risky. The bullet could have gone through him and hit you."

Detective Milano spoke behind them. "Glad to see this softer side of you. Much better than that close-mouthed CIA operative who slunk in the dark for nefarious purposes."

"Hello William, I was never nefarious." Lizzie took in the sweatshirt and jeans and the bare feet. "Nice of you to join us."

Abby revealed a face crossed between bemused and befuddled.

"I came to tell Abby she could go home any time now." He turned to her and said, "I'll go with if you'd like."

The smile which erupted a second later when she looked at him, reflected pure joy. Milano reached out a hand and she intertwined their fingers.

Lizzie walked further down the beach. She'd be happy to report to Delia their new matchmaking business was off the ground, and successful first time around.

She gazed out at the ocean, her thoughts in another place. *I am in disguise again. People look at me and notice an old lady. Maybe one with a bright smile. Inside, I see a lean body and lucid mind. The only wrinkles—internal worry lines.*

As she headed back, the weather front raced across the sky in riotous color. She stopped, scraping her toe in the sand as she watched the ocean reflect the sky. Her time here, despite the murder and threat of danger to friends, proved beneficial. She learned she had friends, could develop relationships that might last, and could work with others. Not bad for the first days of retirement and her beginning effort at moral atonement.

Well God, murder derailed my first efforts at redemption, but I'm getting there. Looking up she saw black behemoth clouds following the rainbow of colors with the big guns. *Looks like Florida isn't perfect after all—like humans.* She raced back through the raindrops to head home.

Readers' Reviews

Formula for Murder: My favorite kind of thriller: fast paced, romantic and filled with humor.

Game, Set, Murder: . . . likeable characters, interesting plot twists and a heroine who loves chocolate and shoes. . .

Murder Most Floral: . . . mystery, delight and humor all intertwined.

About the Author

Judith Mehl parlayed her writing experience and handwriting analysis expertise into a series of mysteries. As former editor of the journal for the American Association of Handwriting Analysts, she learned an appreciation of mind-to-pen revelation that became an important tool in her books.

Protagonist Kat Everitt relies on that science with deceptive charm in the handwriting mystery series, while Mehl's long-time interest in nature and medicinal plants came to the forefront in the third mystery, *Murder Most Floral. A* new character, Lizzie Ort, assists Kat in her detection work. Lizzie charged forward off the pages of the book and found murder in her own series, beginning with *Fountain of Death*.

Mehl has published numerous newspaper and magazine articles prior to her move to fiction writing. Her novels are peppered with gardening and medicinal herb information. A former university publication manager, her fictitious characters are colored with the quirks of her real life world. She lives in the mountains where she explores the relationship of woodland plants to their environment and their medicinal value for humans. She is a member of Sisters in Crime, Pocono Liars, and the Greater Lehigh Valley Writers Group. She is also active with the county Children and Youth agency, the Pocono Herb Club, and the Pocono Mountain Quilters Guild.

In addition to the handwriting mystery series, *Formula for Murder*, followed by *Game, Set, Murder*, and *Murder Most Floral, and* her new herbal detection series beginning with *Fountain of Death*, Mehl's work is included in two anthologies, *A Readable Feast* and *Once Upon a Time*.

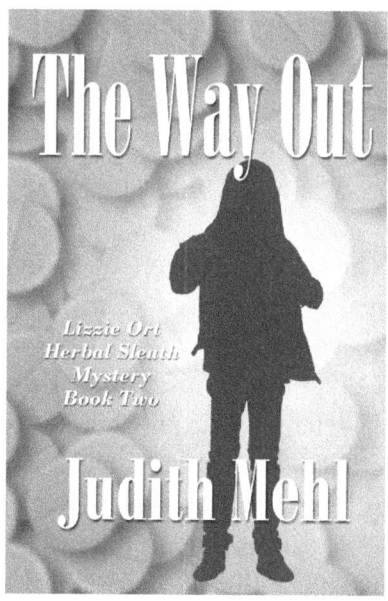

PREVIEW OF *THE WAY OUT*

The Second Lizzie Ort Herbal Sleuth Mystery

CHAPTER 1

Lizzie's powerful fingers strangled the steering wheel. It was a test of will. Of control. To stay on the right side of God she'd have to contain her frustration and let the steering wheel live. If only to avoid crashing the car. She breathed deep, slowing her rhythm, then loosened her bunched fingers. If a run up a mountain couldn't affect Lizzie's breathing, she sure wouldn't let that implacable obstructionist do it.

Stonewalled by a bureaucrat. At a meeting to help teens, no less. Why won't those nitwits recognize the harm teens suffer from opioid drug addiction? Their own, their parents, their friends. A teen center could abate the dangers from all three. Instead the weasel of a principal and his cohorts whitewashed the problem.

Driving home from the meeting, Lizzie wondered how deep their heads dug into the sand. She'd only asked for their backing of a teen center concept, not their gold fillings. Punching her front door in with the flat of her hand, she shoved and grumbled. She hated meetings. And to have no success in her plea transmitted acid into her cast iron stomach.

At home now, the day was on an upswing. Time with Delia, her cheerful and loyal sister, would calm her down. The promise of tranquility through commingling with herbs in the garden would cool her anger. Herbs don't mouth insensitive, shortsighted inanities.

Then she found Delia, just sitting there. Tears jerked her body. Unlike her own wrinkled appearance, Delia's usually unlined face belied her elder status by eleven months at age eighty-three. Now, her face looked ravaged. She sat on the antique sofa, one hand resting on the curlicued wooden arm, polished to a rich gleam. The other held her slumped forehead.

Lizzie knelt next to her. "Delia, my dear, what happened? I haven't seen you cry since you were five and your bike sat mangled in the road."

More composed, Delia raised her head and sniffed. "You forget, I also had a broken leg."

"But I do remember the one thing you moaned, "My bike, my bike. That stupid car ruined my bike."

Delia stood up swiftly and rammed her hands down at her side. "This time it's not a bike. It's a human being. It's little Tyler."

"Little Tyler? Isn't he in his teens?"

"Okay, so he's fourteen." Delia said, then sniffled again. "Somehow I let the friendship fade away and hadn't realized what a horrible situation Tyler's mom, Emily, lived in. Maybe I could have helped and Tyler would still be at home."

Lizzie took her hand, opened her fingers, then gently pulled her to the kitchen table. "I'm fixing tea, then I'll get the full picture and work from there."

Delia succumbed. Not her usual response. Normally, Delia would fix tea for her. The kettle shrieked. Lizzie raced around the sunny kitchen, preparing the weakest, and thus, fastest, tea possible.

Fresh picked herbs sat in a glass of water on the oak table, ready for snipping—a typical Delia move. Over the years, Lizzie had learned most of the herbs and their uses. Her sister's expertise drew many seeking help, but there was such a thing as osmosis of knowledge. These were parsley, oregano, and basil—a sure bet for soup, though the lunch hour passed long ago.

What could have made her sister so frazzled? Delia never forgot meals. They both worked in the garden now that Lizzie was retired, but Delia tenaciously clung to her role as chef. Thank heavens. Lizzie didn't mind dirt on her hands. She'd lived with that a long time. But cooking? She might poison them the first day out.

Tea she could handle. Delia had dried and labeled the herbs. Her own knowledge led to historical usage. Which herbs decorated the mummies for help in the afterlife. Dried and dead. That she could expound on. But even Lizzie knew that chamomile calmed.

The timer rang. Two minutes would have to do. She slid her sister's favorite mug, delicately adorned with spring flowers, into Delia's cold hands. The warmth would help, though the taste might not meet Delia's standards. Sitting down, she yanked her own chair closer, and leaned forward, elbows on the table.

Not a coddler by nature, she instinctively took charge, and spoke with firmness. "What's with Tyler?"

Delia drank her tea and swallowed loudly.

"Okay Delia. Tell me now. What happened to him?"

"I don't know. He's missing. Emily's an old friend, though she's been distant in past years. That jerk of a husband deserted her eons ago. She raised Tyler on her own."

"And?"

Delia looked straight at Lizzie and didn't flinch or hold back. "Emily's afraid he's gone. She confessed she thinks he's been on some drugs. In with the wrong crowd." She sipped more tea.

Lizzie saw that Delia was more collected now, but before she could question her, Delia lifted her head and said, "She's frightened, panicky. He's been gone three weeks and barely stayed at home before that. He's only fourteen. His mom called everyone she could think of from the school phone. They'd disconnected her home phone long ago. But she doesn't know his, you know, his druggie friends."

Lizzie arched her back. Drugs she knew. Kids she didn't. She tried to remember Emily, picture a shape, a blurred image. Nothing came. But Delia had a myriad of friends.

"Did Emily contact the police?"

Delia sniffed again, most of the tears gone now as she bucked up and attempted to address the problem with her usual stoic calm. "She feared calling them. What if they found him with drugs? With little Heather at home, four years old, she didn't know what she'd do if they arrested him. Or her."

"But what if he's in danger?"

Delia sipped the last of the tea. "I tried to tell her that, but she burst into tears again and wouldn't listen." Delia stood to study the newest emerging plants through the large window. Most people didn't have picture windows in their kitchen looking onto a vegetable garden, but Delia and Lizzie defied the norm in many ways. Outside that window new growth spurted from the ground everywhere, portending spring, a bright and enlightening time of year.

Delia turned to Lizzie. "She left a few minutes ago, sobbing, hugging Heather so tight she cried." Her tormented sister's eyes pleaded, "Could you help me find Tyler? I wouldn't know where to begin. But you would."

Lizzie appreciated the confidence in her abilities, but felt it necessary to point out, "I might, if he was lost in some hovel in a foreign country. But here, in safe ole Mountain View?"

Her sister went limp and plopped back into the chair. "Please?" She leaned forward. "They live around those old shacks at the edge of the woods. Nowheres near the big town in stature."

Lizzie barely remembered that area. Maybe it wasn't this nasty back when she explored as a teenager. She didn't have time to reconnect with old haunts since she moved back home.

"Of course I'll help. Did Emily give you any leads? Names of friends we could talk to?"

Delia's frown lines converged. "His mother said there were few. He acted embarrassed to bring them home. She kept the bungalow spotless, as best she could in that bad part of town."

Lizzie sat and bounced her knee in frustration. "There must have been somebody."

"She did mention a friend, Ethan, but she hasn't seen him in weeks."

"Okay. First, I'll nosy around the school. They know me. The principal attended the meeting this morning. Didn't give me any support for the teen center I advocated. Maybe he'll feel guilty and answer my questions."

This time Delia laughed. Quiet, but a distinctive laugh. Warm. Delightful to hear.

Delia said, "Fat chance. That Matthew wouldn't bend if a hurricane blew through. And I'm sorry he didn't support the teen activity center. Still, I can't believe he bashed your biggest foray into helping out the local community."

Occupied with leafing through her book of phone numbers, Lizzie raised her eyes to Delia's sympathetic ones and pursed her lips, appreciating her concern. She paused. "Some bread would be good."

"Wonderful idea." Delia's tall, slim body slid smoothly into action. For her, if it wasn't digging with a trowel and planting outdoors, then cooking took over. She tied on her apron. "Making bread relaxes me. You're right about Matthew though. I hope he helps with Tyler."

Lizzie perused the phone book, a small one, since in her former life, phone numbers were locked in her brain, not written down. She took a minute to respond. "It was a long shot. I don't know teens well enough. Or this community. What I do know is that this area, all of Pennsylvania, is ripe for drug dealers and the forging of new gangs, and worse, victims. These things I know. I can't let our community go the way of the drug-drenched foreign countries where the innocent traveled in fear. Not to mention the filth and shredded shirts and torn pants that flagged the worst of circumstances."

Delia frowned. "We'll get these young lads the help they need. May take a little time." Then she dredged the counter with flour and dug in.

Lizzie sensed bread on the horizon, and imagined the delicious scent of a new loaf in her head before Delia began. She took that as her cue to look for the principal's number, again. Ahh, there it was.

Next time she'd know not to write it under 'D' for dimwit. She called his secretary first. Direct lines were handy, but she'd followed the circuitous route many a time to the answer she needed. Since old Matthew hadn't taken kindly to her forceful overtures this morning, she'd try a maneuver.

Before she dialed, Delia interrupted, shaking flour from her hands before she fiddled with her fingers, and spoke. Slowly. "Umm, tone down the interrogations when doing this. I know you're not used to dealing with normal humans, what with all your years in the CIA."

"You mean, like, just ask them soft questions in a kind manner?"

Delia rolled her eyes at the sarcasm and went back to bread making.

Lizzie debated checking with Tyler's mom first, but Emily seemed the type to need a cooling off period. And Lizzie didn't harbor patience for tearful women. Unkind in some ways, but often necessary. This time, she'd find out more from an unbiased source, before she tackled the mom.

Lizzie grabbed the cordless phone and wound around Delia through the kitchen into the living room. She watched Delia snip numerous fresh herbs, then glide back to the dough, like a ghost, as if her thoughts were mired in more than flour. The pungent scent of oregano, one of her own favorite herbs, followed her. She gave it credit for much of her strong constitution throughout life. Delia's use of it today convinced her that she was sealing a point, thanking her for her assistance. Lizzie saw no need to disturb her. To see her sister, who always radiated enthusiasm and hope, so bothered by this missing child, broke Lizzie's heart.

Finding people was Lizzie's bailiwick. She hoped when it mattered to Delia she wouldn't fall short. All those years serving her country, patriotic. Not helping her sister, unforgivable.

She stood near the front window, inhaled the sweet scent of lavender that reigned in the living room most of her life. She chose a tone of voice and sequence of words to entice Matthew's personal assistant, Elizabeth, into aiding her search for Tyler by finding his friend.

Lizzie moved to the garden to walk around the culinary beds, where green shoots raised their heads through the soil, interspersed with plants already reaching their prime. Swiss chard stood tall, waving in the breeze, ready to pick. What a vegetable. It contained a whole alphabet of vitamins and minerals. The stroll provided time for focus, to compose her words, and begin with chitchat between herself and Elizabeth, easing slowly into her request for restricted information about Ethan.

She said, "Elizabeth dear, I'm glad the new reading program that we set up a few months ago is well underway. I feared we would have to wait until the fall. Great job." Humming in silence while the woman chattered effusively, Lizzie's blunt nature forced her to interrupt, as much as she knew the value of conversation in communication. "Thank you. Good to see it helping. I donated anonymously, remember. I could, however, use your help in an urgent matter."

Upon her request for Ethan's address and information on his whereabouts, the woman reverted to the stalwart guardian of student information. Lizzie prevailed. She asserted, elevated the urgency, wheedled. And finally got what little there was. An address, and a worry that no one had heard from him.

Whispering into the phone, Elizabeth said. "Even Tyler's mother came here asking if Ethan had come to classes. I checked around myself. None of the kids that knew him had seen him."

Armed with the unsaid nuances, and the meager information she imparted, Lizzie thanked her and sat down to plan an attack. Tulip buds popped out on short lime green stems in the last few days, adding spikes of color to the emerging landscape. Deep-rose buds stood firm and strong, tightly woven and waiting for the kiss of the sun to open wide and smile for the lucky few who strolled by. In the many years Lizzie came home for a respite from the dank horrors of her job, she'd never been here when the early flowers bloomed. She snuggled down onto the time worn oak slats in the garden bench, raised her head and sniffed spring.

A huge contrast to the offal of the streets she'd wandered in

Calcutta. She'd been to many sad places, with destitute people. Bucharest, Mali, Macedonia. Of course, her job always took her to the nastier avenues of countries, not the new and gleaming high rises.

This time there'd be no enemy, at least she hoped not. If Tyler'd become addicted to drugs, then these were the immediate danger. How did you fight a pill? Delia could find someone. Once she'd determined where to find the solution if it became necessary, she settled on the more urgent need, how to find a young lad.

Not her normal course of events. Time to change her methods with retirement, and God, her new guide at her side. Somewhat changing. Finding was finding, after all. She lingered briefly, analyzing the flower beds instead of her usual, how to plot murder. Delia had nothing to worry about. She'd already morphed back into a normal human being.

The concept of stillness without purpose was alien to her. Rising, straight and tall, she surged forward. Had Tyler chosen to hide, or worse, no longer controlled the decision?

She must ferret him out.

The Way Out available now at:
https://www.amazon.com/dp/B07C58TC43